The Samurai Cowboys: Book Two

WAY OF THE VIPER

NATE WAGNER

Publishing Services provided by Paper Raven Books LLC
Printed in the United States of America
First Printing, 2023

Paperback = 979-8-9872592-4-5
Ebook = 979-8-9872592-3-8

For Janis, Judy and Debby

The Master and the Viper

Cade Wilson was one member of an elite group of warriors—three orphans of the American Civil War—who were given shelter at Fort Whitmore in the northern New Mexico Territory, and trained by Toshi, a samurai warrior from Japan.

All in the service of their Benefactor, Joseph Whitmore II, these three samurai cowboys were given names that would intentionally absolve them of their former lives—and they became known as Falcon, Scorpion, and Viper.

For years, Whitmore used his samurai and private army of shadow riders to ruthlessly increase his landholdings throughout the territory in advance of the railroad that would eventually connect the expanding East with the frontier of the West.

Everything was going according to plan, until Cade experienced a change of heart and broke from his honor-bound loyalty to his Benefactor. Turning his back against his former master brought swift retribution, as some allegiances cannot be undone.

In the fall of 1876, Cade was the lone remaining member of the three—and the fight for his life had just begun.

"Today is victory over yourself of yesterday; tomorrow is your victory over lesser men."

Miyamoto Musashi
The Book of Five Rings

The Dispatch

TO: BIG GAME HUNTERS

FROM: JOSEPH WHITMORE II

TARGET: CADE WILSON

ALIAS: VIPER

RISK: EXTREMELY DANGEROUS

LAST KNOWN WHEREABOUTS: NEW MEXICO TERRITORY

TROPHY: TWO SWORDS AND PROOF OF DEATH

BOUNTY: $3,000

FINDERS KEEPERS: TARGET HAS $10,000 IN GOLD

CHAPTER 1

Big Game Hunting

The Ramirez gang was on the run just south of Santa Fe, and they were desperate for a place to hide.

Darkness rolled in quickly as the setting sun tucked behind a blanket of thunderclouds. And with the remaining light to guide them, they made their way to an abandoned house at the entrance to a small canyon. The structure itself was barely standing in defiance of whatever fire had taken most of it. But it would do for the night, and hopefully, they could make it through the mountain pass tomorrow and put some distance between themselves and the men on their trail.

Otherwise, it would only be a matter of time before they were caught. Marshal Blackburn had been tracking them since the shoot-out in El Paso, and his reputation as a ruthless and relentless bounty hunter was well known throughout Texas. There was a price on their heads, and the three surviving members of the gang knew there was no quit in his pursuit.

This hideout was new to them, but Julio Ramirez trusted the source of information who told them of its whereabouts. They arrived at the house, quickly tied up the horses, and then surveyed the place while Julio's older brother Carlos tasked everyone.

"Javier, build a fire so we can cook up the last of the bacon and beans. I'm starving," he said while pointing at the charred remnants of the fireplace.

Then Carlos ordered Julio to do the dirty work. "Julio, you have first watch. There's a good spot in the crevice of those rocks over there, under that big tree. If you see anyone coming, howl like a coyote, but don't shoot. It will give away your position."

Julio was reluctant to agree. Carlos was a year older, yet Julio thought he had every right to be the leader after their oldest brother, Ramon, had been killed. But tonight wasn't the time to have that fight.

"Save me something to eat," he replied and walked toward the lookout spot with his rifle in hand. "Why am I always the one stuck on watch?" he grumbled, along with his empty stomach.

It wasn't a long walk to the tree-covered rocks, but it was long enough for the first drops of rain to fall on his coat and hat. Julio ducked his head and stepped up the pace to get under the high desert cedar—even though it wasn't going to offer much protection. "I'm tired of being on the run. Why are we so afraid? There's only two of them. If I were in charge, I'd fight the marshal and his deputy head on," he mumbled to himself.

Then a flash of lightning lit up the canyon, and it illuminated the shadow of someone standing in his path.

He was a mountain of a man, standing over six feet tall with broad shoulders and a blackbearded face. His dark overcoat added to his menacing look, and the distinctive patch over his left eye was a dead giveaway—it was Marshal Blackburn.

Fast as lightning and the thunder that followed, the marshal released his bullwhip, which wrapped itself around Julio's neck. Then, in one quick twist of his wrist, the coiled whip constricted around Julio's throat and left him struggling to breathe and unable to speak.

"Hello again, Julio. That would have been a good spot to see us coming, but I'm a little disappointed you were so predictable," the marshal said in a gravelly voice that sounded like it came from a tomb. "Now drop your rifle… quietly. I have some questions."

• • •

Finders Keepers

The marshal stood over his man and began his interrogation, while Julio dropped his rifle and tried to pull the whip away from his neck with both hands.

"It's no use, amigo. My whip is affectionately named 'Widowmaker' for a reason. And I can ease your pain or tighten the whip and take your head clean off with a flick of my wrist. But for now, all I want you to do is nod or shake your head, yes or no, when I ask a question. Do you understand?" the marshal asked intently.

Julio, still gasping for air, nodded.

"There are only three of you left, yes?" the marshal continued, and Julio nodded. "Good. Ramon Ramirez is dead, so one of them must be your brother Carlos and the other is his friend Javier, yes?"

Julio nodded again and another bolt of lightning lit up the sky. The rolling thunder that followed seemed to open the clouds as the rain fell heavier and harder. But this didn't bother the marshal. The sound of the rain was perfect cover, and he wanted to finish his business.

"Would you like me to release you and ease your pain?" the marshal asked politely, and Julio again nodded yes. Obligingly, the marshal quickly spun around with the whip in his hand and the Widowmaker's coil constricted hard enough to snap Julio's neck. As his lifeless body fell into the mud, the marshal offered an insincere blessing with a wave of his hand and the sign of the cross. "You are released."

Bill Swift, the marshal's deputy, stepped out from behind the big tree and came alongside his partner to hand him a double-barrel shotgun. "How do you want to handle this, boss?"

"Let's rile up their horses and see if we can flush them out in the open," the marshal replied while coiling his whip and taking the shotgun. "You go around and cover the back, and I'll take the front. And let's be quick about it, so we can get out of the rain," he said, chuckling.

Bill nodded and pulled his pistol before stooping down to

sneak around the back of the house. The hard dirt was turning to soft mud, and it muffled the sound of his partner's footsteps.

The marshal stood in the shadows to survey the inside from the open window. He could see the last two men trying to get a fire started in this burned-out shelter, and he could hear them complaining about whatever was left of the roof doing a poor job of keeping the weather out.

"This damn rain," Carlos said, stepping away to try and catch some in his canteen.

"It's better than being out in it," Javier mumbled back as he waved an iron skillet to feed air to the smoking wood.

Assuming his deputy was in position by now, the marshal used the butt of his shotgun to poke the horses. Both men looked up when they heard the sounds from outside.

Carlos turned to Javier with his index finger over his lips, then he pulled his pistol and walked quietly to the door. "Julio, is that you?" he said in a muffled voice, but loud enough to be heard. "What's going on out there?"

Carlos walked slowly to the door and had just pulled it halfway open when the marshal fired a shotgun blast into his left knee, which made him drop to the ground. Screaming in pain, Carlos pointed his pistol at nothing and fired into the darkness. But before he could cock the hammer for a second shot, the crack of a whip snapped the pistol from his hand.

Javier dropped the skillet and jumped to his feet as Carlos continued to wail. Then he pulled his pistol and tried to duck out the back door, but a shot rang out. He stopped dead in his tracks then fell to the floor with a gunshot wound in the center of his chest.

"Bullseye!" Bill said as he stepped in through the back door.

Carlos propped himself up and tried to hobble over to where his rifle leaned against the fireplace. But the deputy was there to stop him as he stepped over Javier's body with his pistol in hand.

When the marshal made his way through the front door, Carlos turned to face the bounty hunter and slowly raised his hands. The soft light of the fire was bright enough for the hunter to see fear in the shadows of his eyes.

"Well now… it seems we finally caught up with you," the marshal began. "We've been tracking you over a hundred miles, and now the Ramirez gang is down to you." With another quick crack of his whip, the Widowmaker coiled around the man's wounded knee.

At first, the marshal gave the whip a right twist to tighten it, and it dropped Carlos to the floor, who then grimaced. Next, he turned it left and released the whip before pulling it back.

"I bet that hurts, doesn't it?" the marshal said. "Trust me. I know Widowmaker's sting. I got a little too careless with it once and put my left eye out. But that's another story. Right now, I need you to sit up and listen to me. Can you do that?"

Carlos just nodded and propped himself up against the wall.

"You stole some horses that didn't belong to you, and your gang killed a group of families moving west out of Texas about a month ago. Do you remember that?" the marshal asked.

Carlos nodded again, still holding his bleeding leg and wincing.

"Good. Because even though the law can't prove you did it, we both know you did. And the man that put a bounty on you wants the gold cross he'd given to his daughter," the marshal said as he leaned in. "Now I don't want to hear what you did to her because I can't imagine it was pleasant. But that man wants the gold cross back, and anything else you stole doesn't matter. That's something we can just keep between us."

Without saying anything else to acknowledge his guilt, Carlos reached into his shirt and produced a beautiful necklace with a cross of gold.

"Here, take it," he said as he pulled it over his head and gave it to the marshal. "And there's over three hundred dollars in cash in that saddlebag. You can have that, too. Please… you can take it all and let me go," he pleaded while pointing to the saddlebag lying next to his rifle.

"Thank you, amigo, but I'm afraid we can't do that," the marshal said while taking the necklace and admiring it in the light of the smoldering flame. "I said the cross was all he wanted back… but he also wants you dead."

"No!" Carlos screamed as he raised his hands, but he could not stop the bullet that went right between his eyes.

"Bullseye!" Bill said as smoke and the scent of gunpowder wafted from the barrel of his pistol.

"Nice shot, Swifty," the marshal shared as a genuine compliment. "Now, can you take a look in that bag over there?"

After holstering his pistol and rummaging through the saddlebag, the deputy pulled out $327 and some other loose items: a silver comb, a nice pocket watch, and an old rusty knife.

"Looks like he was telling the truth, boss. Do you mind if I keep this pocket watch?" Bill asked, assuming it was his now. "Finders keepers."

"Sure," the marshal replied while thinking through what they had to do next. "We're a long way from home, and we'll need to deliver these men to the sheriff's office in Santa Fe. When we do, we might as well stop by a union station and check the dispatch. Maybe there's another bounty in the area."

Bill nodded and started putting the recovered inventory back into the saddlebag.

"Now let's get these bodies outside before they go stiff," the marshal said with a look of disgust. "And let's cook up that bacon. I'd hate to see good food go to waste."

• • •

Sinclair

The man took great care in being meticulously dressed wherever he went. Even as he walked into the dust-covered interior of Pioneer Saloon on the edge of Dodge City.

What most people didn't appreciate about him—unlike the ivory-handled Colt on his hip that most men seemed to covet—was that he didn't care if he looked completely out of place in his tailored coat, bow tie, and buttoned vest.

It was early in the evening, and the piano player was banging away with a lively tune while everyone seemed pleasantly drunk or well on their way. He also noticed that anybody who was drinking, or gambling, wasn't paying much attention to him—which suited him just fine.

The barkeep looked like a reasonably intelligent young man, and he gave his waxed mustache a little twist. "What can I get you, friend?" he asked, sounding somewhat suspicious.

"A glass of your finest whiskey, if you please," the man replied as he casually placed four silver dollars on the bar. Then he looked up from underneath his slim black hat to make eye contact. "I'm also interested in some information."

The barkeep put a glass in front of the man and began to pour from a dark bottle he pulled from the top shelf. "What kind of information?" he asked with an eye on the coins.

"Do you know Sam and Frank Potter?" the man asked before sliding one of the four coins toward the barkeep and picking up the glass.

The barkeep cleared his throat and his eyes darted quickly to his right. "I haven't seen Sam or Frank Potter in weeks. They're probably headed south to Texas."

"That's not what I asked you," the man said before taking a deep, disappointed breath and a sip of the whiskey. "I asked if you know them," he repeated while placing a finger on another piece of silver.

"Look, mister. I don't know who you are, and from the looks of your rig and fancy clothes… you don't belong here," the barkeep said in a condescending tone. "Maybe you'd best finish your drink and be on your way."

"My good sir, maybe I'm not making my intentions clear. My mom named me Oliver, after my grandfather, but everyone else calls me Sinclair," he said calmly and then finished his whiskey. "And if you'll please forgive my British accent, I want it to be known that I have some important business with Sam and Frank Potter. It's my vocation to pay close attention to clues of their whereabouts, and I think they're here. Now if you please, can you top up my drink and point them out to me, so we can conclude our conversation?"

The barkeep leaned back, raised his head, and smiled, even though he didn't appear to distinguish Sinclair's name or reputation. After he refilled the glass with whiskey, he gave a sideways nod and another glance to his right at the poker table in the corner.

"Thank you," Sinclair said with a smile, and he slid the remaining three coins across the bar with his palm.

He made his way to the corner of the room, where four men were playing cards and a fifth chair stood open. Once at the table, he addressed the men who had all taken a slight pause from the game to acknowledge the newcomer.

"Mind if I join you?" he asked, taking a seat and not waiting for their reply. "I do enjoy a bit of cards. What are the stakes?"

"This is a cash game, mister, and we're not big on playing with strangers," said the man dealing.

"Splendid. I have something worth playing for that's as good as gold, and my name is Sinclair. Now we're not strangers anymore," he replied with a dry smile before taking another sip of his whiskey. "Maybe you've heard of me?" he asked while putting his hand inside his vest. Then he produced a folded piece of paper.

Sinclair laid the parchment on the table as if it were

money, leaned back in his chair, pulled a knife from his boot, and began cleaning his fingernails. "So let's get better acquainted. Tell me, who are you?" he asked politely.

At first the men at the table looked at each other as if they all knew this was the end of their game. But then it became obvious that two of the men, sitting next to each other, were the only ones looking down at the table—and these two men fit the description of the Potter brothers.

"Allow me to explain. This bit of parchment is a bounty note, and it's worth two thousand dollars for two men with distinguishable names. And you fine gentlemen do have names, yes?" he asked again.

While the men at the table were still holding their cards, two other men approached from the bar and moved up slowly behind the unwelcome newcomer at the table.

Sinclair decided it was time to force the introductions. He pointed at the dealer to his right, then started going around the table and casually giving the men names. "You look like an Edward… or maybe a James." Then he pointed his thumb at the man sitting across from him. "But you look like a Sam," he said before looking to the man on his left. "And you must be Frank."

Frank didn't answer and instead tried to quickly drop his cards and go for his gun. But Sinclair was quicker, and he stuck a knife through Frank's right hand and into the table.

Then, with a flick of his left wrist, a Remington derringer appeared from up his sleeve and he shot Sam in the neck. Blood slowly covered the table from Frank's hand, and spattered everywhere from Sam's neck as he fell back into his chair and started grasping at the bullet wound and making gurgling noises while trying to breathe.

The two men standing behind Sinclair were a little drunk and reacted too slowly to what had just happened. By the time they did take action, Sinclair had already pushed his chair back, stood up, and pulled his pistol. Then, as one of them took a swing at him, he ducked the punch and shot the would-be attacker in the foot before pointing the barrel of his pistol in the face of the other, who was still trying to pull his gun.

"If you don't mind, this is private business," Sinclair said very calmly over a chorus of men howling in pain. "Drop your guns, if you please," he continued with a smile.

The fourth man in the fight did as he was told; he dropped his pistol and slowly backed away. "Sorry, boss," he said in Frank's direction.

"You might want to get that looked at," Sinclair said to the man with the hole in his foot. Then he turned his attention back to Sam and Frank. He holstered his pistol, then pointed the barrel of his derringer at Frank's temple. "Hold still," he said as he pulled the blade from the table and wiped it on Frank's sleeve before putting it back in his boot.

"Now stand up… slowly, if you please," he said to Frank while glancing quickly around the room and at the other two card players who sat pale-faced and passively out of the fight.

"I assume you gentlemen don't mind if I discuss my business with these two brothers outside, yes?" Sinclair asked, and they just nodded and pushed back from the table to get out of the way.

Sinclair put the folded paper back inside his vest, pulled

Frank's pistol from its holster, and tucked it in his belt. "His neck and your hand are making a bloody mess. You should wrap something around that because I need to chat with you and your brother outside."

"My brother needs a doctor!" Frank said as he pulled off his kerchief and wrapped it around his bleeding hand.

"Your brother looks strong enough," Sinclair responded with a pompous chuckle. "Now let's get him some fresh air. Be a good man and let's help him outside."

The music had stopped long ago, and everyone else in the room cleared a path to the entrance as Frank moved around the table to help Sam out of his chair. Sinclair pulled a few more silver coins from his pocket and threw them on the poker table. "Apologies for the mess. And I'd appreciate that you remember what happened here as a matter of personal business."

Sinclair followed as the two men pushed through the saloon doors into the cool twilight air, then he walked the Potter brothers out into the street and in front of the building. Frank had pulled his brother's arm over his shoulder and was holding a second kerchief over the gunshot wound on his neck.

"Sam and Frank Potter… I have a bit of news for you, and good or bad is just a matter of perspective," Sinclair said before pausing to clear his throat. "There is a bounty for heads, and the gentleman paying it isn't very pleased with you. It would appear that you two have been up to no good for some time, and there was a young man you took advantage of a few months back. And that young man happens to be the son of a senator."

Frank spoke up, "That's a lie! We didn't have anything to do with that—"

"Sorry. That's a moot point. Young Theo was found dead and floating in the Mississippi River, and over five hundred dollars had been stolen from him. You two were the last to be seen doing business with him, over a bit of land I've heard, and that's really all I need to know. I also don't need to know who those other two gents were behind me, but hopefully you've settled up with them," Sinclair said as a lead in to what was to come next. "And now that we've discussed our first bit of business, let's discuss the two thousand dollars I stand to gain from the proof of your death."

"Look! We're innocent, I tell you. We may have sold that greenhorn some worthless land in Missouri, but we didn't kill him. I swear to God!" Frank confessed earnestly and swallowed hard.

"We have about a hundred dollars. It's in my brother's pocket. It's yours if you'll just turn and let us walk away," he said as a distraction while he slowly moved his left hand down behind his brother's back.

"That's all you have left—one hundred dollars?" Sinclair asked with a laugh. "It's quite unfortunate that you don't understand the rules of the game. There's a bounty for your head that has nothing to do with the law, and a little finder's bonus for anything else found on your person. Honestly, I was hoping you still had most of the five hundred dollars with you. But I suppose whatever is in your pockets will have to do."

"What can I say," Frank replied sarcastically as his left

hand found the butt of his brother's holstered pistol. "My brother is a bad gambler," he said as he tried to pull it.

But Sinclair was fast on the draw and four shots rang out as the two Potter brothers dropped to the ground. And as he looked around to notice the people who had gathered to witness the fight, he smiled, hoping his reputation as a quick-draw gunfighter would continue to grow.

"Shame really," he said as he reached down and inspected the pockets of the two dead men. "There's only eighty-two dollars here, and maybe they were innocent."

The people who had gathered around whispered in their respective circles. A moment later, a heavy-set man with a shiny badge on his coat arrived, and he announced himself as a local constable.

"What's going on here?" the constable asked while trying to hush the crowd.

"My fine sir, there has been an unfortunate loss of life here this evening. But do trust that there was a bounty for these men for murder and theft," Sinclair replied as he pulled the folded piece of paper from his vest pocket and handed it over. "In the effort to take these men into custody, I'm afraid they tried to pull a weapon, and I had to defend myself. Wouldn't you agree?" he asked while looking around at the crowd of witnesses.

But nobody in the crowd wanted to get involved; they simply grumbled and nodded at the story. Dodge City was full of wanted men, troublemakers, and people passing through. This was just another shoot-out on any ordinary night, and

Sinclair could sense that the constable was pretending to read the paper handed to him.

After a glance at the two dead men in the street, the constable began to speak. "Well, mister—"

"Sinclair, if you please. And I'd appreciate it if you'd commit my name to memory; for reputational purposes," he replied.

"Take your dead prisoners with you and go about your business," the constable said, handing the paper back. "Alright everyone, it's time to move along now," he continued and addressed the crowd of onlookers by motioning for them to disperse. "There's nothing more to see here."

"Thank you, constable," Sinclair said politely in full agreement. "Your cooperation in this matter is greatly appreciated. But I must be on to more pressing matters. There is another bounty I must urgently attend to… a Mr. Cade Wilson. And these men are not my prisoners," he concluded as he pressed a bloody thumbprint of each brother on the parchment and folded it back up.

Then he walked over to his horse and climbed into the saddle. But before he rode away, he paused to offer one last bit of helpful information. "And constable, there's another gentleman in the saloon who might need a doctor for his foot."

CHAPTER 2

Old Friends

Cade's return across the high desert prairie wasn't as daunting, or as deadly, as his previous journey. Being a little better prepared helped, and heading east with the afternoon sun at his back was nice, too.

Fortunately, navigation wasn't something he had to worry about. The tracks left by Scorpion and his shadow riders were still fresh enough to lead him straight back to the fort, even when they strayed off other well-traveled roads.

He felt uncomfortable returning to Fort Whitmore, knowing he wouldn't be well received. But he had no other choice. He needed to negotiate his fate and future with his Benefactor and to ensure the safety of his sister, Sarah. At best, he was hoping to bargain for their release from servitude in return for sharing the location of the missing gold, or even helping him to retrieve it.

Doubt weighed heavy on his mind. Would his Benefactor

be willing to forgive his betrayal, and the deaths of Scorpion and Falcon, and let him and his sister go? What would he say if, and when, he saw Toshi again? How would he explain to his sensei what happened and that his students were dead? And not just dead—their blood was on his hands. All that wasn't just going to wash away.

He knew this confrontation would not be an easy ask, so he was in no hurry to reach his destination. The days spent traveling gave him plenty of time to think through every possible scenario of how it might play out. And he also enjoyed dry camping under the stars and the crisp scent of September blowing in the wind.

But during his long days on the trail, his thoughts often turned to Lucy and the Johnson family, and he wished he was with them back at Rocky Creek. Hopefully they were managing just fine, and he could go back some day. But the idea of having a normal life seemed like an out-of-reach dream littered with obstacles.

On this day, under a blue sky of puffy white clouds, Cade broke out of his daydream in the saddle when he came to the edge of a creek bed. There was a nice spot to rest the horses under the shade of a big cottonwood tree, and there was a small pool of water that was probably all that remained of the late summer rain.

He found a decent spot to stretch and rest himself. Considering how far he had come, he calculated that he was still a couple of days ride from his destination, and so he continued to trip through his thoughts and feelings associated with the fort. Memories from his past, most of them good, flooded back the closer he got to the place that was his second home.

In the past, whenever he rounded the final bend and the fort was in sight, all his thoughts would turn to being rewarded for a successful mission—being treated like a hero, eating great meals, and enjoying good night's sleep in a real bed. But now everything was different, and for the first time that he could tell, he wasn't looking forward to seeing the fortified gate and the fort's grand spread.

Then something else scratched at his attention. A familiar sound alerted his senses at the same moment he realized he had no time to react. It was the sound of riders approaching.

Cade jumped to his feet just as three shadow riders came into view, coming from the direction he was heading. There was not much he could do, having been caught by surprise, and he certainly felt careless and stupid for being out in the open and out of position to defend himself. Given the vulnerability of the situation, all he could do was stand in the middle of the trail with his right hand on his pistol and his left out in front of him to signal for the riders to stop.

The shadow riders also seemed surprised to see him. Whatever their destination happened to be, they were in a hurry and looked shocked when they crossed paths with Cade. But now, confronted with him at this crossroads, the lead rider put up his hand for the others to slow their horses.

As all three riders came to a stop, the one on the right was the first to speak up and whisper to the others, "Hey, Clark… that's Viper. What should we do?"

The lead rider pulled down his kerchief to reveal his face.

It was Clark, the man Cade rode with from Missouri to the fort over ten years ago. Even though it had been awhile since the two of them saw each other, their friendship had never wavered.

But now they faced each other under completely different circumstances.

"Hold on, Merl," Clark said with a voice of authority over the others. "Let's talk this out. And Tim, don't do anything rash."

Tim had to be the other shadow rider on Clark's left, because that man was ignoring the words of caution. "There's a bounty on the man," he said, holding a twitchy right hand on the butt of his pistol. He also had the look of someone who was already banking on what that hero's reward would be.

"Hello, Clark," Cade began with his hand still on his pistol. "Fancy running into you out here," he added with a smile.

"I'm on my way back to the fort to meet with our Benefactor. How about we keep the peace between us, and everybody stay calm. There's no fight here. Nobody needs to die today," he said, sensing that Clark would agree and could reason with the others.

Cade also assumed that these men weren't necessarily prepared for this moment. But he had to anticipate that something might happen anyway because he could sense that the two men opposite Clark were still twitching and not backing down.

"Our Benefactor wants you dead, mister," Tim said while slowly moving up to the lead position.

That's when Cade could see the dangerous glint in Tim's

eye and sensed he was going to draw. And he expected that Merl, the man on Clark's right, likely would, too.

He tried once more to reason with them. "Don't do it! Whatever you're thinking… it won't end well. I'm asking you again to stand down."

"I'd listen up, Tim," Clark said. "Let's talk this out."

"That's your problem, Clark. You talk too much. And the reward doesn't have to split three ways," Tim said pointedly to make his intentions clear. "C'mon, Merl. He doesn't look so tough. We can take him."

For a moment, it was deathly quiet as all four men stared each other down. And when Tim was the first to pull his gun, he was the first to find out he was no match for the man who had spent years honing his quick draw.

It was over in a moment as Cade pulled his pistol and hammered two shots to Clark's left—and then a third shot to his right. Then he pointed the smoking barrel at his old friend while Tim and Merl fell lifeless from their horses.

"Wait! Don't shoot," Clark said with both hands out in front of him.

"Sorry, old friend. But they should have heeded my advice. I haven't come this far to lose my life at the hands of lesser men," Cade replied as he uncocked the hammer and slowly lowered his pistol. "Now what do we do?"

Clark looked down at the bodies of his two companions and then at one of the horses, which was already wandering away without its rider. Then he lowered his hands and looked Cade in the eye. "Let's talk," he replied.

It was late afternoon by the time Cade and Clark finished

digging shallow graves and laid the shadow riders to rest under the big cottonwood tree. Since the two of them were very familiar with each other, they agreed to camp there for the night. And the last shots fired that day were at a prairie chicken they scared up for supper.

As they watched the bird cooking over the open flame, Clark was the first to start up a casual conversation. "Just like old times, eh? I remember when you were first learning how to master that gun, shooting birds on the trail. Is that the same pistol I handed you at your house?"

The mere mention of that day was both a sad and pleasant memory for Cade. "No, it's not. I changed that one for this Peacemaker. But I still have that old gun in a wood box back at the fort," he replied with a mournful sense of regret. That pistol came from the man who died in the doorway of his family's home back in Missouri. It was likely the gun that had killed his mother—and to this day, he couldn't explain why he kept it.

"You've grown so much," Clark continued. "You were so lean and scrawny when we first met that I could have never imagined that you would become the man you are today. And so quick with that pistol." He smiled. "I've never seen anyone that fast."

"I wasn't always that quick, or aware of who I was becoming," Cade replied with an insightful chuckle, as there was so much more to that story that Clark didn't know.

"When I was allowed to practice shooting, I was only given two bullets a day. Toshi was always teaching me to be precise in all things, and it made me focus on being fast and hitting my targets," Cade continued. "All my skills are a product of my sensei's training and teachings, and learning more about myself along the way."

"I was always curious what was going on inside that building. What was it like being trained as a samurai?" Clark asked.

"It's a long story," Cade replied.

•••

Cade's Tale: The Way of the Viper

One of the most important things I had to learn about the samurai way was that training and pain were closely related.

Toshi was a samurai warrior from Japan—and besides being our Benefactor's personal bodyguard—his purpose was to train us in the way of the samurai. And those lessons would not come without sacrifice, bruises, and scars. When I realized that my mistakes were really just painful lessons to be learned, I focused more on improving my skills and not repeating them.

Six of us were selected from a group of young men the year we built the dojo. At first, we learned how to fight with our hands, and then we progressed to wooden swords, bows, and spears. The following summer, the six of us were pitted against one another to the death until only three of us remained—all because our Benefactor wanted us to prove our loyalty to him. I'll never forget that night or the first time seeing someone's spirit leave their body.

My friend Paul was my first kill, and as a reward, I became Viper. But becoming Viper was only the first step in a never-ending journey. Every day, for the years that followed, I would practice and hone my fighting skills against Falcon and Scorpion when we weren't tasked with a mission.

Many of those missions just involved intimidation because the sight of three samurai cowboys and our shadow riders was usually enough to persuade most people that we weren't there to negotiate. But our Benefactor was also big on sending a message. Sometimes we were tasked with taking no prisoners, and sometimes he'd want us to bring back the heads of people he considered his enemies to further the reputation of his influence and control throughout the territory.

From what I could tell, these enemies weren't always bad people. Most times they were just standing in the way of our Benefactor's ambitions. But all told, we fought and killed everyone from banditos and thieves, to Indians and settlers. As for the territory, we protected his landholdings from Texas to the Mexican border. And sometimes we'd cross the border into Mexico, too.

If we weren't on a mission, we were back at the fort and training. We were always training, and with Toshi there was no such thing as perfection.

On one day in particular, we were training and sparring with our wooden swords when I charged Toshi with an over-aggressive and clumsy attack. He defended the attack and stepped quickly to my left and slashed me across the back—a move I would never forget. But his methods of challenging me were something I would painfully remember, too.

"Move faster. Fight without thinking!" Toshi would often say during our training sessions.

"You move like a donkey. Donkeys are slow and stubborn, and they learn everything the hard way. Are you a donkey or a viper?" he asked, never expecting a reply.

I think calling me a donkey was the closest thing Toshi could offer as a term of endearment. Because compliments were rare, and insults and pain were lessons administered daily.

That day I snapped back at him, still wincing from the lashes across my carelessly exposed backside. "How come you're always harder on me than on Falcon or Scorpion?" I asked.

Toshi stopped our exercise and looked me in the eye. "Foolish donkey… I train you the hardest because you have the most potential. You, above the others, might be able to achieve the fifth ring because you possess strength and skill equal to them, but you do not thirst for death."

"I don't understand," I said.

"The falcon kills without conscience and does not waste its energy. It is relentless in its search for prey, but it only seeks what it can kill. And when attacking its prey, it goes for the kill at first strike," Toshi explained.

"The scorpion also kills without conscience when it uses its sting," he continued. "It will attack prey and anything that opposes it with the same ferocity, and it will sting vigorously at anything when threatened."

"What about the viper?" I asked.

Toshi smiled at me, which was also a rare occurrence. "The viper can control its strike and only kills by choice," he said. "It's as deadly as its brothers, but the viper can decide how much venom to release… choosing the difference between defending itself or striking to kill its prey. The way of the viper is a path wrought with choices, and with avoiding rash judgments concerning good and evil. Those are matters of conscience, and the viper's survival depends on making its decisions quickly and with conviction.

"To arrive at these decisions, you must trust your senses. Do not become dependent on just your vision. Close your eyes and breathe in your surroundings. Listen to the wind and feel everything around you. Your ability to sense danger and where it will come from will allow you to visualize your opponent without seeing him, so you will know how much venom to release."

While I didn't know what he was talking about at first, I started closing my eyes before we sparred—and during the rest of our training that day I began to discover what he meant. I could imagine how he might attack, and how I could defend myself against it. Trusting my senses was a way of removing distraction and focusing on my surroundings and my opponent, and on if, or how, I needed to strike.

It was also an interesting perspective on why the three of us were given our respective names. Maybe our code names meant something beyond just replacing our birth names to become loyal samurai.

But from that day forward, I always looked at Toshi a little differently and approached my training with this new perspective. And every time I sparred against Falcon or Scorpion, I would hear his voice in my head.

"When your opponent underestimates you, that is to

your advantage," Toshi would say. "If your opponent fears you, that is also to your advantage. But any overconfidence will be your weakness."

Falcon and Scorpion definitely wanted their opponent to fear them. They consistently attacked very aggressively, but their overconfidence would eventually leave them open to a counterattack. Watching them, studying them, I applied Toshi's teachings to my fighting style and made better choices in the fire of battle. Fighting against them every day made me the trained killer I am today. That is something I cannot change.

And so it was, for all those years. Toshi continued teaching us the way of the samurai while also learning about us and adapting to some of our ways. He had a coat similar to ours fashioned from his samurai armor, and his was a very distinguishable light gray. He even started wearing a Boss of the Plains Stetson that helped him fit in a little better when he traveled away from the fort with our Benefactor.

Over that same time, I even tried to build a relationship with Toshi when we weren't training. Instead of being the emotionally cold taskmaster he was when he first arrived, he had started to become more like a father figure. He would even make jokes every once in a while.

One night after a hard day of training, Toshi happened to be outside by the fire, sipping some whiskey. As we watched the embers rise and dance from the flames, we talked about the Five Rings when Toshi finally shared part of his story that I had never heard—and I've never forgot.

"I miss Japan, but I know I can never return," he began. "There is nothing for me there. Sometimes it is a good viewpoint to see the world as a dream. When your life and your dreams become more like a nightmare, you can wake up and tell yourself that it was only a dream. It is said the world we live in is not much different from this."

"What happened?" I asked.

"My only son is dead. He died honorably in battle almost ten years ago when ninja assassins were sent to destroy our village," he said after taking a sip of whiskey. Without breaking his stare into the fire, he continued. "I was not there. But I should have been there to fight and die alongside my son. When I did return, I found my home burned and destroyed. And in its remains, I found my wife's charred body clutching a knife in her belly. Instead of giving in to the attackers, she had died with honor.

"My previous master, Yoshinobu, was the last shogun in Japan. And when he surrendered his power to the emperor, I became a ronin… a samurai without a lord or master."

Toshi paused for a moment to look at the house of our Benefactor. "The emperor adopted new weapons and ways from the West, and he turned his back to the samurai. There are no masters left to serve.

"That's why I came to America. In Japan, the time of the sword and the way of the samurai had come to an end. There is no real place for a ronin, and I could not live with that shame. I sold everything I could except the swords and weapons passed down from my father, and his father, and made my way to a village by the sea. It was there I met an ambassador of Japan traveling to America, and he brought me with him to serve as his guardian during the months he was in San Francisco. That's when I was introduced to our Benefactor, and now I'm here.

"In America, I have found a new master and a new sense of purpose. This is where I will accept my death," he continued. "You three are the last of my students, and I will pass down to you everything I know."

Then Toshi finished his whiskey before excusing himself to retire for the evening. "My obligation is here now, and I must accept that. I'm training you so the way of the samurai is not forgotten… and the memory of my son is not forgotten."

I had always wondered why he'd come to America, but I never appreciated or understood what to do with that knowledge. Instead, I came to understand everything he had lost— and appreciate why he pushed me so hard.

Before walking off into the darkness, he stood and stopped to share the final piece of this personal story. "The sword I gave to you once belonged to my son. You should know that," he said solemnly, and I couldn't help but sense the conflict between his pride and his broken heart. It would be the last time he ever spoke of his family or his past again.

But the pain of his story continued to echo in my mind, and then I realized that I would be subject to whatever memories and nightmares my conscience would impose on me for what I've done—and I didn't know if I was ready to carry that burden for the rest of my life.

All I did know was that I wasn't ready to end up like Toshi. I could see the demons that still haunted him like stories painted across the wrinkles in his face. And for the first time, I began to question my path as a samurai and my future at the fort.

• • •

Past to Present Danger

As Cade finished his story, he looked over to his old friend. Clark was staring into the fire as if he was making peace with his own past and life at the fort.

"That explains a lot," Clark finally said. "Everything before arriving at the fort, including the war, seems like a blurred memory to me sometimes. It certainly hasn't been what I thought we were signing up for, and I often think of returning to Missouri."

Then Cade sensed Clark was ready to change the subject back to discussing the events of this afternoon. "I wish Tim would have listened, but he was always a hot head, and Merl was just dumb and greedy. If they wouldn't have been so reckless, we might all be sitting around this fire tonight," he said regretfully.

This observation piqued Cade's curiosity. "There's been something on my mind all afternoon. I didn't expect to run into you, but it seemed like you were somewhat prepared to find me. Where were you headed?" he asked.

"We were sent out to spot you," Clark replied. "The colonel received a wire that Scorpion was dead and that you were headed back to the fort. He sent the three of us to try and spot you," he said, pulling a brass spyglass from the saddlebag next to him.

"There's some high ground about two miles that way," he said, pointing in the direction Cade had come from. "We were racing to get there ahead of you, assuming you were also following Scorpion's tracks. If we spotted you, we were supposed to send Merl back to the fort ahead of you, and Tim and I were supposed to trail behind you without being noticed."

"Jon Cobb," Cade said under his breath while slowly shaking his head.

"Who's that?" Clark asked.

"He's just another pain in my side," Cade replied. "But no matter. His involvement is unimportant, but I think he has some business with our Benefactor. All I've heard is that he's trying to own all the land he can between Santa Fe and the Colorado border, and he's the reason Scorpion tracked me to Rocky Creek."

Clark looked at Cade between the smoke and flames. "I heard you killed Scorpion, and word has it that you killed Falcon, too. The stories going around about you back at the fort aren't good. They say you've killed over a dozen shadow riders and stolen ten thousand dollars in gold coins." After a brief pause, he followed with a burning question, "Is all of that true?"

"That's another long story, my friend, and I have all the scars to prove it. That's all I can say for now. And it's a story that I'd rather tell our Benefactor if you don't mind," Cade replied. "Do you think he'll meet with me if we ride back together?"

Clark snickered. "No, Cade… I don't think so. Even if

he would, he's on his way to Denver for some big meeting about the railroad. He left the day after dispatching Scorpion and a dozen riders to Rocky Creek. All he told us was that Colorado had recently become a state, and he's got some grand vision to expand the railroad from Cheyenne all the way to El Paso. Maybe that's why our Benefactor has business with this Cobb fella?"

Before he continued, Clark poked at the coals and turned the prairie chicken. "The colonel is in charge while our Benefactor is away, and right now he's waiting for you with over forty guns and orders to kill. They want their gold back, but I think they'd settle for knowing you're dead and retrieving those samurai swords. So, I wouldn't advise you to go anywhere near the fort. Even as fast as you are, you're no match for a company of shadow riders guarding the fort," he said in warning.

"That's why we were supposed to come up behind you. We were supposed to drive you to the wolves. But now I don't know what to do. What will I say when I ride back to the fort?" Clark asked earnestly.

"You can tell them what happened, for the most part," Cade replied. "Tell them you saw me and now two more shadow riders are dead. Then tell them that I left you alive so that we can negotiate a truce. I want to speak with our Benefactor and let him know my side of the story."

Cade could sense that Clark was trying to wrap his head around this plan as he mumbled through a simulation of how that conversation would go.

"Okay, then. That's how it will go back at the fort. What are you going to do in the meantime? Our Benefactor isn't expected back until sometime in early October," Clark pondered.

Cade gazed into the fire to think through his options. "I'll wait for you here," he replied. "If you can convince the colonel that I want to return peacefully, I will camp here until you return. How long will it take you to get back to the fort?"

"It's a long day's ride from here," Clark said while mulling over their current position. "But I should be able to make it faster riding alone."

"I'm sorry to ask this of you, old friend," Cade continued. "But I'll wait here for two nights. There's water for the horses and this is as good a place as any to hold up for a bit. Hopefully the colonel will go for it."

Clark echoed that sentiment. "I hope so, too. Because there's something else you should know. There's a bounty on your head, and all the shadow riders know about it. They've been promised a big reward for whoever brings you in. So I want you to promise me there'll be no hard feelings no matter what happens."

Cade nodded silently with a pressed smile across his lips before looking up at the stars in the twilight sky. There was something else still on Cade's mind, and he hoped Clark could help him with it.

"Have you seen Sarah? How is all of this affecting her?" he asked.

"I don't know," Clark replied while slowly shaking his head. "But I do know that our Benefactor has shared some plans about letting some of the shadow riders and girls of marrying age get hitched next spring and moved out of the fort. He says they can start families and work and live on all the land he owns to help keep the peace. It sounds like he wants people loyal to him living everywhere in the New Mexico Territory."

Clark looked at Cade through the flames, then he continued with what was on both of their minds. "Sarah is a fine young woman and definitely of marrying age. The shadow riders have already been coupling up with the single ladies expecting that they can get married and move away to start a family. Something else you might want to think about."

Cade let out the exhausted breath of a troubled man. Worrying about his fate was one thing, but he hadn't even considered his sister being in some form of arranged marriage. And it didn't seem fair that the shadow riders would be allowed to marry and move away from the fort—something he now coveted. With so much at stake, he knew the importance of this plan working. He also realized there was nothing he could do in the moment. But feeling somewhat confident that Clark would be able to get him back into the fort, he turned his attention to the most pressing matter at hand.

"I think that prairie chicken is about ready," he said while sniffing the soft smoky air. "Let's eat."

CHAPTER 3

Red Sky

The morning sun was a little slower to crest over the horizon this time of year, and there was a brisk chill in the air as Cade woke to birdsong and the sounds of nature.

All early indications were that it would be a pleasant day for a long ride, but better to have a little breakfast first. He appreciated having some of Clark's supplies with two fewer men to feed. It made camping a much better experience.

An hour later it was time to get a move on, and Clark told Cade he could be back at the fort before sundown if he rode straight through. Clark mounted his horse and secured a few things from his companions to his saddle, then paused to run through the plan again.

"If I were you, I'd move your camp spot a little farther up this wash. Just in case someone else is happening by," Clark added, sounding like a protective older brother. "And if you haven't seen me by morning on the third day, you might want to ride off and not look back. Chances are things didn't go as planned."

Cade looked up at him and smiled. He appreciated everything Clark was doing for him and hoped he wasn't putting his friend's life at risk. And oddly enough, if there was some sort of reward for bringing him in, there was nobody else he'd like to get it.

"Thank you, old friend," Cade said with a smile and a nod. "Now ride safe, and I'll see you in a couple days," he added optimistically.

"You bet," Clark said with a wink and a smile, but then his eyes opened wide and his face froze.

Cade knew that look all too well, and that's when Clark coughed up the blood that confirmed his worst fear. He took a few steps closer to get a better look, and that's when he saw the arrow sticking out of Clark's back. The next move was purely instinctual, and assuming that another arrow was on its way, Cade ducked behind Clark and his horse just in time for an arrow to hit where he had been standing.

Cade scanned the horizon while remaining hidden behind the shadow of his friend, and he spotted the assassin—a lone American Indian on horseback with a bow in hand. He looked like a warrior ready to fight as he let another arrow loose and rode up the sandy wash on his horse at attack speed.

The arrow stuck in Clark's shoulder and his body slumped forward in the saddle. Cade sensed the horse knew it was time to get out of the way, and his friend's body rolled off and fell to the ground when the horse turned quickly and left Cade exposed.

His attacker loaded another arrow at full gallop as Cade ran quickly up the bank to take cover behind a tree—just in time, as a fourth arrow found its mark in the center of the trunk.

The rider stopped his horse; he must have determined there was no way to flush out his prey, and the element of surprise was lost. After he dropped his bow and slid off his horse in the center of the wash, the warrior stood about sixty feet in front of Cade with a tomahawk axe in his right hand and a long hunting knife in his left.

The warrior stood ready for attack, conveying his unspoken challenge, and Cade was quick to answer the call. At first, he thought about just shooting his attacker where he stood, but there was something oddly mysterious about his opponent, and his intentions for attacking and killing Clark were unknown. Shooting the warrior would lessen his chance to find out, so Cade thought it best to save that option until needed. And if this man wanted to fight with weapons, then he was willing to oblige.

Cade dropped into the wash from behind the tree, pulled his two swords, and took steadily paced steps toward his opponent, who had relaxed, waiting to receive Cade instead of charging. From the looks of him, this man was a fierce warrior and would be a formidable adversary. He was almost as tall as Cade and very lean and strong. He wore a leather vest and his bare torso was adorned with a handsomely beaded necklace. His handmade leather pants flexed with his movements as he squatted down in a defensive position.

"That man was a friend of mine, and you killed him

in cold blood," Cade said as he came into range and close enough to attack.

But as the two began to circle each other, the warrior replied, "You killed my family in cold blood… and I will fight to the death to avenge them." Then, without fear and full of rage, he charged.

Cade was able to defend the first swing of the axe but was surprised at the strength and speed of this opponent. He barely had time to defend his exposed left side as the warrior spun through the attack with his axe and tried to follow with a knife strike.

Cade stepped back to study his opponent's first offensive move, then reset his balance and took more of a defensive stance. Even if the attack was a little unorthodox, it wasn't guided by pure anger. And something about what he said was still lingering in the air when Cade suddenly had to defend the warrior's second attack—an aggressive slash with the axe before he rolled forward on the ground to strike low with the knife.

As Cade jumped over this ground attack, he also had to defend against the back swing of the axe when he landed. Cade stepped back again. Mixing it up with this man was going to be more dangerous than he had originally anticipated.

"You say I killed your family?" Cade asked, trying to get back to what the warrior had first said.

The two men squared off again, and the warrior took a moment to answer. "Yes. The stories of pain and blood are well known. The gray riders and men with swords have killed many, and you killed my family," he said before charging forward again with a slight variation of the first attack.

As Cade defended the strike, he noticed the pattern in his opponent's moves. This man had every reason to want him dead, but he wasn't trained by a samurai.

Memories flashed through his mind. Images of that night at the Comanche camp where he struck the colonel and shot a shadow rider in defense of the innocent women and children they'd been ordered to kill. The memory of that night flooded his conscience, and he suddenly lost any taste for this fight. But he also wanted to know more about the warrior's story, so he decided to press the action and disarm his opponent.

Cade charged forward with both swords moving in concert, leaving the Comanche at a disadvantage and backpedaling while trying to defend with two shorter weapons. This was also the first time Cade had put his speed on display. When he was able to expose his opponent to a physical strike, he used his right foot to kick the warrior in the chest and send him flying backward to the ground.

Cade sensed the Comanche would try to retaliate, so he steadied his defense. When the warrior did get back on his feet, he let out a war cry before throwing the axe as he charged.

Cade blocked the axe throw with his left sword and stuck it into the sand in the same motion. Then he blocked the knife's downward strike with the armor on his right forearm before flicking his left wrist to unleash Scorpion's stinger and punch his opponent in the gut.

The Comanche dropped to his knees, as had so many others after having had the wind knocked out of them by the venomous spike protruding from Cade's left wrist, and suffering the temporary muscle paralysis that followed.

Cade pulled the sword from the sand and returned both swords to their scabbards. Then he disarmed the warrior, and with the warrior's knife stuck in his belt, Cade dragged him to a place where he could sit up under the shade of a tree. Then, after taking a knee, he looked the Comanche in the eyes and started his interrogation.

"I could kill you right now, do you agree?" Cade asked.

The warrior reluctantly acknowledged this truth with a slow blink of his eyes and a slight nod.

"The toxin is temporary, and you will be able to move again, but I want to talk with you first… do you understand?" Cade continued, pulling a handkerchief from his pocket and applying it to the bleeding wound left by the stinger.

Again, the warrior acknowledged with a slow blink.

"What's your name? Where are you from?" Cade asked.

The warrior answered the questions very slowly, still groggy from the toxin.

"My name is Red Sky. I am Comanche… a descendant of Painted Horse. My tribe was camped near the Indian Nation territory after the blue soldiers and white men killed all the buffalo. The forked tongue of the white man brings nothing but death and suffering. While we had to ride for days to hunt, you attacked our camp and took whatever you wanted… and you killed our families without mercy."

Cade could offer nothing to defend himself from that statement or the warrior's interpretation of the events. Many times he had done exactly that at the request of his Benefactor, and he wished he could take it all back. But now another question was pressing on his mind. "How did you follow me here?" he asked.

"There were two sets of tracks from our camp, and I followed the tracks that lead to the great house," Red Sky answered. "Many men guard the great house, so I watched and waited. Then I saw a man with swords and many gray riders heading toward the setting sun. I found a good place to wait and attack, but they did not return. But when three more gray riders headed in the same direction, I followed them here."

Cade knew immediately what Red Sky was talking about and was deeply ashamed. This man was just exacting revenge on the men who attacked his tribe and a camp full of women and children not long ago. An act of revenge he could both understand and needed to avoid as his past kept coming back to haunt him. This man deserved a chance to have his vengeance and to find peace.

"Red Sky… I'm deeply sorry for what happened that night," Cade said while thinking through how to best tell this story.

"I was there. And yes, there were others like me there, too," he continued. "We were there to recover some stolen gold. Nothing else. When our colonel gave orders to kill, I tried to stop him. I shot one of the gray riders and took the gold, hoping they would chase me and stop hurting your people. But the truth is, I never looked back and I don't know what happened after I left."

Red Sky's expression changed, as if something Cade had said made sense to him. Again, he blinked slowly for Cade to continue.

"The other two men with swords are dead now. So are the gray riders that killed your family. They were my brothers, but now our Benefactor sees me as an outcast… and no longer part of the tribe. They were sent to kill me because I stood against them, and they chased me for miles. Do you know what any of this means?" Cade asked, himself a little confused.

Red Sky nodded and started wiggling his fingers with some effort. "Did you kill those two men with swords?" he asked curiously.

Cade didn't want to rehash his past with this man or make a confession in the middle of this desolate part of the territory. But if the two of them shared the same enemy, then maybe his version of what happened may bring some peace between them.

"Yes. I killed the other two men with swords, or they would have killed me. And now I'm going to take my fight to the fort. The place you call the 'great house.'

"There is a man at that great house who is still alive and responsible for everything that happened that night. He's a man we call the colonel, and he gave the order for us not to leave any witnesses alive in your camp after we found the gold. But ultimately, we all take our orders from the man we call our Benefactor, and that's who I need to see," Cade said and then paused when he sensed how callous his words might have been to hear.

Red Sky slowly flexed his arms and wiggled his feet as the toxin from the stinger gradually wore off. "Why didn't you kill me?" he asked.

After pondering this for a moment, Cade answered as

honestly as possible. "Before today, I would have shot you for killing my friend. For many years I have been trained to fight like a samurai. As a samurai, I was honor-bound to serve my Benefactor and do whatever I was ordered to do, including avenging those who fight by my side. But I'm starting to realize that I have a choice. There's a difference between defending and attacking, and I don't have to take a life just because someone else expects that of me. I can accept that I may be a trained killer, but I'm no murderer.

"And there is something different about you. You fight with courage and no fear of death, much like a samurai," Cade continued. "There was just something I sensed about you, and I don't know how to explain it. But now maybe I do, because I needed to hear your story to understand your pain."

"My pain?" Red Sky replied. "How do you understand my pain?"

"Like you, those I loved and everything I once knew was taken from me, and my thirst for blood and revenge changed me. I became an instrument of death. But somewhere along the way I got lost. Revenge didn't bring anyone back, and it did not give me peace," Cade replied.

"Now peace is all I want but there are two men standing in the way of that, and they want me dead. The colonel is guarding the fort and the man we all answer to with an army of those gray shadow riders. So I need to resolve my conflict with our Benefactor or die trying. And that's where I was headed."

As he spoke those words, Cade became aware that the plan he crafted with Clark was now moot. Clark might have been able to get inside the fort and negotiate a truce with the colonel. But without Clark, it would be foolish to ride up to the gates with a white flag and expect the colonel to just let him in.

Cade wandered in a circle, making footprints in the sand. *What do I do now?* he thought to himself while trying to think through his best options. He could return to the church for the gold and just keep heading south to Mexico. Or he could head north and try to intercept his Benefactor away from the fort. There would be men trying to kill him whichever path he chose. But not Red Sky—his intentions were not motivated by his Benefactor or by any reward.

While these thoughts raced through his head, he barely noticed that Red Sky was now back on his feet, as the toxins had worn off. This caught Cade by surprise, but more so because he wasn't attacking. He was just standing there, waiting and listening—and that's when Cade knew what he had to do.

"So here we are," Cade said. "Two men on a similar path. You want revenge. I want my freedom. But the chance of either of us getting what we want by fighting alone is not very likely. And as my sensei once shared in his teachings, 'To become the enemy, see yourself as the enemy of the enemy.'"

Red Sky stared at Cade with a very puzzled expression.

"Come with me," Cade said plainly and sincerely. He knew he needed to make it clear to Red Sky why he would even say such a thing. Five minutes ago, they had been about to kill each other.

"Look, we're both after the same two men, for different reasons. The colonel is currently well defended in the fort and is expecting me. And he is in charge of the fort while my

Benefactor is traveling north to Denver. There is no way either of us could attack the fort alone or try to get to the colonel without being killed.

"But if we could get to my Benefactor while he is away from the fort, we could intercept him where he is less protected," Cade said as he continued to formulate the plan in the moment. "Then we could all travel back to the fort together and the colonel couldn't fire on us. Then you could challenge the colonel to a duel once he's out in the open, and he should be honor-bound to accept. This way, we both have a chance to get what we want. I can negotiate my freedom from my Benefactor, and you can fight the colonel to the death to avenge your family."

Then Cade handed Red Sky his knife back as a gesture of good will. "What do you think?"

•••

The Pact

Red Sky was both surprised and intrigued by the proposal; it was unusual for someone he had been hunting and trying to kill to ask if he wanted to journey together.

But after having tracked the first party back to the great house, he agreed that it would be death to try and attack it alone. The description of the colonel commanding the others was similar to what he'd heard from some of the survivors. If that man was still alive, then so was the threat to his tribe.

"What do they call you?" Red Sky asked curiously.

"My name is Cade. Cade Wilson," the man replied.

Red Sky looked at Cade very skeptically. He didn't fully trust this man, or understand him. But he also knew that the man with swords was a deadly warrior. His quickness with his weapons was too much to overcome, and so it was likely better to join him to get his revenge.

Because what mattered most to Red Sky was avenging the deaths of his family and protecting his tribe. He was nomadic by nature, and the proposed journey was less concerning than understanding *why* he should go. But the idea of capturing the chief, this Benefactor, away from the great house, made sense. Confronting this man, or killing him, would fulfill his sense of purpose.

Red Sky also sensed something deeper that he may have in common with Cade. There was nothing more dangerous than fighting a warrior who had already accepted death as an outcome. Fighting alongside such a man would make them stronger together.

Red Sky stepped forward, cut the palm of his hand with his knife, and presented his bleeding palm to pledge an oath. "By the blood of my ancestors, I will fight alongside you," he said, handing the knife to Cade.

When Cade made a similar cut and raised his hand in kind, Red Sky clasped Cade's palm firmly and they made their pact. Then both men stepped back to acknowledge the ritual and the bond they had just formed.

Red Sky nodded as he took his knife back from Cade. "*Haitse,*" he said.

CHAPTER 4

Vision Quest

The midday breeze was warm and dry as the events of the morning imposed their mark on Cade. He continued to struggle with Clark's death even though he understood Red Sky's motives—and now he would need to make the most of the bond with his new companion.

They took inventory of the three horses, supplies, and the weapons and coats that had been removed from the three dead shadow riders. They weighed their options, then decided to adopt it all as it gave them something of value to trade. It would also afford them time as they plotted their course. If a wandering horse returned to the fort, there would certainly be more shadow riders hot on their trail. But for now, Cade figured they at least had the advantage of a two-day head start.

After burying Clark near the other two graves, Cade presented Red Sky with Clark's holster belt and pistol.

"Clark would have been okay with you having this," Cade

said of his old friend. "That's how we met, and you're probably going to need this someday." Then Cade also presented Red Sky with Clark's gray coat. "It's also going to get cold where we're going. You're about the same size as my old friend, and you'll probably need this, too."

Red Sky accepted the gifts and Cade showed him how to properly fasten the gun belt. With the gray coat on, his new Comanche friend almost looked the part of a shadow rider.

The two sensed it was time to get a move on, so they agreed to start riding north. As they made their way up the wash, they were more focused on not being seen than on trying to ride at a brisk pace. And one of the first things Cade appreciated about Red Sky was that he knew how to use brush and tree branches to cover their tracks.

As they traveled farther up the wash, they eventually had to work their way up to level ground and a view of the vast expanse of prairie and the distant mountains that lay ahead of them. Red Sky took the point while Cade led the four horses and trailed behind. This made for slow travel, and by late afternoon they decided to find a good place to camp for the night.

After gathering some wood to build a fire, Red Sky pointed beyond the mountains silhouetted against the western horizon as the setting sun cast its shadows. Its remaining glow cut through some clouds to produce golden beams of light.

"The Comanche once roamed this land. We fought many times with the Apache, then alongside the Apache when the white man came. They, too, recognized the white man as a common enemy. But there has been so much death… now we are so few," he said.

Again, Cade felt ashamed of his past. Too many bad memories crept through his conscience, the more he thought about all the faces that had crossed his path. At the time, it had been easy to forget the deaths of those who stood in his way because he had been trained to believe that all moral conflicts were absolved by loyally serving his Benefactor. And since he had grown up in his Benefactor's care and beliefs at the fort for so many years, he really didn't know any different.

As both men gazed into the fire and chewed on some smoked rabbit meat, Cade broke the silence over the crackle of the flames. "I don't know what it is about meeting you, this place, or what I've been through the past couple weeks, but it's making me remember everything I've done. Some parts of my past are horrible things that I'd rather not remember, but then I imagine other things that seem more like thoughts or dreams of things that haven't happened yet.

"We were so close to the fort, and before you came along, it was my plan to return. My friend was going to help me surrender myself, and I hoped they might take me back for who I once was. Because there was a time that I was respected there. I was treated like someone very important," Cade said.

"But the funny thing is, the more time I spend away from the fort and my Benefactor, the less I miss it, if at all." Cade looked up at the increasingly starlit sky. "The only thing I care about now is making sure my sister is okay, and that I can be free. I promised my mom on the day she died that I would look after Sarah, and I'm grateful for our time and everything we received at the fort. But now things have changed, and I'm ready to stop all the fighting—especially on someone else's orders.

"Over the past month or so, I've also been thinking about all the innocent people who needed someone to protect them from men like me, and men like my Benefactor," he concluded.

"It sounds like you are on a vision quest," Red Sky offered with a thin smile and a nod. "Visions from the spirit world can heal the pain of your past, and they can show you a new purpose in life."

Then he produced a sleek wooden pipe from a small leather pouch and packed it with some tobacco. After pulling a burning twig from the fire to light the pipe, he puffed the smoke into the warm rising air over the fire and produced a small ring that hovered just for a moment.

"You should be open to your visions during your quest. Some visions may come as dreams, or as animals, or forces of nature. But you must be patient. Your true purpose will be revealed in time… when you are open to receiving it," he said.

Cade smiled back at Red Sky. Their conversation reminded him of Toshi in so many ways. There was a quiet wisdom in this man that he would have never known if he had acted impulsively.

The two sat quietly around the fire for the rest of the night, each of them lost in their own thoughts—and it was the perfect night for sleeping under a peaceful sky.

• • •

The Old Woman

When they broke camp in the morning, the two companions continued heading north without breakfast. Cade knew it would be a good day to put some miles behind them and not worry about covering their tracks—and early morning was a good time to hunt.

Entering the tree line beneath some low mountains offered cover and some prospects for their next meal. Red Sky was still in the lead with his bow in hand, on the lookout for other riders and anything that might be good for supper.

Cade was busy bringing up his packhorse and the three others in tow while also on the lookout for food. He was using Falcon's old weapons and tried to show Red Sky how the samurai used a bow and arrow. If they were lucky, maybe a pheasant or another prairie chicken would turn up—and the bow's silence wouldn't give away their presence.

But the most important thing was finding the next source of water, so they tracked around the north side of the low mountains, looking for a spring or creek bed that could be a good spot to rest by midday. Instead, they were surprised to happen across a small cabin next to an equally modest barn.

Oddly enough, the most remarkable thing about the scene was that there was no obvious trail leading to or from the property. The two structures seemed built into the trees and were overgrown with shrubs, as if they had been designed to blend perfectly into the landscape. But there were definitely signs of life, as a faint waft of smoke was coming from the chimney.

As they drew closer to the cabin, both men noticed a scattering of chickens, a couple of cows, and a small flock of sheep milling about. There was also a sheepdog lying casually on the porch without barking at their arrival.

Carefully and cautiously, the riders dismounted and approached the cabin, moving toward the only door they could see. They assumed it was the front, but not wanting to take any chances, they spread apart and walked up behind their horses. The uninvited appearance of two strange men approaching could provoke something equally unexpected from whomever lived inside.

There was still no sign of anyone the closer they got to the cabin, so Cade motioned to Red Sky to stay back while he walked up alone. The weathered wood of the front porch creaked under his weight with each step, but the dog just yawned at him and continued paying him no mind. With his right hand on his pistol, he stepped to the side of the door and gave it a little knock.

"Hello. Is there anyone home?" he asked in a calm and unthreatening tone.

On the other side of the door, a woman's voice quietly answered, "Hello, death rider. You may enter if you mean no harm."

Cade looked to Red Sky with a curious expression and shrugged. Still proceeding with caution, he remained on the side of the wood plank door and reached over to the latch with his left hand. After giving the latch a quick pull, he pushed the door, and it swung open quite easily.

When no gunfire followed, Cade slowly stepped into the doorway and the shadow cast behind him was swallowed by the dimly lit interior. As he squinted to peer into the room, a pig ran past his legs and gave him a start.

"That's alright," the woman's voice assured him. "He needed to get outside anyway."

"Is that pig your pet?" Cade asked with a sarcastic chuckle.

"Grimly?" the woman replied matter-of-factly. "Of course he's a pet. All my animals are pets. But Grimly decided he was king around here. Now how about you step inside so I can get a better look at you, and tell your friend he can come in, too."

Cade turned to Red Sky and waved for him to come in after he tied up the horses. Then Cade proceeded inside the cabin and was surprised to find, as his eyes adjusted to the light, that it was really one big room. In the middle of the far wall was a fireplace with a kettle hanging from an iron hook, with a dutch oven resting just above the coals. The only other pieces of furniture were a bed in the opposite corner and a hutch along the wall in a space that must have served as a kitchen.

There was something really odd about this place, but whatever was inside that cast iron pot smelled like food, and it was producing an aroma that could trigger anyone's hunger. Next to the fireplace was a table with a couple of chairs, and over in the corner was an old woman in a rocking chair carving a spoon out of wood.

"I'm almost done with this one, and then your friend will

have a new spoon. It's been a long time since I've had guests. Please come in," she said, putting the final touch to the spoon and placing it on a little side stool next to her.

"Excuse me, ma'am, but it almost sounds like you were expecting us?" Cade asked, raising an eyebrow. When Red Sky entered, he also seemed curious about how the old woman would answer.

"Of course, I knew you were coming," she said, looking at Cade. "But your friend here was a bit of a surprise, and that's why I had to make him a spoon. Been a long time since I've had guests," she repeated, pointing her thumb at Red Sky.

"But how did you know?" Cade asked. "We don't even know where here is!"

The old woman laughed, and it crackled like brittle twigs underfoot. "Still much to learn, death rider… much to learn… if you'll open your mind," she said with an accent Cade couldn't recognize. It was also hard to tell how old she was, but her thick gray hair was pulled back into a braided bun, revealing the soft wrinkles around her eyes and face.

Cade gave Red Sky a confused look and then turned back to the old woman. "Are you some kind of witch?"

"Heavens no, child… but I've been called that once or twice. I knew you were coming the same way you see things, too," she said rather intuitively as she offered Cade a warm yellow-toothed smile. "Would you like some tea?"

She motioned for them to take a seat around the table as she remained standing and shuffled around the place. Then she pulled some cups from the hutch and fetched the kettle. The table was small but accommodating, and a random collection of herbs and other plants in pots hung from the ceiling near the windows in the kitchen. After picking some of the herbs and putting them into a bowl to mix together, she added the collection to the kettle to steep.

The two men sat in silence as the old women hosted them. When she finally took a seat at the table and poured the tea, Cade could sense that there was more to this woman's story, and he was very curious to hear.

She took her first sip and gave a gentle nod of approval before beginning. "My name is Moira. Our family was one of eight that came to America from Ireland many years ago. Some decided to stay in Pennsylvania, but the rest of us moved out west to avoid the war. We never made it to California, but we decided to stake out this spot of land to have a place of our own. We battled dust, disease, and disaster every step of the way, and we were the only ones to make it this far. My husband built this place with the help of my sister's two boys. But he passed about two years ago, and my two nephews went to find work for the railroad. So now it's just me, and my pets. My sister Erin and her husband, Patrick, live in Trinidad, and they come to check on me every now and then."

Then Moira abruptly changed the subject while looking at Red Sky. "Are you Comanche?"

"Yes. My name is Red Sky," he replied with a nod. "The Comanche roamed these lands and hunted the buffalo, elk, and deer that were plenty… but now we are strangers here, and we are the hunted."

Moira winced. Even though she seemed to know his story, it was still clearly painful to hear it.

"Pleasure to meet you. My sincere apologies to your family and your people. They all deserved better than what they got. And I would say that your friend here did something completely unexpected by letting you live. I did not have clear sight of you until this morning, and it shows that there's some hope for him yet," she added with a wink and a smile.

"And you, death rider, what name better suits you? The name you were born with, or the name they gave you?" she asked.

"Please call me Cade," he replied in stunned amazement. How did a woman he'd never met seem to know so much about him?

After another sip of tea, Moira nodded at Cade and continued as if she could read his mind. "The light is something everybody has, but it is brighter in some and it allows them to see things others cannot. For those others, they either don't see what the light shows them or choose not to. But the light is very bright in you. Do you know what I am speaking of?"

Cade took a sip of tea and shook his head. "No, I don't know what you mean. What is this 'light' and what does it have to do with me?"

"Oh, child," she said, smiling back at him. "Do you ever have dreams that you can't explain? Visions of things that are yet to come?"

As her words hung in the air, Cade slowly grasped what she meant. "Yes. Sometimes I have dreams and visions of things to come. But it mostly happens when I'm asleep. Is that what you mean?" he asked, seeking clarity.

Moira looked back at him with the patience of a mother.

"Can you think of other times when you've had foresight? When you close your eyes, can you sense things around you?"

Cade felt suddenly connected to everything around him. He also felt foolish and empowered at the same time. His cheeks became flushed from something very warm inside him. He looked down at his tea, wondering what may be in it, as everything in the room now seemed very vibrant and alive.

"Toshi, my sensei—my teacher—taught me that a samurai must be able to see his opponent and visualize the fight with all of his senses, not just his eyes. And over the years I have been honing my fighting skills by closing my eyes to sense the energy and movements of everything around me," he tried to explain.

"This 'light' is something I've never been able to explain, but it's been growing stronger since I left the fort and began discovering other things about myself. Things that were of less importance when I was in the service of my Benefactor," he continued.

Moira nodded, turned her eyes to Red Sky, and took another sip of tea. "How about you? What do you see when you dream?"

Cade listened as Red Sky described the 'light' to Moira a little differently, and in the way he'd learned since childhood. He could sense the good or bad in people, and he could sense when he was in danger. But he had also learned how to look to the earth and sky for direction. This was a skill that came naturally to him and he used it daily to survive, hunt, and guide him across the vast open landscape.

"Everything speaks, and their story can be heard in the wind… if you are listening," he added.

"How interesting," Moira said. "The two of you will make good travel companions."

Then she looked back at Cade and asked a question that caught him completely by surprise. "What is it you want, Cade Wilson?"

At first, he hesitated to answer, trying to better understand the question. But then he offered up the obvious answer. "I want to be free of my Benefactor."

Moira laughed again. "You're already free of your Benefactor. You just don't know it yet. But he may not be free of you, and that's a problem."

After pouring a little more tea into Cade's cup, she asked the same question but added a condition he could understand. "Close your eyes and open your mind. Now take a deep breath and tell me what you see. What is it you really want?"

Cade did as she asked and visions soon appeared. Images of Lucy flooded his mind. The memory of her smile and their kiss created their own luminescence. These images quickly blended with other pleasant memories of Johnson Ranch, Rocky Creek, and a normal life of morning chores, sun-filled afternoons, family dinners, and feeling loved.

That is what he really wanted, and what he was the most afraid of. These things would come at a cost, and that cost was being free. Until he had his freedom, he would continue to look over his shoulder and put the Johnson family at risk. He could also see that freedom was only a small piece of what he really wanted. When he opened his eyes to look back at the old woman, he sensed she already knew what he was thinking.

"Welcome to the world, Cade Wilson. You've just been born for the second time," she said with a smile. "Knowing what you really want will give you both focus and purpose. And don't worry about sharing your vision. Love gives off a light of its own."

Then she cocked her head to one side and squinted to peer deeper into his eyes. "But I would ask you to remain open-minded. There is something else I see in you… a girl. You will save a girl, and someday she might even be as strong as you."

Cade smiled and nodded back. "Yes. It's my sister, Sarah. I'm very concerned about her. Hopefully, I can free her from the fort as well."

Moira hesitated. "Possibly. This is unclear to me. But that's why I would ask you to remain open-minded. Your path will be filled with many obstacles. If you are fortunate enough to survive, the vision will reveal itself."

"Now to you, child of the earth," she said to Red Sky. "Revenge may fill your heart today, but I hope that you will be able to love again. Your path is righteous, but very narrow. I see that your heart will open again someday. That your people will look to you for leadership. And for now, it's good that you two are on this journey together."

She took the last sip of tea from her cup, sniffed the air, and said something that didn't require any further explanation. "I think that stew is ready. Who's hungry?"

• • •

The Marshal Arrives in Rocky Creek

Across the expanse of land and mountains of the New Mexico Territory, two riders approached a quiet little town from the southern road.

As the marshal and his deputy passed idly by the arched sign for the Johnson Ranch, they hesitated for a moment and took notice of its location before proceeding into town.

Some bounty hunters have a sixth sense when it comes to rumors and stories about dangerous men. The whispers tend to grow louder the closer they get to the source, and the details from actual witnesses start to add up, too.

Marshal Blackburn was on the trail of one story in particular—one going around about men with swords and the deaths of two dozen men in Rocky Creek. That same story also involved a man worth a lot of money. And when they tied up their horses in front of the Five Point Saloon, their presence did not go unnoticed by the folks in town.

Inside the saloon, the marshal made his way to the bar and he didn't bother to look at anyone other than the man standing behind it.

"Can you tell me where I can find Cade Wilson?" the marshal asked the bartender without any pleasantries. He was typically straight to the point when it came to tracking, so he made sure his first question was an easy one.

"Mister, that's what everyone wants to know. You're not

even the first person to ask me that today," the bartender replied with a wry grin. "But I'll tell you the same thing I told the others. That man is a stone-cold killer. The whole town saw him take down thirteen men in one night, and he was already in jail for killing eight others. The judge ran him out of town last week, and the word is he was last seen heading east." The bartender polished a glass, put it down, then added, "And if you're looking for Cade Wilson… you must have a death wish."

Blackburn could tell the bartender may not be the best person to ask, but he had confirmed that Cade Wilson was here and that some of the stories he'd heard were likely true. The next person who stood out to him might be a little more helpful, and now he just had to wait for that person to come forward. "Well then, how about a whiskey for me and my friend," he said very casually in response to the warning.

While the bartender grabbed a bottle and poured two shots, the swinging doors opened, and a troubled-looking man stepped into the saloon.

Blackburn just smiled. "There's our man, Swifty. Let's have a word with him," he said as he grabbed the shot glass and raised it to his deputy. Then he took the shot and placed the glass back on the bar with a loud pop that seemed to call the attention of everyone in the room.

"You! What's your name?" the marshal asked while pointing at his person of interest.

"Uh, my name's Hicks," he said, stammering. "I work for Mr. Cobb."

"I don't know who that is, but I bet you know something about the whereabouts of Cade Wilson, don't you?" Blackburn followed while also looking around for an open table. The marshal spotted one with a man sitting alone and fixed his gaze on the man's face—as he often did to commit a face to memory—and for whatever reason, that man quickly finished his drink and left his chair on the way to the door.

Blackburn motioned to the now empty table. "How about we take a seat over there."

Hicks looked like a man who didn't appreciate what he might have stumbled into, but he slowly made his way over to the table.

"You serve food?" the marshal asked the bartender.

"Yes. Our lunch plate is steak chili with a roll," the bartender replied.

"Sounds good. We'll take two of those and bring the whiskey," the marshal said, then he followed Swifty over to the table with Hicks.

After they all took their seats, the rest of the room uneasily resumed whatever they had been doing. The marshal carried on being very direct; he looked at Hicks and repeated the earlier topic of conversation. "What can you tell me regarding the whereabouts of Cade Wilson?"

At first Hicks struggled to say anything, but eventually he began telling the story of when Cade Wilson arrived in Rocky Creek and everything that had happened as a result. He talked about how Cade had been working out at the Johnson Ranch and how Lucy Tucker and her boy, Eli, were very fond of him.

"He killed five of my men and over a dozen others," Hicks added spitefully, just before the food arrived. He stopped there, and the lunch plates provided a little interruption from the conversation, but the marshal took the opportunity to explore other details.

"How did those other men know to find Mr. Wilson here in Rocky Creek?" he asked curiously. "It's not like this place appears on a map. And all of this happening in just two weeks sounds like too much of a coincidence."

"My boss, Mr. Cobb, had me send a wire to Mr. Whitmore asking for help. Then he had me send a second message a week later to explain that a man named Scorpion and twelve others with him were dead," Hicks said.

As he listened to Hicks answering his questions, Blackburn knew there was truth to his story. Mr. Wilson's connection to the man issuing the bounty, and his potential whereabouts, were all beginning to make sense.

Then the marshal took everything in and summarized to his deputy what they'd just been told. "It sounds like Cade Wilson knows Mr. Whitmore, or worked for him, and now there's bad blood between them. So Whitmore sent this Scorpion fella and a dozen other men to kill Cade Wilson, but this man got the best of them. That means he's a very dangerous man, and it explains why Whitmore put a bounty on him. Does that sound about right?"

Swifty nodded and the marshal turned his attention back to Hicks, who also agreed.

Then Blackburn changed his tack and pressed an urgency to leave. "If he was heading east and back to wherever he came from, then he's got at least four or five days head start. We better finish eating and get a move on."

"Can I go now?" Hicks asked nervously.

"Yes. You can go. And you can tell your boss that Marshal Blackburn and his deputy were in town. But I would appreciate that you would keep the information about where we're headed a secret from anyone else. Do you understand?" he said with a glare.

Hicks just nodded and got up to leave. When Hicks was out of earshot, Bill Swift turned back to his partner.

"You know he's not going to keep that a secret, don't you?" Swifty said, with a chuckle that expressed how predictable he was sure Hicks was.

Blackburn finished chewing a bite and chased it down with a shot of whiskey. "Yes. I know that worthless jackass is heading back to his boss right now to tell him everything about our conversation. I'm counting on that," he said sarcastically.

"The story of Cade Wilson continues to grow. And now we know a little more about how our target is connected to the man who placed the bounty. But what we don't know is why our target would head east and back to where he came from if he's been on the run with ten thousand dollars," he continued, then took another drink.

"We know he's not heading south because we just came from there, and he has a pretty good lead on us if he's heading east… or maybe that's where he wants people to think he's heading. The chance of us heading east and catching him before he gets wherever he's going, or killed by someone else, seems unlikely," Blackburn said with a shake of his head.

"If I had that kind of money and bounty hunters after me, I wouldn't be heading in the most likely direction to be followed either. No, Swifty, I think Cade Wilson is smarter than that, given all he's survived so far. Something in my gut tells me he's heading north."

"Then what do we do next, boss?" his deputy asked, sounding a little confused.

"Let's finish up here and get some supplies at the general store. We're heading north," he replied.

CHAPTER 5

Accommodations

The conversation with Moira continued into the late afternoon, and while Cade may have felt like pushing on earlier, it was also comforting spending time with this mystic woman. Talking with her calmed his soul and reminded him of being at the Johnson Ranch. And as the two travelers felt obliged to be considerate, there was an unspoken assumption that a home with this many animals doesn't take care of itself.

In return for the hospitality, Cade and Red Sky offered to help with some late-day chores. Even though the random collection of animals basically had free range of the land surrounding the little house and the barn, they wondered how she managed alone as it still took two of them to make quick work of splitting some wood, topping off the water troughs, corralling chickens back into the coop, and gathering grass and feed for the three cows and their horses.

As Cade became more attuned to his surroundings, this

place felt hidden from the world—everything about it was beyond the normal. Much like the house, the barn seemed larger inside than it appeared from the outside. Besides all the animal stalls situated along the east wall and flaps leading outdoors to the pens, there was a big open area and plenty of space in the loft or on the opposite side's bunk room for some bedrolls. The potbelly stove in the corner looked a little dusty, but it was there to provide heat for whoever may be bunking out here.

After the hearty meal of slow-cooked stew, Cade and Red Sky agreed to make an early start tomorrow, and they were ready to set up their overnight accommodation in the barn. But Moira baked up some sweet cakes and put on another kettle of tea for the evening. As the three of them sat around the evening fire, she mentioned how this collection of herbs would "put you to sleep like a baby," as she poured the tea.

When it was time to turn in, the two made their way to the barn and lit a fire in the stove. And true to Moira's claim, within moments of Cade lying down, he felt the heaviness of sleep start to take over. When he finally made his bed in the bunk room with Red Sky, he was asleep in no time and dreamed of meditating peacefully in the sun on Flat Rock.

● ● ●

Honoring the Way

Cade breathed in the fresh morning air along with the scent of woodsmoke from the chimney. Fall was beginning to show its colors and it would be a great day to ride strong if they could shed some weight. So, after some morning chores and a hearty breakfast of fresh eggs, he hoped Moira would agree to his proposition.

"Can we please leave some of the horses and our things behind?" he asked. "We have many miles to go, and we need to travel fast and light."

"Oh, child, where you're going… your journey will not be the destination," Moira said mysteriously, and Cade assumed her sense of humor was as strange as everything else about her. "Maybe you'll be back. Maybe you won't. But of course, your horses can stay."

After they packed up what they could carry on their two horses, they said their goodbyes for now. Hopefully, they would be back along this way, and if not, the four horses they left along with everything else was hers to sell or make use of them.

The last gift the old woman had to offer them was a makeshift map of Colorado and some tips on how to navigate their way to Denver.

"Thank you, Moira, for everything. Meeting you has been a blessing," Cade said graciously. "Wherever my path leads, it seems to be filled with good people. Hopefully, that's a sign, as I do hope to see you again."

Moira smiled back. "Best be on your way, Cade Wilson."

There was nothing else to be said, and Cade knew it. If she could see the future, it was probably best that he didn't know. He needed to remain clear and focused if he was to successfully intercept his Benefactor—because he did know that anything could happen between here and Denver. So he just tipped his hat and turned his rested black horse away from the rising sun.

As anticipated, the two were making good time traveling without pack horses and being less cautious about leaving a trail of tracks behind them for anyone to follow. They mapped out a route that would take them west and then north along the base of the mountains. And from there, they would plot out the best course to Denver while traveling along but not on the main trails.

By early afternoon, they could see mountains looming in the distance and had just picked up their pace after a short rest to water the horses. That's when Red Sky raised his hand with a motion for them to slow down and listen.

"Do you hear that?" Red Sky asked after they almost slowed to a stop.

That's when Cade heard gunshots in the valley ahead. "Yes, but they're not shooting at us, and they don't sound like hunters. The shots are too random."

"We could go around," Red Sky said plainly. "But this valley is our best path."

Cade nodded and pointed forward. "Let's find a place to take a quick look. I'd rather not go out of our way just to try to stay clear of whatever is going on. Hopefully, we can pass by unnoticed and avoid any trouble."

They pulled up on a small ridge and found a vantage point between some trees to survey the scene. Up ahead, they could see four people in a clearing, so Cade pulled the spyglass he got from Clark to get a better look.

"What do you see?" Red Sky asked.

Cade carefully considered what he was about to say before sharing the news, as he knew it was trouble. "I see a girl in a standoff with three cowboys who have her surrounded."

What he didn't tell Red Sky was that she was holding a knife and the reins of her horse while the three men took turns shooting at her feet and laughing about it. While Cade couldn't hear what was being said, he couldn't imagine it was anything pleasant.

"We need to help her," Red Sky whispered.

"Yes, I know," Cade said reluctantly. "This is an unfortunate distraction, but there's no getting around it. I don't like the looks of those men or what they're doing."

Cade gestured for Red Sky to take the high ground and cover his back. After giving him a long minute to get in place, he tugged on the reins and walked his horse slowly toward the commotion. Once he was close enough, he pulled his pistol and fired a single shot in the air.

The single gunshot was enough to get everyone's attention. The three men stopped laughing but kept their pistols pointed at the girl, and she looked at Cade without lowering her knife.

"Gentlemen, I don't know what's going on here, but this is no way to treat a lady. Why don't you holster your pistols and let's try to settle this without anyone getting hurt," Cade said very calmly, with the hammer of his pistol cocked and pointed in their general direction.

"What should we do, Dale?" the farthest one asked the man in the middle.

"We should do as he says, boys," Dale replied sarcastically as he slowly holstered his pistol. "But keep your hand on your gun."

Cade appreciated that the leader of this rabble had been identified. Now he could address him and just be mindful of the other two.

"Would you like to tell me what she's done to deserve this?" he asked.

"Mister, there's a bounty for this woman, and we're claiming it," Dale began to explain. "We've been chasing her for a country mile and finally caught up to her. So now we're just having a bit of fun before we take her in."

Cade looked at the girl. She seemed a little young to have a bounty on her head, but the fire in her eyes was bold enough to show she was not going out without a fight. "What do these men want you for?" he asked her directly.

"She cut a man… down there," the man farthest from Cade said flippantly while grabbing his crotch and then chuckled at his little joke.

"Is that true?" Cade asked the girl, brushing off the interruption.

The girl's face was covered in dirt and sweat, and her hair was a mess. She looked like she had been on the run for days and was weary of whatever she'd done to deserve this, but she stared at Cade and simply nodded while keeping her knife held firmly.

As much as he didn't like it, Cade didn't know what to do.

When she admitted that she'd done whatever she was accused of, it wasn't necessarily his place to get involved. So he slowly eased the hammer of his pistol and holstered it in an attempt to de-escalate the situation. He was about to motion for Red Sky to come out and for them to continue on their way when the man closest to him finally spoke.

"Dale, that's Cade Wilson," he said shakily.

Everything then changed as the three men perked up and turned to face off with Cade from their respective positions. As they turned, Cade could only wonder how they knew his name and why they looked ready for a fight. But satisfying his curiosity would have to wait, as it became increasingly evident that he had just become their new target.

"If you know who I am, then you might want to just let me by," Cade said to break the silence while also trying to size up which of the three would draw first. "I have no business with you, and I'd just as soon be on my way without any trouble."

He tried to warn them, but could sense the tension was still rising. All three men were now focused on Cade with hands on their pistols, and then Dale licked his dry, chapped lips. "He can't be that fast. Nobody is fast enough to get all three of us," he said with a tone of false conviction.

Cade barely heard the arrow flying loose before he saw it stick in the chest of the man farthest from him. But the arrow didn't kill the man instantly, and he pulled his pistol as a reflex and fired a shot in the dirt before collapsing.

That gunshot snapped everything into place, and there was no turning back now. As their friend collapsed, the other two instinctively pulled their pistols. But Cade was faster, and now he had one less man to worry about.

Cade drew his Colt and hammered two shots into the man closest to him, but didn't lose focus as the man blew back about five feet and fell to the ground. And when Dale's shot at him missed, Cade carefully aimed and fired a round into Dale's right shoulder. The shot caught him in the upper part of his chest—and Dale lowered his arm, groaning in pain.

"Now drop your gun!" Cade ordered, and Dale let it fall from his hand.

"That wound likely won't kill you, but you should know that I still might. It all depends on your willingness to answer some questions. Do you understand?" Cade asked while dismounting his horse. When Dale nodded, Cade started with the most pressing thing on his mind.

"How did you know my name?"

Dale pulled a kerchief from his pocket and held it to his bleeding gunshot wound. "If you're Cade Wilson, then there's a bounty out for you, too."

"Who ordered the bounty?"

"Some fella named Whitmore," Dale continued. "He put out a dispatch to all the big game hunters. The kind that chase very dangerous men. You're worth three thousand dollars dead, and it said you have ten thousand dollars in gold that belongs to whoever kills you."

Cade remembered his conversation with Clark, and that he had mentioned something about a bounty on his head. Now he knew it wasn't just among the shadow riders—some of the deadliest bounty hunters out there would be after him, too.

"Is it true what he said?" Red Sky asked as he came riding up behind Cade.

Cade pursed his lips but nodded just the same. Then he looked over to the girl, who was still just standing there, watching him. She hadn't run off or done anything after the shooting started. Was she waiting there to say something?

Cade turned back to Dale. "Can you ride?" he asked.

"Yeah, I can ride," he replied.

Cade holstered his pistol and pointed the man toward the closest horse. "Then I suggest you leave your gun and ride on. Consider this your lucky day, because it didn't have to be like this. But for some men, the way is always death."

Dale walked slowly and then painfully mounted the horse, using his left arm. And as he rode off to the west, Cade turned his attention back to the wild looking girl still holding a knife.

"Now what are we going to do?" he asked aloud.

•••

Joanna Carter

Cade sensed a little tone of disappointment in his friend. "You should have killed him," Red Sky said very matter-of-factly. "He could tell others what happened here."

"Maybe so," Cade replied. "But at some point, I have to stop killing men just for personal gain or convenience. And thanks for having my back. How did you know to go for that one first?"

"He looked the most anxious," Red Sky said with a smirk. "Besides, I figured you could get the other two."

"Those bastards deserved it," the girl said in a soft voice, but she would not lower her knife.

"You're probably right," Cade said, a little surprised to hear her speak. Now that he was really noticing her, everything about her seemed to be a perfect blend of dangerous beauty.

He guessed she was about five foot six and strong for a girl her size. Her dark hair was pulled back in a single braided ponytail, and the stray frazzled ends perfectly framed her naturally pretty but not-so-innocent face. She had fashioned a bit of rope round her waist to serve as a belt, and her blue paisley dress was stained with dirt and blood—which didn't appear to be hers.

"What's your name?" he asked.

"Joanna Carter," she replied somewhat defensively, as if she didn't want to say it. "I appreciate what you did. And what those men said about me is true, but that bastard deserved it, too," she continued.

"Are you talking about the man you cut?" Cade asked suspiciously.

"Yes. His name is Spencer Carmichael, and his father owns the railroad company my family works for. The Carmichaels think they can own everything and everyone they can buy. One day he went too far, and I pulled his own knife and put it between his legs," she explained while gently waving the knife in her hand. "Now he wants me dead, and I've been on the run ever since."

"I can certainly appreciate your point of view. Working

for someone trying to own everything and everyone seems to be a problem we both have in common," Cade said as he raised an eyebrow and glanced at the two dead bodies lying on the ground. "But hopefully you can find your way to wherever you're going, and it looks like those two might have left you a couple horses and some supplies to help you get by. I wish you the best of luck."

"You're just going to leave me here?" Joanna asked, sounding a little confused. "Where are you going? Because if you're headed west, you're just going to run into more of them."

Cade shook his head. "We're headed north toward Denver. And no, you can't come with us."

"Why not?" she asked defiantly.

"How old are you?" Red Sky asked. "There has to be some place you can go. Because you're a little young to be riding north with strange men."

Joanna slipped the knife into her belt and Cade sensed she was puffing herself up in a display of pride. "I'm sixteen years old, and I just came from the north. I bet I know the way to Denver better than you, and I'm an excellent shot with a rifle. My dad taught me how to shoot. I can take care of myself."

Cade couldn't help but laugh as he mounted his horse. "Is that what you were doing when we found you? Was that you taking care of yourself?" And while he could tell from her expression that she didn't appreciate the joke, it was the truth she needed to hear. "I'm sorry, Joanna. But we can't take you with us, and we've lost enough time already."

He turned to Red Sky and signaled that it was time to move on. As the two men were about to ride off, Joanna walked over to one of the dead men's horses and pulled a Spencer rifle from its saddle strap. She actioned the bolt to load a round into the barrel and took quick aim.

Cade heard the shot and saw the tree branch next to him fall to the ground. He pulled his pistol, reared his horse, and shouted at the girl. "What do you think you're doing? Is this how you repay people for helping you… by shooting them in the back?"

Joanna reloaded and kept the rifle pointed at Cade. "I could have killed you, but I didn't. Now we're even. I wanted to show you that I can shoot. I can take care of myself, and I want to go north with you."

"Why do you want to come with us?" Cade asked. If he was going to entertain the girl's request, he had to know.

"I didn't get a chance to say goodbye to my mother, and I'm worried about her," Joanna said very convincingly. "She still works for the Carmichaels. They are building a rail line from Cheyenne all the way through Colorado. If I could ride back with you, there's a good chance I might see her again," she replied with confidence, and sounding well-informed.

"Take me with you to Denver, or as far north as you'll go, and then we can go our separate ways. Otherwise, I'll just shoot you right now and claim the bounty on you for myself," she said while fixing her aim.

The ungrateful boldness of this girl frustrated Cade. He had saved her life and now she was threatening to shoot him—but then Moira's words ran through his mind: *You will save a girl, and someday she might even be as strong as you.*

"Maybe you were supposed to save her?" Red Sky said aloud. Was he thinking the same thing?

Cade looked to the sun to try and gauge the time. He thought about Sarah and then about Lucy. Both were strong women, but not like this girl. He could tell she was a fighter. Yet the old woman hadn't said anything about taking the girl with them.

The only reason that made sense to him was that she knew the way north and was somehow connected to the railroad. Two things that could help him intercept his Benefactor. Not knowing what else to do, he eventually shrugged at Red Sky and motioned for her to come along—and not just because his choices were limited to shooting her or giving in to her ultimatum.

"Well, come on then," he said begrudgingly, holstering his pistol. "I'm Cade, and this is Red Sky, and daylight's wasting."

CHAPTER 6

Denver

Joseph Whitmore II had a reputation among his peers as an ambitious man; he'd been casually reminded of this character trait many times.

He was also quick to remind any critics that he learned everything from his father when it came to the expansion of his landholdings—take what he wanted and figure out the details later. It could take years to argue over who owned what, and by then he could just sell it off, be it land, cattle, or his interests in the railroad companies laying track across the wide-open landscape.

Eventually, he knew these railroad companies and the United States government would be interested in his land because there were only so many ways to carve new trails that connected Denver to Pueblo to Santa Fe—and then through the New Mexico Territory and on to California along the southern border. And when they came to him to build on his land, he would make them pay.

"How long do they expect us to wait here?" he asked Bruce Aker, the businessman and legal arbitrary who had brought him to Denver to meet with Victor Carmichael and the governor of Colorado.

"Just another day, I'm sure, Mr. Whitmore," Bruce replied. "Even with train travel, unforeseen challenges can add time to make it here. Please be patient. We're about to make a deal that's going to make you a very rich man."

"That's easy for you to say." Whitmore replied with a side-eye glance. "You're brokering part of this deal. You stand as much to gain as I do, my friend. And as long as we can prove that the best way to connect Colorado with Texas in the New Mexico Territory flows through my land, then we'll all be happy."

"Well, until then, I suggest we take advantage of the hotel amenities and find a good place to eat around here," Bruce said, in an attempt to soothe the situation.

Whitmore snapped his fingers at the barmaid. "Bring us another round of whiskey and tell the hotel manager we'd like a word."

A few moments later the barmaid delivered the drinks, and she was followed by a fidgety man in a tight suit. "Hello, Mr. Whitmore, and what can I do for you today?"

"Where can we get a good steak around here?" Whitmore asked.

"Well, sir, we do offer a fine supper here at the Frontier Hotel. But the Crystal Star is just down the street and they'll have something on the menu you should enjoy," the hotel manager said.

"Thank you kindly. That is all," Whitmore said with a wave of his hand.

As the hotel manager walked away, another gentleman at the bar turned to acknowledge the men at the corner table.

"Hello kind sirs, my name is Sinclair," he said while offering up his hand as he approached. "Did I hear the manager address one of you as Mr. Whitmore?"

Whitmore looked at the man with suspicious curiosity. He could tell the man was British just from his accent, and because his father still had ties with the old country. "Yes, that's me. Do you know my family?"

"Oh no," Sinclair replied. "But I do know about the bounty you put on a man by the name of Mr. Wilson that's worth quite a bit of money, and it's my vocation to stay informed of such things."

Hearing that name caused a wrinkled line to form across Whitmore's forehead. Knowing that Viper was still out there after taking his gold and killing his revered samurai cowboys was enough to make him drink the full glass of whiskey in his hand.

"Anyway," Sinclair continued, "I heard you might be heading to Denver and thought I would try to meet up with you here."

"I appreciate that you have an interest in the bounty I put on that treacherous scoundrel, but what is your interest in me?" Whitmore asked while gritting his teeth.

"Well, sir, I assure you that my interests lie solely in

finding this man for you and collecting on his death. And it's sort of a calculated gamble on my part. See, I think everyone from Kansas to California will be after that man, and that he will eventually be driven up this way. He might even want to come after you, knowing you put the bounty on him," Sinclair said.

Whitmore gestured to the man sitting alone in silence at the opposite table. "I assure you, Mr. Sinclair, that man is a samurai warrior from Japan. His name is Toshi, and as my personal bodyguard he is sworn to protect me with his life. If the man we once knew as Viper decides to come after me, we will be ready."

"Just Sinclair, if you please. Mr. Sinclair is my father, and he's a wretched old soul," the bounty hunter corrected. "But I absolutely agree, as I will be ready, too," he replied, looking at a spiderweb in the sunlit corner of the window. "It's a fairly simple strategy, really."

•••

Campfire Stories

Joanna was tired and very hungry, but she wasn't going to complain. She had been riding for days on the first saddled horse she could jump on after stabbing Spencer. Now she was just grateful to have someone else to ride with—especially someone as deadly as these two men.

As she followed behind them, she appreciated not having

to worry about being alone. Joanna also thought about how she might see her mother again, and riding north with Cade and Red Sky was her best shot. Hopefully, she could sneak her way into the work camp and convince her mom to leave the family they had been serving all these years. There had to be a better life away from the Carmichaels, as she knew there was no way she could go back.

But for now, the grumble in her stomach could not be ignored. So she tried a subtle tactic to appeal to her new companions.

"We should probably find a place to camp. It will be getting dark soon," she said to Cade, who ignored her.

Joanna spoke up a little louder. "If we're heading toward Pueblo, we should be there by tomorrow. From there, it's a few more days to Denver. I don't know how much farther we're going today, but I can lead us back to the place I camped last night. It's tucked away in a little wash with some water for the horses."

"That sounds like a good plan. Show us the way," Cade replied and whistled to Red Sky in the lead.

Joanna sensed this was an opportunity for her to offer something of value to her travel companions, so she followed Cade's direction and took the lead along with Red Sky. In less than an hour, she guided them back to a spot with a little pool of water and a fire ring of ashes from where she slept last night.

They made camp without much of a word, but Joanna sensed they were happy to have a place to rest and eat. "We'll have to ration our food a bit," Cade said while inspecting their supplies. "We only packed for two."

Joanna was grateful to hear him say that, because she'd be happy to have any food tonight. It was also nice to hear Cade say "we" and consider her as part of the group. She started to think that maybe he wasn't a bad man—and maybe shooting at him wasn't the best way to get his attention.

After a modest supper of jerked beef and a few carrots, Joanna found herself watching the two men through the flames and the smoke of their fire. Everyone sat in silence, just as they had while moving about and making camp.

"What happened today is likely a sign of things to come," Cade finally said. "I just want you to know that this journey will be long and dangerous. If you want out, I'll understand. Because I don't want anyone else to get hurt because of my past and what I've done."

Joanna looked at Red Sky and then back at Cade. She knew what he was saying, but not why he was saying it, or everything he had done to have a bounty on his head. From what she had witnessed of him so far, she could only imagine that it was pretty bad and something else about gold. But she really didn't have many other options—she was also on the run and riding with him was better than riding alone.

"I'm not afraid," she said ardently. "If it's all the same to you, I'll keep riding with you."

Joanna caught Red Sky looking at her as he gave a nod. His confidence in her was a welcome gesture to end the day.

Then Cade changed the subject with a curious question. "Alright then, we'll head out tomorrow and put in a good ride. Now how about you tell us a story, Joanna?"

"What do you want to know?" she asked, a little bewildered.

"Well, for starters, you could tell us how you learned to shoot like that?" he asked.

Joanna didn't know how to answer at first, but the dancing glow of orange and yellow flames helped trigger some memories.

"Working for the railroad was a way of life for my family," she began. "I was born in Pennsylvania, and my father served in the Union army during the war. And even then, he told me that his job was helping build and repair railroad track.

"After the war, my father worked for railroad companies that were expanding west. He was a surveyor, and he worked with the crew that mapped and cleared the land ahead of the crews laying track. My mother and me would work in the service tents mostly cooking and serving the men as we moved slowly across the country.

"Over the years we went from Indiana to Illinois, and then from Iowa to Wyoming. My father worked for the Central Pacific company that was building what he called 'the transcontinental railroad.' He was very proud of his work, and my father would tell me what a big deal it was that there was train track that connected California to New York, from coast to coast, and that we were part of it," she said with a smile.

"But as a soldier, my father also knew how to shoot. And when I was ten years old, he taught me how to shoot a rifle. We would also go out hunting for a little something for ourselves, as most of the food we served the work crews wasn't very good.

"My mother educated me for years, because she grew up

in a boarding school. She was hard on me to learn because she wanted me to marry well and have a good life. My father was very proud of me, and he was hard on me in other ways. But he raised me to be tough and said I was a better shot than he ever was."

Joanna looked a Cade for a moment and noticed he was smiling for the first time. It was a pleasant smile, and something she didn't necessarily expect from a man who appeared dangerous and unapproachable. But there must have been something he appreciated about her story. "Go on," he said.

She looked over to Red Sky, and he also seemed content to listen to her chatter on—so she did.

"My father eventually went to work for the Carmichael family. They were expanding the railroad into Kansas and then Colorado, and they hired my father for his experience. And just like before, my mother and I went to work for them, too. But since the Carmichaels started using immigrant labor to lay railroad tracks, we basically traveled with them and worked as their hired servants.

"Then, one night, my father was playing cards in a saloon in Cheyenne. The sheriff said he was caught cheating when someone shot him dead. That man's name was Remy Chandler, and I will never forget it," she said bitterly. It was a very painful memory, and she didn't know why she brought it up. But now that it was out there, she continued.

"I watched that man lie to the judge. Him and his two friends. They said it was self-defense when they accused my father of cheating and that he was the first to draw his gun. But my father was a well-respected man. He had his vices—whiskey and gambling—but with God as my witness, I know that he would never cheat at cards or shoot someone over a game. The pistol he carried around was just for protection, even though he told me that he'd never shot anyone. Not even during the war.

"Then that bastard smiled at me when the judge set him free. I watched as Remy and his friends rode off, and I could hear them laughing. That was almost a year ago, and I swore on that day that if I ever saw that man again… I would get justice for my father," she said scornfully.

It had been a while since she had conjured up the images of those men and that event, and the anger that came with them caused her to pause for a moment.

"Sorry to hear about your father," Cade said through the glow of the flames. "I know what it's like to lose your family and want revenge. We both do," he continued with an acknowledging look to Red Sky. "So what happened between you and the man you cut?"

Joanna was surprised by the question, and she cleared her throat and swallowed hard. She had never spoken about what happened that day to anyone—the day she ran out of the Carmichael family tent, covered in Spencer's blood. But she also felt like everything about what happened that day was bottled up inside her.

She began to rub her fingers with her thumbs. It was a nervous habit, and her mother always teased her about it. It was something that always gave her away when she was lying or anxious about something.

But after a deep breath, Joanna brushed some wild strands of hair from her face and looked at these two men. As she considered how to tell this story, she decided that it didn't really matter that she didn't know them. Instead, it almost made it better that she didn't, and if she was going to ride with these men, then she thought they should know her side of the story about why those bounty hunters were after her.

"After my father died, my mom cried for three days. When she finally stopped, she was just never the same. She always had a distant look in her eyes, and she seemed more than willing to just take care of the Carmichaels, who had sort of adopted us," she began. "My mom said we were lucky they were taking care of us when they eventually stopped paying us. I guess with my father gone they thought they were doing us a favor.

"As we always worked with the family either on the train or in their big tent, Spencer Carmichael had taken notice of me for some time. A lot of men took notice of me, and I always hated the way they stare, but Spencer was different. He was a few years older than me, and sometimes he would try and catch me alone and put his hands on me. But I never welcomed his advances.

"It's not that Spencer wasn't handsome, and my father had always told me they were a good family with a lot of money. But that didn't matter to me, because I liked another boy who was part of the work crew. Tommy was his name," she said.

"When Spencer saw me with Tommy one day, he had one of the rail bosses move Tommy up the line to do demolition work. A few days later, I heard that Tommy had died in a dynamite accident, and I never forgave Spencer for that."

Joanna looked back into the fire and took a casual moment

of silence for Tommy. Seeing his smiling face after a long day's work was how she always wanted to remember him.

"But that never stopped Spencer from coming after me," she continued, rubbing her fingers again. "And one afternoon, he was drunk on whiskey when I came into the family's tent to prepare the table for supper. The tent was bigger than everyone else's, and it was where we would all eat and sleep, when Victor, his father, and other members of the Carmichael family would come to the front of the line. But on that day, we were alone in the tent together and he came at me."

Joanna paused and looked away from the fire for a moment. Everything she was about to say next was both embarrassing and personal. The lump in her throat sank into her belly and she felt a little nauseous. Thankfully, she had eaten something, or she might have gotten sick. But she felt comfortable enough to tell them after furiously rubbing her fingers again. And when she found her resolve, she continued.

"First, Spencer came up behind me and grabbed my wrist. He kept going on about how pretty I was, and he wanted to know why I didn't like him. When I told him that I would never be with him and that I blamed him for what happened to Tommy, he slapped me across the face," she said and stopped to touch her cheek. Somehow she could still feel the sting of his hand hitting her all over again.

"Then he pulled my wrist and tripped me to the ground." She cleared her throat, then continued. "Before I could get up, he jumped on top of me and pinned me down while I tried to fight him off. He grabbed both of my wrists to stop me from punching at him. When I screamed for him to get off of me, he just laughed and said I should stop fighting. He was so close that I could smell the sweat in his clothes and the whiskey on his breath.

"When he did let go of my wrist, he had a wild look in his eyes as he reached down to unbuckle his belt. But while he was doing that, I stopped hitting him and reached down to his waist. My hand found the handle of the hunting knife he wore on the opposite side of his pistol holster," she said, using her hand to imitate the moment.

"When he reared himself up on his knees, I could tell that he wasn't going to stop, and he just laughed again as if there was nothing I could do about it," she said coldly. Remembering that moment, her eyes narrowed and her tone darkened as she unintentionally emphasized the burning memory of that afternoon and the emotions that were full of humiliation and spite.

"But what he didn't know was that I had already pulled his knife. And when he saw it in my hand, he wasn't laughing anymore. Because that's when I stuck him," she said, making a forward stabbing motion with her hand. "I stuck him in the place he was so eager to show me. And then he screamed like I've never heard a man scream before. When he rolled off me, I could see the blood on the knife, and on my dress, and he wouldn't stop screaming. Then I could hear voices outside coming to find out what was going on, and that's when I got up and ran out of the tent. I ran because I stuck Spencer Carmichael with his own knife, which I still have," she said, tapping the handle of the knife sticking out of her rope belt.

Joanna looked down at her dress. It was a simple blue

dress and similar to other simple dresses she'd worn as a servant for years. But this dress was stained with sweat, dirt, and blood—and she hated it. She hated how it looked, what it stood for, and everything it reminded her of.

"'Get her!' was the last thing I heard Spencer say as I jumped on that horse over there and rode off as fast as I could. I didn't know where I was going or what to do, but I knew it would be foolish to stick around or try to go back. There was no way he was going to let me live after what I did to him, even though he deserved it. And I knew that his family wouldn't have me back either."

Joanna felt her chest swell with all kinds of emotions. She was still very upset about what had happened and full of resentment for what Spencer had done, but she felt a little relieved to have shared her story. As she looked at these two men, she also felt some respect toward her in their glances.

"Then what?" Cade asked.

"I just kept heading south, trying to figure out what to do and where to go. I didn't have any money, and I had to steal some food from a store in Pueblo. Some men chased after me for about a day, but I haven't seem them since," she said and then let out a deep sigh. "I thought if I headed south far enough that maybe I could find some church or something to take me in and let me hide out for a while. But then those bounty hunters started chasing me, and the rest you already know."

Telling her story felt good, and not just because of the way Cade and Red Sky were looking at her. They hadn't said a word while she told her story, and they genuinely listened without judging her or apologizing for Spencer's behavior like her mother probably would have. Her mother was always making excuses for him or talking about how nothing was ever his fault.

"Thanks again, for helping me," Joanna said sincerely. "I know you didn't have to bring me along with you, but I promise not to slow you down, and I really am a pretty good shot with that rifle."

"I bet you are, Joanna Carter," Cade said with a tip of his hat. Then he leaned back against his blanket and closed his eyes. "Keep pointing us toward Denver and we'll be just fine."

•••

Trinidad

The twilight sky was filling with stars as Marshal Blackburn and his deputy tended a small fire. After taking the mountain pass from Rocky Creek, they were dry camping just north of a small town across the Colorado border.

"How are those beans coming along, Swifty?" Blackburn asked his partner while he cooked their supper.

"Anytime now," he replied. "They needed a little more water."

Then a voice cried from outside the glow of their camp. "Help me, please."

Bill set the pan down on a cooking rock and pulled his pistol. "Who is that? What do you want?" he hollered back into the shadows.

"Settle down, Swifty," Blackburn said to ease his deputy. "Save your shot unless you need to. No sense in bringing attention to ourselves. Whoever's out there doesn't sound like much of a threat."

A few moments later, a lone rider came into view, and he was slightly hunched over in the saddle.

"Stop right there!" the deputy shouted as he cocked back the hammer of his pistol.

"Please don't shoot! I need help," the man replied. "I've been shot in the shoulder and I can't raise my arm."

"Come slowly into the light and keep your hands where we can see them," Blackburn said, and the rider did as he was told. Once in the light, the marshal stepped over, grabbed the reins of the rider's horse, and took a closer look. "That looks like a gunshot alright. So tell me, mister, who are you, and who shot you?"

The rider slipped slowly out of the saddle and slid down to the ground. He walked gingerly over to the fire to sit down, then began to answer the marshal's questions.

"My name is Dale Harris," the rider said. "I was chasing a bounty with my two partners… a girl some rich family wanted alive. That's when we came across Cade Wilson. He's the one that shot me. Him and his Indian friend killed my partners."

Blackburn perked up. "Cade Wilson, you say. Are you sure it was him? How long ago was this?" he asked as he shot a glance to his deputy and motioned for him to lower his pistol.

"Yes. It was him alright. He's a very dangerous man," Dale replied and then turned to the marshal in desperation. "Do you have any whiskey?" he asked, still holding his wounded shoulder.

The marshal shook his head. "Sorry, friend. We can't help you there. But you say he had an Indian friend, too?"

"Yeah, I don't know who he was. He looked Comanche," Dale said. "Look, mister. I really need some help here. Have either of you ever cut a bullet out?"

"That I can help you with," the marshal replied as he pulled a knife from his belt and moved the blade toward the fire. "But before we do, are you absolutely sure the man that shot you was Cade Wilson?"

"Yes. He was ready to pull his pistol the moment we said his name. This all happened just a few hours ago," Dale said, pointing in the direction he had come from.

The marshal studied the man and arrived at an intuitive conclusion. He sounded quite impatient and exhausted, but not like a man who was lying.

"I know it was him. He was wearing a brown coat… the likes of which I had never seen before. And he had two swords strapped to his back. But his big mistake was letting me live, because I'm going to get that son of a bitch. Now can you please cut this bullet out. I need to stop the bleeding," he said urgently.

"Sorry about you and your partners. That's some unfortunate news, friend," the marshal said very coolly. "I could try and cut that bullet out, but it's going to hurt like hell, and we'll still need to get you to a doctor. But there is an alternative," he said as he stepped toward Dale.

"Alternative? What is that?" Dale asked as his eyes darted between the two men.

"It means that if nobody else knows that you crossed paths with Cade Wilson, then nobody ever will," Blackburn replied as he cut Dale's throat in one stroke with his knife.

Bill finally holstered his pistol. "You know what that means, boss?"

"Yes I do, Swifty," Blackburn replied as Dale's throat bled out in front of them and his body fell to the ground.

"While every other big game hunter is searching east or south, our target is heading north. Just as we suspected," he said with a smile. "And we're right on his tail."

CHAPTER 7

Crossing the Bridge

Cade and his companions headed north, and they avoided any trails that may attract unwanted attention. To keep their horses fresh, they switched between hard riding when the terrain permitted, and walking when it required a more sure-footed pace.

Around midday they came across a little creek and stopped to rest. It was a good time to reflect on how far they'd come and plot out the remainder of the day. Since his companions had heard about Whitmore and the gold from the bounty hunter, Cade also thought it might be his turn to share some stories about his past and why he was riding to Denver.

Cade spoke about his life and samurai training at the fort. Then he tried to explain how he met his Benefactor and his sensei, and he thought back to when he'd told the Johnson family these stories. Joanna seemed very interested in hearing more about Toshi and the way of the samurai, but he stopped short of telling them about Scorpion and Falcon—or any details about the gold or his time in Rocky Creek. But as he concluded his tale, he emphasized how important it was to reach his Benefactor away from the fort, when he would be the least protected. It was the only way Cade believed he'd get a chance to reason with him.

When they mounted their horses to continue their journey, Joanna stayed closer to Cade than she had the previous day and asked so many questions about his swords and training that she reminded him of Eli. And with her questions' random persistence, she eventually tripped into territory that was a bit more personal.

"Have you ever been in love?" Joanna asked.

"You have a very curious nature," Cade replied without addressing the topic. He could tell it was an innocent question, even if he didn't know why she asked it. But he wasn't prepared to lay bare his feelings to her or anyone else. Not today.

"Well, I've never been friends with a strange man before. I just thought I'd ask," she said.

Cade nodded but still didn't answer. He found some odd wisdom in her words. He had never been friends with a strange girl before, so it made sense that he'd never been asked about matters of the heart. But his silence seemed enough for Joanna to take the hint, and for the rest of the afternoon she just rode quietly beside him.

By late afternoon, Cade could see the outline of a town on the distant horizon. "Is that Pueblo?" he asked Joanna, and she nodded. "Good," he said to acknowledge the surrounding landmarks without needing to know more. This was as close as he wanted to get, so they maintained their course until they arrived at the banks of a steady-moving river.

"You didn't say anything about crossing a river," Cade said to Joanna while trying to estimate the breadth and depth of the new challenge before them.

"I'm sorry. I forgot about the river," Joanna said with a flush of embarrassment in her cheeks. "I went through town because I was desperate for food, but now I remember riding across a bridge."

Red Sky looked at Cade. "It would be hard to cross here," he said plainly. "The water is fast and deep. We'll have to go downstream."

"But for how far?" Cade asked, knowing there was no easy way to answer. "We could be backtracking for days."

"I don't think we should go into town," Joanna said. "Someone might recognize me, and there could be trouble."

Cade just smiled at the girl. She was young and spirited, and her decision-making showed why she was a survivor. But she still had a lot to learn about being hunted and the dangers that lurked around every corner. "I think we all have a pretty good reason not to go into town," he replied.

"We could cross the bridge in the dark," Red Sky said. "Less chance of being seen."

Cade removed his hat and ran his fingers through his hair—and the wrinkled lines that creased his forehead didn't subside as he thought through what his companion had just said. Crossing the bridge at night still meant going into town, and going into town would definitely increase their chances of being seen. But the alternative was likely worse. If they lost another day or two trying to cross the river, it could mean that they make it all the way to Denver for nothing.

"Let's wait until dark and cross at the bridge," he finally said. "We can wrap our blankets around us and try to disguise ourselves. And if we split up instead of riding all together, maybe it will draw less attention."

The plan was risky, but they all agreed and looked for a nice place to rest and wait for a few hours. While they sat by the river's edge, Cade gave Joanna a stick and asked her to draw what she could remember about getting to the bridge in the dirt.

When the sun dipped below the horizon, they mounted up and cautiously made their way into town. Cade was surprised to discover that Pueblo was more densely populated than the smaller towns he was more accustomed to, and the scent of woodsmoke mixed with the smell of industry.

He was also unfamiliar with the layout, so he looked to Joanna to help them navigate through the darkened streets and in between the buildings. But once the bridge was in sight, he told his companions to stop so they could survey the scene.

Much of the landscape was just as Joanna had described, but there were some other details she had forgotten. Oil lamps illuminated the four corners of the bridge on both sides and the river walk leading up to it. There were only a few trees on both sides of the river, so there was limited cover. Only a few townsfolk were still milling about when it should have been suppertime, but enough for them to be seen.

Cade considered all this and thought of everything that could possibly go wrong. The obvious conclusion was that crossing this bridge unnoticed was going to be a bigger challenge than he had anticipated.

"It's time to split up," he said looking at Red Sky. "You and Joanna should go first. It may look out of place if either of you is traveling alone. Once you make it across, I will follow behind you and we'll meet up on the other side," he concluded and confirmed the plan.

Red Sky nodded and the two pulled ahead while Cade stayed back in the shadows to watch. As they made their way across, two people were leading a one-horse wagon across the bridge from the opposite direction. But these people didn't pay his friends any mind, and Red Sky and Joanna blended right in. When they reached the other side, Joanna looked back to signal they were okay. So far, everything was going according to plan.

Before Cade made his way to the bridge, he caught sight of four cowboys on horses coming up the street. They were headed to the bridge, and he was likely to cross paths with them at the same time. He quickly figured he had two options: he could either quicken his pace and get ahead of them, or hold back and try to let them to pass ahead of him. Being caught out in the open was an awkward spot to be in, but he didn't like the idea of having four men behind him. So he pulled back a little and decided to follow them instead.

The four cowboys were talking loudly and laughing among themselves, and they didn't really pay any attention to him. But Cade couldn't tell what they were talking about as he continued to put some space in between them before following their lead. He was back about fifty feet but still close enough to hear them laughing about something one of them did. It didn't matter. As long as he could keep a safe distance behind them, he would be across the river, and they would be none the wiser.

As the four riders finished crossing and turned to the right, Cade glanced at his companions waiting for him in the distance. What he hadn't seen was the large man who had emerged from the shadows on the left and was now blocking his path.

"Hello there," the man said while addressing him very casually. "My name is Marshal Blackburn, and I'd like to have a word with you."

Cade didn't like the look of this guy, but once again, he was caught out in the open and in the middle of town. And with those four cowboys still within earshot, he thought this wasn't the time to draw more attention to himself.

"What is it you want?" he replied.

"I think we both know what I want, Mr. Wilson," the marshal replied as he took aim with his double-barrel shotgun. "You are Cade Wilson, I suspect," he said before taking a moment to spit.

"I also figured that we might catch up with you at the river crossing. And just so we further understand each other, my deputy is near that building just over my shoulder with a rifle trained on you, and he has you dead to rights. They don't call him 'Bullseye' Bill Swift for nothing, so I'd advise you don't try anything, or he'll start shooting."

Cade felt vulnerable and foolish, and he studied the marshal while thinking through his best options. But since he couldn't make out where the deputy was hiding, he could only assume by the look of this man that he wasn't bluffing. So he decided to go along for now and showed his hands—and he hoped that if this was a legal misunderstanding, he'd have an opportunity to explain.

"Good. Now why don't the two of us make our way to that building over there and talk things over in private," the marshal continued and motioned with a tip of his head that Cade should take the lead. "No sense in involving others in our business, including your Indian friend and the girl. We'll leave them out of this, for now, if you cooperate."

Assuming the marshal was an agent of the law, and given his recent entanglements in Rocky Creek, the last thing he wanted to do was gun down a marshal and his deputy. He was in enough trouble as it was, but Cade was definitely curious as to why the marshal referenced Red Sky and Joanna. How did he know about them?

He surveyed the building the marshal was directing him toward, which looked like some sort of factory. There were smokestacks billowing the results of whatever was being manufactured inside, and there were sounds of activity coming from within. Cade approached the building with the marshal trailing behind; he walked toward two large doors that were slightly ajar with a dimly lit glow coming from inside.

When they reached the building, Cade saw a man emerge from the shadows with a rifle pointed at him—just as the marshal had described. "Easy now, mister. And keep those hands in front of you," he said.

"How about we go inside," the marshal instructed as he

dismounted his horse and pointed the shotgun back in Cade's direction. "Nice and slow now… get off your horse."

Cade did as he was instructed, although it seemed odd that they would be going inside this factory instead of a sheriff's office. He didn't like this one bit, and recalculated his options if this started going sideways. These men carried themselves like professionals, and he figured it was going to take some element of surprise or a moment of lapse if he was going to gain the upper hand.

The deputy pushed one of the big doors open and motioned for Cade to enter. As they walked in, there were a few men working and tending to something that looked like a smelting pot. Whatever was inside that pot smelled very industrial, and it produced heat and an orange glow that lit up the room. Besides the hot metal, some oil lamps were hanging from the posts and rafters.

A burly-looking fella who must have been the foreman approached. "What do you want? You shouldn't be in here," he said, clearly surprised that Cade and the marshal had just walked inside their place of work.

"Why don't y'all take a break?" the marshal said without seeming to pay any mind to the foreman or his authority. "We have some business to discuss. It won't be but a moment."

Cade could see the confusion on the faces of the men at work, but none of them looked willing to challenge the marshal. So they all quietly stopped what they were doing, laid down their tools, and shuffled outside.

"Looks like we're alone now," Cade said to the deputy, who still had a rifle pointed in his direction. "I can assure you that I'm not looking for any trouble with the law. So how about you lower that rifle and we can discuss whatever is on your mind—"

A whip cracked and coiled painfully around Cade's neck before he could finish his thought. The attack had caught him by surprise, and he struggled to breathe as the whip strangled him. As he tried to reach for his neck, the whip tightened even more and he fell to knees. The lack of air was dulling his vision and other senses, and it was hard to think about how to defend himself while he was doing his best not to panic.

"Who said we were the law?" the marshal asked, sounding amused at Cade's naivety. "Now that I've introduced you to my whip, I'm going to loosen up ol' Widowmaker and give you a breath. But don't try anything, or I'll twist her back and snap your neck."

Cade could feel the whip loosen just a little, and he quickly took in a deep breath to fill his burning lungs. Suddenly blackness wasn't all he could see, but he still didn't have his wits about him enough to fight these two men.

"You're a wanted man, Cade Wilson," the voice of the marshal rang out through the blood pulsing in his ears. "There's a bounty for proof of your death, but we're also interested in the gold you should have in your possession. Now where would that be?"

Cade didn't have the air in his lungs to answer the question, but he could hear the the deputy speak up from somewhere behind him.

"Maybe he hid it somewhere?"

"Maybe so, Swifty. But why don't you go out and fetch

his saddlebags just to be sure," the marshal replied. "And if anyone tries to stop you… shoot 'em."

•••

Haitse

Joanna could only watch along with Red Sky as Cade was ushered into a building that looked like a factory.

"Who are those men?" Joanna asked while trying to muffle any sound of fear in her voice.

"I don't know, but it doesn't look good," Red Sky replied with a grim look on his face. "They look like bounty hunters."

"We should hide," she continued. "They look serious, and there might be more where they came from."

"No, we're not just going to leave our friend," he replied sternly in an attempt to settle her down. "I want to see what's going on in there," he added pensively.

"Cover me from behind that tree," he said and pointed to a spot that would make a good vantage point for Joanna to set up with her rifle. Then Red Sky pointed to a series of windows on the building's upper level. "I'll get on the roof and take a look from up there."

Joanna looked from the tree to the roofline, and Red Sky's plan made sense. But then she imagined the worst. "What happens if they come out shooting?"

"Shoot back," Red Sky replied with a chuckle. "But don't hit me."

"I've never really shot anyone before," Joanna confessed. Her cheeks blushed; the tough exterior she tried to present still had its cracks. But she knew it wasn't time to be prideful. It was time to be honest.

Red Sky looked her in the eye and Joanna sensed that he already knew the truth, but he believed in her anyway. "Me neither," he said with a smile. "I prefer arrows and blades."

He hesitated to resurvey the situation. "Just cover me until I have time to take a look. And if anyone comes out shooting, shoot back and give me a chance to get out of there." He gave Joanna a pat on the shoulder then crept into the shadows.

Joanna felt somewhat assured while she tied up her horse and grabbed her rifle. Red Sky's sense of humor reminded her of her father. Just as dry, but he used it well when she was upset. She still didn't know if she was ready for this, but being part of this group and contributing was also something she wanted to prove to herself.

It was a short walk to the tree, and the trunk was just wide enough to hide behind. Once she felt situated, she caught a glimpse of Red Sky making his way to the building without being seen.

He eventually reached the corner of the building where there was a ladder to access the roof, but now he was out in the open. The men who must have been working inside were now standing around outside, and they began pointing at Red Sky while talking among themselves.

Joanna couldn't hear what the men were saying, but from the tone of their voices they sounded pretty frustrated with their situation. That's when one of the big doors swung open and a man emerged with a pistol in his right hand and a kerosene lantern held high in his left. With the big door wide-open, she was able to look inside and was surprised by what she saw.

Cade was on his hands and knees, and there was a large man standing over him with something that looked like a rope around Cade's neck. It was not what she expected at all. Seeing Cade on the ground, and Red Sky about to be found out, she knew she had to do something but feared she had to choose which one to help.

Nobody had come out shooting, but she knew she couldn't wait for the man with the pistol to see Red Sky on the roof. If he did, he'd probably shoot him, or worse—they would both get lynched. So she steadied her rifle and took aim. The first thing she could get a sight on was the lantern in the man's left hand. And just before he turned to see what the workers were pointing at, Joanna squeezed the trigger.

The bullet must have pierced the tin bottom of the lamp as kerosene splattered all over the man holding it. Joanna hid behind the tree as the workers all scattered at the sound of the gunshot.

The man turned and pointed his pistol at the dark. He was trying to aim at wherever her shot may have come from, but the kerosene must have blurred his vision. He dropped the lantern and rubbed his eyes, with his pistol still aimed at nothing. Then he slowly backed into the building.

Red Sky was on the roof, looking down through the windows. And if the man with the pistol was going back inside, then maybe there was a way to keep him in there. So she reloaded, took aim at another lantern hanging from a post just inside the door, and squeezed the trigger again.

•••

Fire & Darkness

Inside the building, Cade heard the first rifle shot and the deputy cursing whoever shot at him. From the sound of his footsteps, the deputy was sliding his feet as he backpedaled into the factory.

Then he heard a second shot, and a lantern that must have been hanging from a post tumbled down and the glass shattered on the floor. Cade watched the fuel in the lamp spill out onto the floor, and the kerosene puddle that continued to grow.

But that was the least of his worries as Cade felt the whip tighten again around his neck. "Don't you think about going anywhere," he heard the marshal say, then he called out to his deputy.

"Who's shooting at us, Swifty?" the marshal shouted out loud enough for anyone to hear. It didn't sound like he appreciated being on the other side of a fight.

"I don't know, boss. It must be the Indian or the girl," the deputy replied. "But I can't see. My eyes are burning."

Cade could hear the marshal and his deputy continue to talk over him about his friends, and he gathered that Joanna must have shot the lantern. It wasn't much, but it could be the distraction he needed to try and free himself. But the coiled tightness of the whip around his neck had not changed, so he closed his eyes and focused on taking a slow, deep breath to keep his wits about him.

When he reopened his eyes, Cade could see the puddle of kerosene seeping under some crates and canisters next to the post. While the deputy was still retreating but looking outside to see who was shooting at him, he had blindly stepped back to where he was now standing in the fuel. And that's when Cade saw the small bead of flame slowly drip from the lamp into the puddle of fuel and ignite it.

The wave of flame immediately spread across the floor like a pool of fire, and then some of it jumped up the deputy's left leg. He screamed as parts of his pants caught fire, and he tried to pat it out with his hand. But whatever he did, it had the opposite effect—and in less than a second, his left arm went off like a fuse, and suddenly the deputy was engulfed in flame.

"Swifty!" the marshal yelled out as his friend ran in circles and randomly fired his pistol. "The river! Run to the river!"

Watching the deputy on fire as he ran out of the building was the next distraction Cade needed. The fire around them engulfed anything the fuel touched, and it spread so quickly that the marshal stepped away from it and close enough for Cade to reach him. He seized the opportunity and flexed his wrist to release his stinger. And with a quick lunge, he threw an unbalanced punch but stuck the venomous spike into the marshal's leg with all the strength he could muster.

The marshal was a large man, but Cade's punch was

enough to knock him off-balance. And as the paralyzing toxin did its work, he groaned and fell to the ground.

Cade was still on his hands and knees, and he hoped his enemy was no longer a threat. As he desperately clawed at his neck, a shadowy figure emerged from above. As the shadow came into focus, Cade could see it was Red Sky. How he got there didn't matter as the two of them tried to free the coiled whip from his throat. But as Red Sky twisted the whip, it got even tighter, and Cade slapped his foot to stop.

He made a circle motion with his finger, and Red Sky twisted the whip in the other direction. The whip loosened, and Cade's first big breath was a mix of dust and smoke that burned his throat. He coughed violently as Red Sky helped remove the rest of the coil, then helped him to his feet.

"What did you do to me?" the marshal asked, groaning and still lying on the ground.

Cade, barely able to speak, just flexed his wrist and retracted his stinger. "You're temporarily paralyzed," he replied. "Hopefully it will wear off before this place burns to the ground."

As the two men emerged from the building, they found themselves somewhat surrounded as Cade continued to cough from the smoke. The workers, the four riders from the bridge, and some townsfolk had been drawn to all the commotion.

But nobody tried to stop them. Instead, the people gathered outside the building had started to organize a fire brigade, while others just stood and stared at Cade and Red Sky as they walked through the crowd. So they pushed their way through and Cade saw his beloved horse standing there, waiting for him. The horse was stomping his feet like he was ready to be done with this town, too.

Cade grabbed the reins and climbed in the saddle. Now sitting above the crowd, he could see Joanna waving to them—she was already on her horse and waiting with Red Sky's. As his friend ran off to mount, he took one last look behind him. The townsfolk had formed a human chain, passing buckets down as the fire was growing inside the factory. Then Cade noticed the shadow of the marshal starting to sit up from the soft glow inside.

"That's Cade Wilson. Somebody shoot him!" the marshal shouted to anyone that was listening. It was the last thing Cade heard him say before something inside the factory must have reacted violently to the fire—and a loud boom produced a fiery ball of smoke that billowed from the open doors and windows.

The urgency of forming the human chain resumed, but that's when Cade heard the first gunshot. Then a second. Someone was shooting at him, and he didn't know who or where from. But he wasn't going to stick around to find out, and so he pointed his horse north and into the darkness of an unfamiliar road.

A moment later, Red Sky and Joanna came right up behind him and the three were riding as hard as they could when a few other shots followed from the distance. But whoever fired them wasn't in pursuit, and they pressed on as fire bells rang out throughout the town.

Riding into the cold night, they followed a well-traveled road to put as much distance behind them as possible. Cade hoped they were heading in the right direction, but it was hard to tell. The one thing he did know for certain was that his whereabouts were no longer a secret—and that meant the fire they were running from probably wasn't as daunting as the one they were headed into.

CHAPTER 8

Half-Moon

A frigid wind was blowing over the mountains, and the half-moon in the cloudless sky offered little light to navigate across open terrain. But Cade had no intention of sticking to the trail.

Once they were a few miles north of the town, they looked for a place to sleep for the night. About a half mile off the trail, they came upon a thicket of trees streaming out from the base of the mountains. It wasn't perfect, but it would offer them some cover from the wind and anyone looking for them—and they took one last look to make sure they weren't being followed.

Joanna began gathering wood, but then Red Sky warned against it. "No fire," he said, and Cade reluctantly agreed. They didn't need anything to draw attention to them tonight.

"Is anyone else hungry?" Joanna asked, shivering under her blanket.

Cade didn't answer. His throat was still very sore from

the marshal's whip, and the leather burn had left a nice welt on his neck. The pain made it hard to even swallow a drink of water, but he knew they should eat something and feed the horses, so they could all be ready to ride at first light.

"How much jerky do we have left?" he asked.

"Some for tonight, but not much for tomorrow," Red Sky replied while rummaging through the saddlebag of supplies.

"Well, tomorrow is another day, and right now I could use something to eat," Cade said optimistically.

They ate quietly in the moonlit darkness until Joanna spoke up, "Do you think they were able to put that fire out? And that man who was on fire… do you think he's still alive?"

Cade shrugged. "Hard to say. But everything that happened back there is sure to raise some attention," he replied. Then he added, "Thank you for saving my life. Those men were trouble, and I should have been more aware of the dangers." He glanced at Joanna and felt foolish for critiquing her naivety earlier in the day.

She smiled back and Red Sky gave a nod. Then, the three of them laughed, as if the inside joke was funny now that the ordeal was over. They were now travel companions with a shared experience that created a new bond between them, and they took turns at exchanging their respective versions of what happened.

"You really are a good shot with that rifle," Cade said to Joanna with a wink and a smile. "But there is something I need to know. Why did you shoot at the lanterns? That was a pretty clever diversion."

Joanna shook her head. "I can't really say. They were

something easy to aim at, and I figured that the man wouldn't be able to see Red Sky if I shot out the light."

Cade laughed and looked over to Red Sky. "Sounds like she had you covered. I'm just glad I didn't burn up in there."

"How did you get out?" Joanna asked Cade. "I saw Red Sky open a window and go in after you, but that man had a rope around your neck."

"It wasn't a rope, it was a whip," Cade said as he rubbed his neck again. He didn't like being strangled or feeling suffocated. This was the first time he felt powerless to do anything since the time when he was stuck and immobilized from Scorpion's stinger. Then he flexed his wrist, and the stinger sprang out from under his sleeve.

"This was a gift to a friend of mine from our Benefactor, and now it belongs to me. When you shot at the lanterns, it caused enough of a distraction that the man who called himself Marshal Blackburn stepped close enough for me to use it. This stinger has a venom that renders a person temporarily paralyzed," he said, looking to Red Sky for his silent validation.

Still looking at Red Sky, Cade continued. "The marshal referred to that whip as Widowmaker, I can understand why. When Red Sky first tried to free it from my neck, he turned it the wrong way and it tightened. But luckily the stinger worked and the marshal was paralyzed long enough for us to figure it out and escape before that explosion.

"Which reminds me, I need to reapply some of the resin," Cade realized while finishing his story and thinking out loud.

"What kind of venom is it?" she asked.

Cade appreciated her curiosity, even if he wasn't up for

sharing too much about his past and how the stinger became his after Scorpion's death. "I don't really know. The resin sticks to the stinger, and it's in a little leather pouch inside my saddlebag. I have to reapply a little bit to the tip after I use it."

"It's snake venom," Red Sky said in a confident tone. "There are painted snakes in the desert that can incapacitate a man with a single bite."

"You're probably right. And we both know what that feels like," Cade said. "But it sure does come in handy, and I think we're going to need every trick up our sleeve to get where we're going."

"Yeah, I suppose so," Joanna said. "The next stop on the way to Denver is Colorado Springs, and hopefully we won't have to ride through the middle of town. But it's going to be a long day tomorrow. We should try and get some sleep."

"I hope Mr. Whitmore is still in Denver when we get there. If we get there," Cade said, feeling a little more aware of the dangers that lie ahead. "Because now I need him to call off the bounty, too. Being free from his servitude won't mean squat if I'm still running from bounty hunters like that."

They all agreed and decided to turn in for the night. It was going to be bitterly cold without a fire, so they found shelter from the wind, huddled a little closer together than the night before, and wrapped themselves in their blankets.

Cade had not meditated in days, but he was feeling the need to recenter and recount what had happened today. The confrontation with Marshal Blackburn needed to be a learning experience. There would be deadly men out trying to kill him, and they wouldn't all have the same respect for battle that he once shared with his samurai brothers.

He gazed up at the night sky and was amazed at how many stars he could see in complete darkness. Then he closed his eyes and thought back to memories of the fort, Toshi's teachings, and how to fight dangerous opponents.

•••

Cade's Tale: Shadows of Tomorrow

We affectionally called the center of the dojo "the fighting pit" over the years. Weapons fashioned out of wood hung along the walls of the big open room, and there were four training dummies made from tree stumps in the four corners. And it was where the blood from our knuckles and cuts during sparring exercises permanently stained the floor.

One of my least favorite training exercises was sparring against Scorpion. He was stronger than me and easily out-weighed me by about thirty pounds. While I was quicker than him, it would only take one good punch or kick to put me off-balance or on the floor.

As we took our positions in the fighting pit and bowed to each other, I had already planned to use speed to my advantage. We were training with our wooden swords, and my plan was to attack high and sweep his legs.

"I'm on to you, Viper," Scorpion said with a sly grin. "I know what you're trying to do… and it's not going to work."

"How can you be so sure?" I replied with a chuckle. My plan may have been a little obvious, but that didn't stop me from trying.

Scorpion easily blocked my high strike and raised his knee to prevent the sweep. Then he did something completely unexpected and spun around to deliver a roundhouse kick to the side of my face.

The force of the kick sent me flying backward, and I struggled to regain my balance. True to his nature, Scorpion pressed the attack. When he advanced, my best move was to avoid the charge. So I ducked and rolled out of the way and was able to come up on my knees and block his next strike with my sword.

Then I popped to my feet and backed up to put some distance between us. I needed to collect myself, and the stinging hot pain in my ear would be a nice reminder not to be so sloppy next time. But the immediate concern was my opponent charging again.

Our wooden swords clashed as we parried and exchanged strikes and counterattacks. Then we got locked in close and mixed hand fighting with our swords. As we traded some arm grabs and knuckle punches, he continued to press and tried to use his size to his advantage. His aggression caused him to overreach, which presented an opportunity for me to step to his left and deliver a solid right-hand punch to his left eye.

Now we had both scored a strike against the other, and blood was streaming from the cut above his eye as we squared off again. But instead of feeling good about scoring a punch,

I could tell that all I'd really done is provoke the rage inside a man who didn't need anything more to be angry about.

"Strike your opponent's face," Toshi said from his spot against the far wall. As our sensei, this mat was where he would sit and watch us train while occasionally shouting instructions. "When you strike your opponent's face, he must defend or move his head… either will make him vulnerable."

Toshi was right. When it came to fighting, he was always right. My first attack was too high, and it was easy for Scorpion to defend and counter with the roundhouse kick.

So when Scorpion charged again, I modified my plan. I defended the strike and countered by poking my sword toward his face. When he defended my thrust, I was able to crouch down and spin quickly to sweep his legs with a kick that dropped him to the floor. Once on his back and caught off guard by my attack, I jumped on top of him and abruptly stopped short of a death strike with my wooden sword at his neck.

"Do you yield?" I asked victoriously and smiled down at my fallen opponent.

Scorpion looked at me with disgust. "If I had my stinger, I would have finished you before you got that lucky punch."

"Good," Toshi said from his spot. "Very good. A samurai should focus on the fight and minimize the number of moves to finish an opponent. It's nice to see that even donkeys can learn."

I reached down to give my defeated friend some help up. But as Scorpion picked himself off the floor, Toshi stood up from his spot then walked over to us, holding a wooden sword. He extended his hand to take Scorpion's sword and excused him from the floor.

"Now you'll fight me, Viper," Toshi said and squared off. "Let's see how you defend the same attack."

"But you have two swords, sensei," I said a little defensively. "How can I fight you?"

"That's up to you," Toshi replied. "Are you a Viper… or a donkey?"

The only thing I hated more than sparring against Scorpion was going against Toshi. He was the best sword fighter I knew or had ever met. He was also a little shorter than me, but whatever advantage I had in reach, he could overcome with his skill and being low in his attack.

After we faced each other and bowed, Toshi quickly pressed his attack and poked at my face—just as he had instructed. I anticipated the second attack would come after I defended the thrust, but I barely reacted in time to spin and block his strike. Now we were in close, and I was feeling very clever, using my defense to pin down both of his swords. That's when he dropped the sword in his right hand and backhanded me across the face.

"The sword is not the only weapon of the samurai," Toshi said as the pain in my cheek became flush with embarrassment. "When close fighting, you cannot underestimate your opponent or the element of surprise."

Then Toshi motioned for me to square off. "Again!" he commanded, without picking up the second sword.

This time I charged and became the aggressor. I guessed that he wouldn't mount the same defense, so I lunged at his face with my wooden sword and waited for the block to counterattack. But instead, he leaned backward and grabbed my wrist, and before I could regain my balance, he turned to pull me over his shoulder and flipped me onto my back.

As my body hit the floor, he gave me another little reminder of his superiority—he rapped my head with his wooden sword so hard that it rattled my teeth and shook my senses.

"Clumsy donkey," he said, sounding both irritated and amused. "An off-balance attack will put you on your back."

I closed my eyes to regroup and took a deep breath. But when I opened them, everything in the room had become very dark. And when I rose from the floor to face Toshi again, he was silhouetted in shadows as if we were no longer in the dojo.

"Again!" Toshi shouted at me. But this time he was holding two swords. Real swords.

As I looked at my hands, I was also holding two swords— mine and Falcon's. Then I turned back to Toshi and tried to understand what was going on and what my sensei had just tasked me to do.

"Why, sensei?" I asked. "I don't want to fight you."

Toshi just looked back at me with an expressionless face. "We stand apart... and the time has come for one of us to welcome death."

• • •

Spirits

Cade shook himself awake. He must have fallen asleep and his memories tripped into a dream. A horrible dream—or maybe another vision of what was to come. *Damn that old witch*, he thought to himself. The images in his mind seemed more vivid now that Moira had told him what they may mean. It was something he appreciated about meeting her, but he could also sense the curse of the light she spoke of and was beginning to understand his visions.

But nothing from his vision was going to happen tonight, and all he could think about now was being cold and completely out of his element. He was traveling through unknown parts of Colorado, with two people he barely knew, on a quest to confront his Benefactor. And to confront his Benefactor, he knew he would eventually have to face Toshi.

"Bad dream?" Red Sky asked from the shadows.

Cade looked into the darkness and the direction of his voice. The only light between them was the soft red glow of Red Sky's pipe, and he was looking right back at him.

"Yes," Cade replied. "It started as a fond memory and turned into something much darker."

Red Sky began humming a song as he blew smoke rings that dissipated into the wind and the star-filled sky.

At first his song started out low, but then it broke into a very tribal cadence. Whatever ritual was going on in Red Sky's mind was being played out in a very symbolic way. Then he stopped and spoke quietly as not to wake Joanna.

"The Comanche warrior lives beyond death," he said. "When we attack, we fight to kill. There is no other way. But a warrior never dies… he comes back as a spirit. And the spirits of my ancestors surround me. They whisper to me during the darkest times to give me strength.

"Our journey together is a dangerous one. Death is the shadow that will be ready to take us both. I can accept that," he said.

Then Red Sky drew from his pipe one final time and blew another smoke ring in the air. "Tell me, Cade… what spirits surround you?"

•••

Ashes

"Are you okay, mister?" the factory foreman asked the large man who slowly emerged from the charred interior of the factory building.

Marshal Blackburn had gone back into the building to retrieve his deputy's hat. The fire was out, but much of what had been burning was still smoldering and producing a foul smoke. He coughed and tried to spit it out while dusting himself off. But he was not at all interested in answering the question, and instead had one of his own.

"Where's my deputy?" Blackburn asked.

"If you mean the fella on fire that jumped in the river, I think he was taken to the infirmary," the foreman replied.

"Where's that?" Blackburn followed. As the worker pointed and gave directions, he put the crease back in his partner's hat and brushed away the ashes and soot. If his partner was still alive, he was going to find Swifty and give it back to him.

"What else did you see?" Blackburn asked curiously as he coughed again and spat. "Did you know who that was… the man who caused all this when we tried to take him into custody? There's a bounty on his head, and a lot of people would be very interested in hearing about what happened here."

The foreman shook his head with the look of someone who didn't want to get involved. "No, sir. I don't know who that man was. Some say his name is Cade Wilson, and that he's a ruthless killer."

"One and the same. This was all his fault, and you best be sure that I'm going to find him again. But if anyone else comes through here, I'd appreciate if you didn't mention me or which direction he was headed," Blackburn said before he looked back at the smoldering building. "Did you see who shot out those lanterns and started the fire?" he asked curiously.

"I think it was a girl," the foreman said, stammering. "She was behind the tree over there, with a rifle. And there was an Indian on the roof. He was looking through the window up there, but he didn't do anything. When your deputy came out to investigate, she shot the lamp out of his hand. Then she shot the second lamp and all hell broke loose."

"Yes, it did. And we wouldn't want that to happen again,"

Blackburn said with a glare as he walked toward his horse. "As for everything else we discussed, and just in case anyone comes asking… you don't know me, and this conversation never happened."

CHAPTER 9

News of the Day

Breakfast at the Frontier Hotel wasn't particularly fancy, but the dining room's ornate decor certainly added some flair to the overall experience. The smell of coffee and bacon filled the room and it paired perfectly with the early fall breeze coming in through an open window.

But Joseph Whitmore II was not hungry for a plate of eggs as he sat alone at the table. He wanted to get on with his business deal and make it back to the security of the fort. For whatever reason, the interaction with Sinclair made him feel uncomfortable and unsure of his safety until he knew for sure that Viper was dead. And that uneasy feeling continued to grow when the hotel manager walked toward his table holding a small piece of parchment.

"Did you hear about the fire in Pueblo, Mr. Whitmore?" the hotel manager asked very excitedly. "You wanted me to let you know if I received any news that might be odd or out of the ordinary. Well, there was apparently a shoot-out in Pueblo yesterday, and an iron factory caught on fire as a result. Word is that a man named Cade Wilson was responsible, and his current whereabouts are unknown."

Whitmore just looked at the manager in disappointment. After taking a sip of his coffee, he put out his hand to take the parchment from the manager. "Is that all?" he asked.

"That's all I've really heard so far this morning. But it did sound like Cade Wilson might be heading north, and he may not be alone," the manager added.

Over the manager's shoulder, Whitmore could see Sinclair making his way into the room and taking a seat at a corner table. As he did not know how he wanted the bounty hunter to hear of this news, Whitmore opted to keep it to himself for now. Because the feeling that this information was somewhat predictable to a dangerous few was unsettling.

"Thank you. Please keep me posted, and let's be careful of who else knows about this," Whitmore said, flipping him a silver dollar. Then he dismissed the manager so he could read the announcement.

As the manager was walking back to the lobby, Bruce Akers entered the room and passed him along the way. "Looks like it's going to be a beautiful day, my friend," he said with a big grin and pulled up a chair at the table. "I've heard that the Carmichaels are heading to town and are ready to meet later this morning."

Whitmore was still reading the parchment; he barely acknowledged his business partner. The good news Bruce had just shared was not good enough to change his mood in that moment, and Whitmore's long face piqued his companion's curiosity.

"What's wrong?" Bruce asked. "I thought you'd be happy to hear we're meeting today."

"I am, thank you. But there's something else I need to address, too," Whitmore replied and pushed away from the table. "Assuming we're meeting down at the train station, I need to gather Toshi and my shadow riders and meet you outside."

"But I haven't eaten breakfast yet," Bruce replied, surprised by the sense of urgency.

"Have mine, I haven't touched it. But I'll be outside with my men in five minutes," Whitmore said impatiently, and then made his way toward the man sitting alone at the corner table.

"How did you know Viper, I mean, Cade Wilson, was heading north?" Whitmore asked the bounty hunter.

Sinclair just smiled and pushed back in his chair. "Good morning to you, too. And I didn't know that Mr. Wilson was heading north, but I certainly suspected it was a possibility. Are you confirming that to be true?"

Whitmore didn't want to debate with this man. Sinclair's fine-tailored clothes and snappy comebacks were a bit much to deal with this morning, but he also knew when it was time to hedge his bets. There was too much at stake, and he didn't care who killed Viper. At this point, he just wanted him dead and out of his affairs.

"I'm saying there's news out of Pueblo that Cade Wilson was spotted there, and there was a shoot-out that resulted in a fire. And yes, reports are that he's not alone and he's heading north," Whitmore said before hesitating.

"I'll make you a deal, Sinclair," he continued. "I have some business to attend to while I'm in Denver, and you're welcome to follow along as an observer to provide security. You are not to interrupt this business, and I would appreciate it if you could keep Mr. Wilson from interrupting it, too. Do we understand each other?"

"Indeed," Sinclair replied. "So where are we off to this morning?"

•••

The Plan

They started riding before the sun broke the horizon and had already put some good miles behind them as it climbed higher in the sky.

Cade was keeping an eye on the surrounding landscape and on Red Sky, who had taken point as the three riders made their way north. Anything could hit them between here and Denver, and they had to be cautious. They continued to avoid the main trail, and according to Joanna, the next town along their current route was Colorado Springs.

He noticed that Red Sky was also looking out on the horizon and then behind them unusually. "What's wrong? What do you see?" Cade asked.

Red Sky didn't immediately answer. Instead, he stopped his horse, turned to the south, and motioned for them to stop. Then he listened for a moment before issuing a warning.

"Riders approaching from the south. They're riding hard up behind us. We should take cover!"

Red Sky pointed to a small patch of overgrown sagebrush and high grass, then he led the way to the best spot they could hide behind and encouraged them to dismount. Once he was off his horse, he pulled it down to get it as close to the ground as he could—and he instructed Cade and Joanna to do the same.

Cade loved his horse, but right now he was acting like a stubborn mule. He refused to lie down, but there was no other choice. A beautiful black horse would have been easily spotted on the sparse horizon.

"Turn his neck and lower him down gently," Red Sky said while motioning with his hands, and Cade did as he was told. He did so just in time, too, when six riders came into view as they crested a small hill about a half mile behind them.

The riders were kicking up a fine cloud of dust in their wake, and they were evidently trying to get somewhere fast—or catch up with someone. Either way, they looked like trouble as they rode past.

"More bounty hunters?" Joanna whispered.

"Most likely,'" Cade replied just as quietly. "But no sense in asking them."

As the riders faded into the horizon, Red Sky was the first to help his horse rise and mount up. "They're gone now, and riding too fast to look back. We should be able to follow their tracks without them noticing."

"There's just going to be more of them," Joanna said. "We

can't keep ducking and hiding every time some riders pass by. We'll never get anywhere."

She was right, and Cade knew it. They had already slowed their pace from earlier in the day, and now they were running low on food and water—and they were still no closer to Denver.

As they all mounted their horses, Cade looked to the clear blue sky and then closed his eyes to listen. After what Red Sky had told him last night, he wondered if there were spirits surrounding him. And if there were, he hoped they had something to say because he was open to ideas.

"How can we make it the rest of the way to Denver and reduce our chances of being caught out in the open?" he asked.

For a long moment the three of them just exchanged glances. Cade knew it was an impossible question to answer, but he had to ask. At this point, and after the events in Pueblo, his companions had just as much at risk as he did if they all got caught together.

"We can catch the train to Denver in Colorado Springs," Joanna said. "If you have money, I know where the train station is. I've been there before. Once we're on the train, we won't be out in the open, and we could make it to Denver in less than a day."

Cade looked to Red Sky as he casually cocked an eyebrow. "That's an interesting idea. I've never been on a train. How about you?"

Red Sky shook his head. "The iron horse would be faster, but there could be danger," he replied, and Cade shared his concern.

But there was something exciting about the plan, too.

Cade smiled back at his friends and his horse kicked up a small circle of dust as they prepared to ride. "Yes, there could be danger. But time is of the essence. And besides, I've always wanted to ride a train."

•••

Sharing a Vision

Whitmore waited impatiently at the train station in Denver.

The station wasn't a large building, and he heard talk of the city constructing a bigger one in the town center, down by the river. Still, the station that currently served as one of the new railway hubs for Colorado offered one office space for Whitmore to conduct his meeting with the men he needed to influence. As he watched a train roll in with just a few passenger cars through the dust-covered window, he finally felt like this business trip was about to pay off.

"It's about time," he said to his business partner.

"Patience," Bruce cautioned. "Let's not get ahead of ourselves. These are important men and we need them to see your vision… not just your ambition."

Whitmore ignored his partner's concerns, and instead began watching the people stepping off the train in the late morning sun. There were men in fine suits and women in pretty dresses, and everyone seemed pleased to be at their destination. *This is the future of the West, and I will be at the center of it all*, he thought to himself.

Then he saw two men disembark with a small entourage that appeared to work for them.

"Is that Victor Carmichael?" he asked.

Bruce stepped to the window and peered out. "Yes, it is, and that's his son Spencer with him."

"Excellent, now we can get down to business," Whitmore said and traipsed off toward the platform receiving the passengers and their luggage.

As Victor and his son entered the building, Bruce stepped forward to make the introductions. "Mr. Carmichael, I would like you to meet Mr. Whitmore," he said as the two men exchanged pleasantries and handshakes.

"Our apologies for being a few days late, Mr. Whitmore," Victor said, both casually and unsolicited, but in a sincere tone. "We had a little trouble, and my son Spencer needed some medical attention. But I wanted him to be here, and so we had to wait a bit."

"Not at all, Mr. Carmichael. It's nice to meet you, too. And I hope you're on the mend," Whitmore replied, shaking Spencer's hand. "We've made the most of our time in Denver these past couple days, and now we're looking forward to meeting with you."

"We're anxious to meet with you, too," Spencer said flatly. He didn't seem happy to be here but was relunctantly present to fulfill his role in the family business.

"Well, if you don't mind, I think we should adjourn ourselves to the humble little office space the building offers, so we can discuss things with a bit more privacy," Whitmore said. And with a smile and a wave of his hand, he pointed out the only closed door at the far side of the building. "I've been told that the governor is on his way, and I've asked the porter to deliver some coffee while we wait."

The gathering of businessmen made their way toward the office, and the respective groups of people employed by Whitmore and the Carmichaels began to follow, with their travel trunks in tow. The luggage dragging across the wooden floor made a very unwelcome scratching sound, and Whitmore cringed with a glance at Toshi and the four shadow riders who accompanied him everywhere.

"Can you please give them a hand with their bags," he said, somewhat annoyed that they were just following him around doing nothing.

"Yes, boss," one of the shadow riders responded and stepped forward to help.

Victor and Spencer entered the office and took positions on the far side of the large oval table in the center of the room. The clean white tablecloth and place settings were very welcoming, and the porter entered with a tray of coffee and white china cups. As Victor sat down, Bruce took the far chair opposite the Carmichaels.

"Why don't you have a seat?" Whitmore said to Spencer, as they were the only two still standing behind their chairs.

"That's okay," Spencer said with a slight grimace. "I prefer to stand since my—"

"No need to bother these gentlemen with unimportant events. Now how about some coffee?" Victor said as if to change the subject. Everything about him suggested he was an overindulging and controlling father. Something Whitmore knew a lot about.

"Indeed." Whitmore nodded and smiled after taking one last glance out the office door. He could see two more well-dressed men in black and brown suits walking across the boarding platform—and they were coming toward the office.

Whitmore stood in the doorway to receive them and extended his hand to introduce himself. "Governor, it's a pleasure to meet you. I'm Joseph Whitmore II, and I thank you for coming."

The man in the black suit looked back at Whitmore and received his handshake, but then politely shook his head. "Nice to meet you, too, Mr. Whitmore," he replied. "My name is Bradley Stanwick. I'm one of the administrators for the state of Colorado, and here to represent the governor in his absence. This is my assistant, Mr. Tobin."

Whitmore stepped aside to welcome the men into the room but was likely having a hard time disguising his dissatisfaction. He felt insulted that the governor would send this representative and his valet to such an important meeting, and especially after everything he had invested in setting it up.

"Is there something wrong?" Stanwick asked.

"Why isn't the governor here?" Whitmore snapped. "Because even though you may represent his interests, I hardly think you also represent his authority—"

"Gentlemen, welcome!" Bruce said as he stood, and his wooden chair made the same annoying sound as it scratched against the wooden floor. "This is Victor and Spencer

Carmichael," he said while making introductions around the table. "Have a seat and enjoy some coffee."

After everyone had acknowledged one another and taken their respective seats at the table, Whitmore noticed Bruce give him a wink, presumably to calm him down and segue the conversation. "We're glad you're all here, as there is much to discuss. And without further ado, I'll give the floor to Mr. Whitmore."

Whitmore gathered himself while he closed the office door and took a rolled-up map from his leather strap bag in the corner of the room. As he untied it and placed it on the table, he glanced at Bruce to give him a hand moving the coffee platter, so he could unroll it and begin his presentation.

"Gentlemen, this is a survey map of the New Mexico Territory. You'll notice that on this map, we have proposed the ideal line for the expansion of the railroad from Denver to Santa Fe, and this second line from Houston and Fort Worth to Santa Fe. Then this third line extends south and along the border with Mexico… and all the way to California." Whitmore motioned with his hand beyond where the image of the map ended.

"Today, I would like to propose that we formalize a plan to lay track across the vast expanse of the New Mexico Territory to connect Texas with Colorado and continue on to the coast. Because of the lack of navigable rivers and waterways, the railroad will offer the single biggest opportunity for us to connect the largest cities and make way for future trade and commerce," he said, then paused briefly. "What do you think?"

"Very interesting," Victor said aloud as he studied the

details of the map. "I have some business partners that think Pueblo would be the perfect place to build an iron factory to produce rail line. And with that operation centrally located in Colorado, we could build as we go. But I have to ask, why are you suggesting to take the Cimarron Route instead of following the Santa Fe Trail through the mountain pass?"

"Fair question," Whitmore replied, expecting that a challenge to his proposed route might come up. "My father and I share a vision. I would assume it's much like your family business, Mr. Carmichael. We see an opportunity to come south from Kansas City and skirt the northern edge of 'No Man's Land' and the Indian Nation. And the line coming from Texas runs through protected land here all the way to Santa Fe. These routes will connect every city from Missouri to Texas right through here and intersect at Las Vegas," he said, then pointed at the map and the expanse of land he had acquired over the years.

Bradley Stanwick sipped his coffee and leaned back in his chair. "I can assure you, sir, the governor believes we are still at the beginning stage of planning… and we're not at all prepared to formalize plans at this time."

"Is there a problem with the proposal?" Whitmore asked.

Stanwick gave a thin smile. "The governor is concerned about the big-picture benefits of the railroad and connecting our growing cities and towns. But with all due respect, the path you have carved doesn't look like any land worth building on," he said in an apparent reference to Whitmore's land in the New Mexico Territory. "Wouldn't that be adding an incredible amount of time and cost to go around the mountains at the southern border instead of through them at the pass?"

Whitmore hadn't liked this Stanwick fella from the moment they met, and even less the more he shared his opinions. "I can assure you, Mr. Stanwick, I own the majority of the land in the proposal. It's easily accessible by train and the surrounding areas, and it's well protected from bandits and train robbers. So whatever costs may be incurred in track will be made up for in not having to cut through a mountain pass and deal with every homesteader that may have taken root in the path of progress."

"So your proposed route would largely stand to benefit you?" Stanwick asked with a sarcastic chuckle.

"It would benefit all of us, Mr. Stanwick. Because I shouldn't have to tell you how difficult it was to lay claim to this territory and protect it from those willing to steal and destroy it," Whitmore replied. "It's taken years to assemble men that were former soldiers of the war and give them new purpose. These men are loyal and unbound by the rules of the military when it comes to protecting our business interests and keeping the peace.

"This may sound ambitious to an outsider, but that's exactly what I've done to put this deal in motion. And I further intend to disperse them across this expanse of land to take up residence in every little town and outpost along the way to ensure that we not only lay track but also keep commerce moving securely through the northern part of the territory."

There were some looks of concern around the table, and

Whitmore could feel his temper rising as he glanced at Bruce for some assistance.

"I think what my friend is trying to say is… the New Mexico Territory is still very wild and untamed," Bruce said in an attempt to keep the deal on track. "But with Mr. Whitmore's resources, it does offer an opportunity to connect with Kansas, and Texas, and then ultimately with the Santa Fe Trail at Fort Union. It's not deviating too far from the mountain pass—"

"Sorry to interrupt you," Stanwick said, a little bemused and not sorry at all. "But I'm just not seeing it. By taking the most direct path, the rail line can go through Colorado City and Trinidad, and then through the pass to Santa Fe. I think the governor would agree that the path through the pass would be in the best interests of Colorado."

Whitmore was growing more frustrated by the minute. He didn't like where this conversation was going, nor did he own or control any of the land on the route that Stanwick was proposing. Ironically, this was the same area that his business associate Jon Cobb owned, and it was the crux of his ire as the place where his elite samurai cowboys were killed.

"Could we hear this from the governor himself?" Whitmore asked, openly challenging Stanwick's authority.

Stanwick paused, checked his pocket watch, then offered up his best suggestion. "Well, that train outside leaves for Colorado Springs in twenty minutes. If you want to hear this news from the governor himself, my suggestion is that we be on it."

Whitmore looked to Bruce and then back to Stanwick. "Are you saying the governor is in Colorado Springs?"

"Indeed he is. He's a very busy man, and the mining

operations of this state are also very important to him," Stanwick said. "So this meeting being postponed was why he isn't here today. But we can meet up with him there to discuss your plan, if it's that important to you."

Whitmore turned to the wall. He didn't want anyone to see the look of concern on his face, as the last thing he wanted to do was travel south. But he wasn't about to get this close to a deal to lose it arguing with an administrator or because of any worries that he may cross paths with Viper.

"Is there a problem?" Stanwick asked.

"No. No problem at all," Whitmore replied. "I assume this would be an overnight trip," he continued while addressing everyone else in the room.

"But we just got here!" Spencer said. "Dad, we have all of our bags and people waiting outside that door."

"That's enough, son," Victor said curtly. "What do you want to do Mr. Whitmore? Because I feel that part of this is our fault. And if we need to head to Colorado Springs to make it right, that's what we'll do."

Whitmore looked to Bruce, and he nodded back. Then, as if the man had confirmed the obvious to protect his interests, he announced his intentions to the room. "Let's get on that train."

Whitmore excused himself, opened the door, and exited the office. Then he called Toshi and his shadow riders over.

"We're getting on this train to Colorado Springs," he said, pointing out the window to the engine billowing smoke and steam. "There's no need to pack anything. We're only staying the night, and we'll figure out our accomodations when we get there."

Over Toshi's shoulder, he saw the well-dressed man who was quietly standing in the corner and cleaning his fingernails with a knife. Assuming the bounty hunter overheard their conversation, he just cocked his head as a steam whistle on the train echoed through the building, announcing the train's imminent departure. "You, too, Sinclair."

Sinclair tipped his hat and picked up his saddlebags. And as he walked over to the ticket window, Whitmore wanted to know if he predicted this, too.

"You're already packed and ready? Did you know we were heading south?" he asked.

"Oh, these? These bags come with me wherever I go," Sinclair replied with a smile. "It's my vocation to be prepared for anything."

CHAPTER 10

The Train Schedule

It was getting late in the afternoon and the long shadows of fall blanketed the three riders as they approached the outskirts of Colorado Springs. The plan to follow the pack of men had worked, as they had made up the twenty plus miles without being noticed—with the exception of a small wagon train going the opposite direction that didn't seem to pay them any mind.

Joanna began to recognize the landscape leading into town; it offered plenty of cover, as the mountains in the distance gave way to trees and wash-cut canyons. And just like when they had arrived in Pueblo the day before, but even more cautiously given what had occurred there, she took the lead and found a spot from which they could survey the scene before advancing.

She also felt like this was another big opportunity for her to help. She had some knowledge of the town and knew where the train station was, and so she confidently suggested a scouting plan to her companions.

"I think I should go into town alone and check out the train station," she said very matter-of-factly. "You guys stand out like a sore thumb, and the three of us together would likely make things worse."

Red Sky looked to Cade. "She speaks true. The three of us are sure to get attention."

"Agreed, but what are you going to do when you get there?" Cade asked.

Joanna stiffened up in her saddle. "I'll find out when the next train to Denver is leaving, and I'll map out the best way for us to get from this spot to the station. That is, unless you have any better suggestions?"

Cade paused but eventually shook his head. Then he pulled two gold coins from his coat pocket and handed them to Joanna.

She was surprised at first, as she'd never seen or held a twenty-dollar gold coin before. The shiny glint of two of them in her hand was beautiful, and the weight of them seemed to add to their value.

"What are these for?" she asked.

"It would be a shame to ride all the way into town and not be able to purchase tickets for the train," Cade replied. "Besides, I think it would be best to be prepared. We need to get us, and our horses, on a train to Denver as quickly as possible."

Joanna smiled. Cade's gesture not only showed that he trusted her, but that he respected her ability to make decisions, too. "Thank you," she said with heartfelt sincerity. "Wait for me here, and I'll do my best to get us taken care of."

"And if you don't return?" Red Sky asked.

Joanna hadn't considered that, but now realized it was a possibility. "Well, if I'm not back before dark, then assume something went wrong," she said without waiting for a response.

She turned her horse, then made her way into town at a steady gallop. The sun was just above the mountains, and it would be getting dark in a couple of hours. She had to make the most of the remaining daylight, and there was no sense in taking it slow when it may be easier to go unnoticed if she rode in fast.

It took her a moment or two to remember her way through town, and she had to try and retrace her path from when she was passing through in a hurry not that long ago. She took the side streets and did her best to avoid eye contact with anyone, but it didn't take her long to be casually riding through the center of town. That's when she noticed a few familiar-looking landmarks and buildings, and she eventually found her way to the train station.

The building itself seemed under construction, but it was still quite welcoming compared with what Joanna had seen in her years of traveling through smaller railroad towns with her father. In many ways, train stations were all the same in her mind. The trains would come and go no matter how nice the building was. It was the people who mattered, and very few people she met while working on trains were nice. Or decent.

And right now, all that station represented was the hope of seeing her mother again.

She tied up her horse, then she used her hand to brush the lone stragglers of hair out of her face in an effort to make herself presentable. It had been a long time since she'd had a bath or washed her hair, and her dirty blue dress was not very becoming either. But she didn't have time to waste on superficial things, so she stood up straight, puffed herself up, and walked straight into the train station and toward the ticket window at the entrance of the grand lobby.

The mousy little man in spectacles behind the glass didn't even notice her, as he was busy tapping away on some device and taking notes. So Joanna subtly cleared her throat and knocked on the window to get his attention.

"Oh, pardon me. I didn't see you standing there, miss," he said, looking up for a moment. "I'll be right with you." Then he went back to what he was doing. When the device stopped tapping, he made some final notes and pushed his work to the side.

"How can I help you?" he asked.

"When is the next train to Denver?" Joanna asked. "I need tickets for three people and our horses."

The ticket agent smiled. "The train from Denver should be here any minute now, and the next train back leaves tomorrow morning at eleven o'clock. I'll be happy to sell you three tickets tomorrow because I was just about to close up for the evening, and I've already locked up the cashbox."

Joanna was a little disappointed, feeling that she'd risked

coming into town and would have to return empty-handed. But the next best thing was some information to share.

"What time should we be here tomorrow?" she asked.

"The ticket window opens at eight o'clock in the morning," he said with a smile, and Joanna nodded back just as the whistle of the inbound train announced its arrival at the station. Then she watched as the agent turned to look at the big steam engine pulling into the station. "See, miss? Right on time," he said. "Miss?" He looked back to the ticket window—but Joanna had already gone.

•••

The Stockyard

Cade watched as Joanna came riding up to make sure nobody was following her. The sun was behind the mountains now, but its silhouette outlined the bold features of the rugged backdrop. There was still plenty of light aglow to see that she was alone, and she would indeed make it back safe.

"Welcome back," he said without trying to sound surprised. "What did you find out?"

Joanna looked a little tired and out of breath from the ride, but happy to have returned safely from her scouting mission. "The train leaves for Denver tomorrow morning at eleven o'clock, and I think I've found the best way to the station. But I couldn't buy tickets tonight, so here's your money back," she said, handing the two coins back to Cade.

"Thank you," Cade replied as he accepted the coins. He appreciated her courage and honesty. He also didn't know of any young woman who would ride into a town alone, with a bounty on her head, and do what she just did.

"Does that mean we'll have to camp out again tonight?" she asked.

"Reckon so," he replied. "Red Sky, how much food do we have left?"

Red Sky shook his head. "We're out of horse grain, and we just have this little bit of jerky left," he said after unfolding the leather food pouch.

"I saw a place that looked like we could get some food for us and our horses," Joanna said. "I rode past it on the edge of town, and I didn't see a lot of people there."

Cade was tired of all the running, ducking, and hiding. At this point, he would welcome a head-on fight if he could also get a warm meal and a place to sleep. And since they were taking a much bigger risk by just riding into town tomorrow and getting on a train, they might as well do so with full bellies.

"What do you think?" he asked Red Sky. His companion's furrowed brow said enough, but he also looked persuadable and ready to go along for the ride.

"Alright, Joanna, lead the way," Cade said as he mounted up, and he let her take the point. It was getting darker by the minute, and now they were committed to getting to this place and escaping the cold air coming over the mountains that would soon follow.

After a short ride to the outskirts of town, they arrived at a collection of structures with large fenced pens for corralling herds, and a house situated behind a barn with light coming from inside. A sign above the entrance read "The Stockyard," and there was smoke pouring out of a chimney pipe, which smelled like cooked meat. Just like Joanna had said, there were only four other horses tied up out front.

Red Sky led them to the side of the barn and behind the only tree, so they could tie up there. Cade appreciated the fact that Red Sky was ever the cautious one, always looking to cover their tracks.

When they pushed their way through the big front door, Cade saw four men standing around a makeshift bar at the back of the big room—and they all turned to see who had just walked in. The big room was the inside of a barn, but instead of animals and stalls, there were four large tables with a collection of various chairs around them. A crossbar chandelier with lanterns was suspended from the ceiling, and there were buffalo pelts hanging on almost every square foot of the walls. There was a fireplace in the back corner of the room with meat on a spit slowly turning over an open flame, and the big, burly fella standing by the fireplace was likely the owner.

Cade assumed this was some sort of frontier saloon, similar to a dozen random outposts he'd been in before. He led the others to the table closest to the door and sat down. Since all the tables were open, better not to be too far from the door, so they could make a quick exit if they had to.

A young Mexican girl appeared from a side room, but the owner stopped her with his hand, then just grumbled as he slowly made his way across the room. When he stopped just short of the long end of the table, he pulled the chewed-up cigar from the corner of his mouth and looked Cade up and down like he was guilty of some crime.

"We don't serve his kind here," he said, pointing at Red Sky with the chewed-up cigar.

Cade didn't want any trouble, but he wasn't going to back down, either. He didn't appreciate this man's attitude toward his friend, which was all too familiar from his time at the fort.

"What exactly do you serve here?" he asked sarcastically.

"This place is for ranchers and buffalo hunters, and both don't take kindly to savages. So if he's with you… you'll have to go," the owner replied, then put the cigar back in his mouth.

The Mexican girl looked to be coming toward the table to calm the situation, but one of the men at the bar grabbed her arm to stop her. She pulled away, and in doing so, she caused the man to spill his beer, and she fell off-balance to the ground.

As the owner walked back to the bar and cursed at the girl to mind her business, Cade heard Joanna whispering to him, "I hate men like that. It's not right."

"There's a lot not right here. We should go," he whispered back and cocked his head toward the door at Red Sky. "Go gather the horses. I'll be out in a minute."

They all stood from the table, then Red Sky and Joanna made their way out while Cade walked to the bar to speak to the owner.

"I don't expect you'll change your perspective on my friend, but I have money and I would like to leave here with some food and a sack of grain for our horses tonight. Can we reach a compromise?" Cade said, hoping the owner would be more agreeable, if just dealing with him.

The owner said nothing back and instead looked unamused and unwilling to compromise. So Cade produced a gold coin from his pocket. And when the owner saw the coin, his throaty laugh and tobacco-stained smile showed that his bigotry may have its limits when it came to money. But he still seemed determined to prove this was his place, and they would do business on his terms.

"Hey, Zeke, get a load of this guy," the owner said to the man who had grabbed the Mexican girl. "He's paying in gold, and he has a servant girl and an Indian. He must be somebody real important," he said and laughed again in Cade's face.

Then he spat on the floor and put the cigar back in the corner of his mouth. "How about you turn around, Mr. Important, and show yourself out the door," the owner said with a glare. Then he pulled a hefty meat cleaver from a cutting block and held it like a weapon while Zeke and the fella standing next to him took positions around Cade. "Or we'll be happy to kick you out on your butt."

Cade slipped the coin back in his coat pocket and slow blinked to calibrate his senses. He needed to gauge the proximity and presumed intent of these men who had become the unnecessary focus of his attention. And that's when he heard the door to the establishment reopen.

"Riders are coming. We need to go—" Joanna began to say.

For a moment, the owner and the other two men were distracted, and Cade seized the advantage. He quickly pulled his right sword, then cut the handle of the cleaver out of the owner's hand along with part of his thumb. Then he took one step back, crouched low, and spun around with his left leg to sweep the third fella's legs out from under him.

With the third man flat on his back, Cade pulled his left sword and confronted the other two. As he thrust forward, he brought the edge of each blade against the necks of Zeke and the owner in a T formation.

"Do I have your attention now?" Cade asked while abandoning the pleasantries and treating them like misfits who mistakenly thought they could threaten him.

The owner stopped chewing on his cigar and stood perfectly still. He was holding his bleeding hand with a look of complete surprise, and Zeke could only swallow hard against the sword at his throat. "And you on the floor," he said, addressing the third fella. "Don't try anything, or you and your friends will regret it."

Sensing that he had control of the situation, and that time was still a matter of importance, Cade continued. "Good. Now I would appreciate if we could get some food, and I would expect that we can renegotiate the terms, yes?" he asked the owner, who only nodded in response.

He glanced over to the Mexican girl, and spoke clearly and firmly, "I'll take what's left of that sack of grain in the corner, there. And put some of that jerked meat and a loaf of bread in that bag hanging on the wall," he ordered after doing a glancing survey of what looked available in the side-room pantry. "Quickly, please!"

The girl cinched the sack of grain and grabbed the drawstring bag from the hook on the wall and did as she was asked. After she wrapped something that was likely buffalo meat in some cloth, she put that and a loaf of the bread inside the bag and presented it all to Cade.

"Thank you," she said softly.

Cade flipped his wrists and slid both swords back into their scabbards. Then, after taking the sack of grain and the bag of food, he reached into his opposite coat pocket and pulled out three silver dollars he had separated from the gold. After tossing them on the bar, he tipped his hat and turned to leave.

As he made his way to the door, Cade locked eyes with Joanna. She stared unblinkingly at the scene before her, and then she mumbled something barely audible that only Cade could hear. "Can you teach me how to fight like that?" she asked.

Cade just smiled as he remembered something she had said earlier, and then he turned to address the owner one last time. "Oh, and one more thing. Be mindful of how you treat people, or it won't be as pleasant the next time we meet."

•••

False Pleasantries

Whitmore looked around and began to regret his impetuous decision to come here.

The Prairie Moon Hotel & Saloon was not as comfortable as their previous accommodations in Denver, and the smell of something burning in the kitchen only made the lack of decor in the saloon more noticeable. But the hotel was directly across the road from the train station, and he was more concerned about meeting with the governor.

From the window, he could see another hotel on the other side of the tracks in the fading light. It was the best hotel in town, and that's where the governor and his administrators were staying. It was also where Stanwick had gone to meet with the governor after they arrived in town.

"I don't know if we can trust this Stanwick fella," Whitmore said aloud, glancing at Bruce, who was sitting at a table and busy wiping his spectacles clean. "It's been over an hour and still no word."

Bruce readjusted his spectacles and went back to looking at the map Whitmore had presented at the meeting. "Maybe so, but he makes a good point. The more direct route is through the mountain pass and then on to Santa Fe."

"Not you, too!" Whitmore snapped. Then he dismissively waved his hand at his business partner, and his wrinkled brow further animated his growing anger. "I brought you here to help broker this deal, not side with some political nobody who suggested we lay track through the mountain pass instead of south to Madison and then through the middle of my land. It's taken me too long and cost me plenty to control the northern heart of the New Mexico Territory. My father will not appreciate it if I can't make this happen, and we didn't come this far to lose this deal now."

"Fair enough," Bruce replied. "But you might want to be prepared for the alternative. Who controls that land south of the pass at the border?"

"Jon Cobb owns most if it, but not all of it," Whitmore

replied through gritted teeth. "This so-called associate of mine wants to get in on everything I'm trying to build. But all he's done lately is add to my frustration, and now two of my samurai cowboys are dead."

"Assuming this Cobb fella won't know what get's decided here, what would it take for you to buy him out?" Bruce said.

Whitmore looked over at Victor and Spencer Carmichael standing over at the bar, and then back out the window to see what appeared to be Stanwick and his associate Mr. Tobin approaching the Prairie Moon—alone.

"I don't know," he said quietly, almost to himself. "But I don't want to think about that right now, and I don't see the governor."

Stanwick and Mr. Tobin entered the hotel saloon, then they made their way directly over to the table where Whitmore and Bruce were waiting for them.

"Gentlemen, I'm here to extend a pleasant greeting from the governor and to let you know that he looks forward to meeting with you tomorrow morning," Stanwick said without seeming at all sincere about it.

"What do you mean tomorrow?" Whitmore replied. "We just traveled all the way down here. Why isn't the governor meeting with us here tonight, or over at his hotel for that matter?"

"Be assured, the governor is a very busy man," Stanwick said loud enough to address everyone in the room, and the Carmichaels walked over to join the conversation. "Schedules must be maintained, and I've told you that he's here in Colorado Springs to meet with companies about their mining interests in our great state. But he is prepared to meet with you tomorrow morning at the train station, and we'll have plenty of time to discuss details on our trip back to Denver."

"That sounds fine, Mr. Stanwick," Bruce said. "We'll meet you at the train station after breakfast."

"Works for me," Victor Carmichael replied and finished the shot of whiskey in his hand.

Whitmore didn't like it, but it was probably for the best. He would have plenty to think about tonight and could approach his conversation tomorrow with a clear head. And besides, knowing that they would be on the train back to Denver together would give him that much more time to negotiate.

"Please tell the governor I look forward to meeting with him tomorrow," Whitmore said through a forced, thin smile.

CHAPTER 11

Fire in the Sky

Everyone was up early in anticipation of catching the train, but it was too soon to head into town.

Red Sky sat silently with Joanna as they both watched Cade doing some stretches on an open patch of ground in the crisp morning air. The more he watched, the more Red Sky imagined himself being able to mimic the way Cade was setting his feet and balancing his movements in his warrior's dance—and with the same deadly intent as he wielded two swords in a fluid motion.

The dawning sun was aglow with red and yellow hues pushing against the darkness as they stretched across the sky. This was a sign, and Red Sky took notice that Cade's silhouette was stark but slowly fading against the light.

His father had told him that a red sky in the morning was an omen and how he got his name. The elders would say it was a sign a storm was coming, and every sign he could interpret from the sights and sounds of nature around him told Red Sky that this omen would speak true today.

Cade finished, relaxed from his stance, and stood straight up before taking a deep breath and sliding his swords back into their scabbards. When he walked over to join Red Sky and Joanna sitting by a small fire, he half smiled as he approached.

"Do you feel the spirits around you?" Red Sky asked.

"Something like that," Cade replied confidently. "I needed to clear my mind today. My dreams were a little fuzzy and unclear last night, so I wanted to spend some time this morning renewing my sense of focus."

Red Sky nodded. His friend spoke true, but it also seemed that Cade was trying his best to assure everyone else. And without saying it out loud, both knew they were riding straight into trouble today—and they would need their wits about them.

"It's likely that we will cross paths with those riders today. We've almost crossed paths with them twice now," Cade said firmly. "Once on the trail, and again last night. Even though we were lucky to make it out of The Stockyard without being seen, that hardly matters now. I'm sure those men inside let them know we're here."

"Likely so," Red Sky said. "That's why we put some distance between us last night… so we could avoid more trouble and get some rest."

"It's a few miles back to town. Do you still want to catch the train?" Joanna asked politely. "Because we could always go around and keep heading north."

Red Sky looked to Cade to hear what he'd say, even though he thought he knew the answer. There was courage and strength in his friend, and he was not afraid of death. And he would likely choose the way that was death, but he would not be the one to choose that way for others.

"Yes. That is my path. I can't keep ducking and running, and something tells me that we need to be on that train today," Cade replied sincerely. "I'd rather ride straight into a fight than get ambushed by bounty hunters."

"But I worry about you two," he continued. "This simple plan to catch my Benefactor away from the fort has become quite complicated… and deadly. Again, I wouldn't hold it against either of you if you want out."

Red Sky looked over to Joanna, and the determination in her expression said it all. "I've come back this far; I have to find my mom. I need to see her again," she said.

"The warrior spirit is with you," he said to Joanna. "But now you must be ready."

"Ready for what?" she asked.

"Ready to fight to the death for what you want," Cade replied. "The warrior walks the path of death, and that path starts with your first kill.

"You need to know that there are powerful men that want us dead, whether for revenge or pride, or both. And the man that comes for you will not hesitate to kill, and so neither can you.

"Make your shot count," he continued. "And from now on, we've all got to assume that anyone who knows our name has a motive or something to gain. This means that where we're headed, and everywhere in between, we won't be able to trust anyone."

Joanna looked puzzled, but not afraid. Red Sky patted her on the shoulder and she smiled.

"You'll be fine. Have courage," he said to assure her.

"Then let's load up, and make sure your guns are at the ready," Cade said calmly yet sounding like a warrior preparing for battle.

As Red Sky turned his gaze to the sky, the colors had softened to yellows and lighter blues. When he listened to the wind through the trees, it was as if he could hear his father's voice whispering in his ear, *I will be with you.*

Then the Comanche turned to Cade. "The warrior spirits are with me, and I will be with you," he said as he showed Cade the scar on his palm.

●●●

8:30 a.m.

Joanna took the lead into town, but much slower than yesterday. This time they were all together, and anything could happen along the way—or when they got there. As the lead, she was very anxious about the plan and about being responsible for getting them to the train station. Her spirits were definitely higher than her confidence, and there was no turning back now.

The anticipation of getting to the station and what they were doing was also very exciting to her. Never in her life of servitude to the Carmichaels did she imagine she'd be doing something like this or riding with men like Cade Wilson and Red Sky.

As the three riders cautiously made their way through town, she was mindful to avoid The Stockyard and take them down the backstreets as Cade and Red Sky followed behind in single file. Still, the town seemed very peaceful and quiet this morning. So peaceful that she actually started to believe that everything might go smoother than planned.

They eventually arrived at a main street that was wide-open and lined with small business buildings on both sides. The train station was in sight at the end of the street, but still a few blocks away, and a dozen or so people were milling about near some of the businesses. They would not be able to go any farther without being seen, so they paced themselves as they rode down the merchant boulevard to avoid drawing any unnecessary attention.

"Stop," Red Sky said quietly but loud enough for her to hear.

"Why?" she turned and whispered back. "These people aren't going to pay us any mind, and we're almost to the train station."

"There's something wrong," he replied. "The way is not clear."

"Let's pull up here for a second," Cade said while looking up the road to the station. "I agree with Red Sky. This seems too easy."

Joanna guided them to a spot between a small, gated corral and a white-painted building that was likely a general store. As they tied up, a few customers emerged from the store with a crate of whatever they purchased and gave them a brief look—but then continued on their way. After they dismounted their horses, the three riders ducked behind the wood fence of the corral to peek around the corner.

They could see their destination in the distance, and Joanna felt a sense of urgency to reach the station.

"We're so close. Why don't we just ride hard up to the station and tie up there? We'll be safe once we're inside," she said.

Then a clock chimed very peacefully from somewhere in the distance, and it sounded as if it was coming from inside or near the train station. Cade pulled the spyglass from his saddlebag and extended it.

After the clock finished chiming, Joanna counted on her hand and marked the time. "It must be nine o'clock," she said. "What do you see?"

Cade moved the spy glass around then lifted it up. "I see some people leaving the hotel carrying luggage. They must be catching the train," he said.

"Can I see?" Joanna asked impatiently.

Cade handed her the spyglass. She was eager to use it, and she appreciated how he handed it over without question. But having never used one before, it took her a moment to focus one eye through the little spot and realize what she was seeing.

Victor and Spencer Carmichael were standing in front of the hotel, and she instantly felt a pit in her stomach when she saw them again. They were followed by two men carrying their trunks, and then she saw the woman with the familiar blue dress and her hair tied up neatly in a bun, walking behind them—just as she always had.

"My mom is here!" she said before realizing how loudly she said it. But then Cade gently patted her shoulder, and it reminded her that they were trying to keep a low profile. They all watched from afar as seven others walked out of the hotel behind the first group.

"Who else is with them?" Cade asked curiously but somewhat expressionless. "Let me look again."

After she handed the spyglass back, a look of surprise spread across Cade's face when he took it and peered in the same direction.

"What's the matter?" she asked.

"My Benefactor and my sensei are here, too," he replied.

•••

Convergence

The gray coats of the four shadow riders were unmistakable as they poured into the street from the hotel. Cade's Benefactor was right behind them, along with Toshi and some other man in glasses, who Cade had never seen before.

As he lowered the spyglass and collapsed it into itself, Cade was overcome with an odd mix of feelings that he couldn't seem to process in the moment. The pursuit of his Benefactor wasn't supposed to end here, was it? But equally, this was also a fortunate coincidence.

"Looks like they're all heading to the train station," Red

Sky said from over Cade's shoulder. "Our journey has been rewarded."

"I reck'n so," Cade said sarcastically. "We should probably let them get to the train station so we know where they are… and no innocent people get hurt."

Even though they all seemed to silently agree, Cade knew that hiding in this spot, converging on the train station, and confronting his sensei and Benefactor were completely different things—and he felt completely unprepared for any of them.

"What's the plan?" Joanna asked.

"Well, going to Denver is now the least of our worries," Cade replied with a chuckle. "But we need to keep my Benefactor from getting on that train, and hopefully your mom, too," he said over his shoulder to Joanna.

Then he knelt down on one knee and faced his friends. He didn't really have a plan, but he remembered that Joanna said the train would leave at eleven o'clock. So luckily, they still had some time—or that's what he thought before he saw the six familiar-looking riders coming up the street and heading their way.

"Damn! Those bounty hunters are not giving up," he warned, and Red Sky and Joanna turned to see. The riders were slow-walking down the middle of the street, looking around in every direction.

"We've got about two minutes before they stumble upon us," Cade said as he quickly assumed command of the situation. He surveyed their surroundings, and he knew they had to avoid getting pinned between the bounty hunters and the station. The best scenario was to go unnoticed and just let the hunters pass through. And for that to happen, they couldn't all stay here.

"We need to split up," he said, looking to his warrior friend. "Red Sky, take your bow and get on the roof of this building, or the one in front of it, without being seen. We'll try to avoid the fight, but if it comes… be ready.

"Joanna, I want you to stay right here and hide. Let them pass. I'll slip into this general store and sit tight until they ride past both of us," he said, nodding at the building next door. "Hopefully, they will ride on. But if I do have to face them, I'll lead the fight toward the station. When the fighting starts, fire a couple shots from here to scatter and confuse them," he said in the best way he could—and because he needed her to know he was counting on her. "Do you understand?"

Joanna nodded, but she had a puzzled look on her face. "Then what?" she asked.

Cade just smiled back. He couldn't help but appreciate her optimism. "After they ride on or the fight is done, you'll need to bring our horses up to that hotel," he said, pointing to a spot with a tie-up post. "The same hotel from where everyone we came to see just left. That is our next stop," he said with a little tip of his hat to Red Sky. "Now, let's go!"

Joanna sank down into the corner behind the fencing and clutched her rifle across her chest. Cade hoped she really understood, as there hadn't been enough time to get into details, and Red Sky was already making his way past the horses with his bow.

Cade moved from behind Red Sky to get as close to the wall as he could. Then he climbed the two steps to the platform in front of the big window and opened the door to the general store.

As he made his way inside, he looked out the window to see if he had been noticed. But the riders kept advancing down the middle of the street, seemingly unaware of his hiding place, so he quietly looked around to see who else was in the store. The storekeeper and the only other customer inside just stood there looking at him, so he put his index finger to his mouth and gestured for them to go about their business.

Cade glanced back out the window; the riders had slowly passed the store and then turned right at the first of two intersections between them and the train station. Once out of sight, Cade waited about another minute before exiting the store.

"Thank you kindly," he said to the storekeeper. "Have a nice day!"

But after he opened the door and stepped out onto the platform, he saw another familiar-looking character step out of a place across the street that looked like some sort of brothel. And when that man turned around, Cade immediately recognized the patch on his left eye and the bullwhip on his right hip.

Marshal Blackburn and Cade just stood there for a moment, staring each other down. The marshal seemed equally unprepared for this surprise, and so there was no clear advantage either way. And even though there was the expanse of the street between them, they were locked eye to eye in anticipation of who would make the first move.

Cade wanted to focus his senses and feel the distance between them, but he wasn't about to close his eyes. He could smell the fresh pile of horse crap in the street and smoke from woodfires in the air. He could also hear people walking around and the general activity in the street around him. As he set his balance on the wood planks underneath him, he was now ready to face this enemy. Even though the marshal had not moved and inch, Cade could still feel the burns on his neck from that deadly whip.

Then the sound of an approaching stagecoach broke the silence. It came from the opposite direction of the same road the bounty hunters had turned down, and out of the corner of his eye, Cade could see it make a sweeping left turn and come to a stop in front of the hotel they were headed for.

Even with this distraction in their peripheral view, Cade and the marshal had not stopped staring each other down. But this standoff couldn't last forever. It was time for Cade to press this fight and maintain his path toward the hotel.

Cade slowly sidestepped to his right and in the direction of the train station—and the marshal followed along on the opposite side of the street. If he kept sidestepping, Cade saw that he would eventually be behind a wooden signpost that could offer a bit of cover. The marshal must have realized that, too. And when Cade saw the marshal go for his pistol, he quickly pulled his first.

Cade got off a shot as he moved quickly to duck behind the signpost. And even though his shot missed, it made the marshal duck a little, and his shot missed, too.

But the marshal was quick to shoot again and then ducked behind two horses tied up front. There was no advantage for Cade to get a clean shot, and the idea of shooting at each other from across the street didn't make sense either.

Down the street, the passengers who got out of the stage-coach started running to the train station, and anyone else on the street quickly scattered to get out of the way.

"Looks like I caught up with you again, Mr. Wilson!" the marshal shouted from behind the horses. "And this time I've got a score to settle, too," he said, firing another shot that split the wooden sign and cut Cade's cover in half.

We all have scores to settle, Cade thought while he crouched low and looked for an attack position. But there was nothing between him and the marshal, and he found himself out of places to move. There was nothing but the building on the corner of the intersection, which looked like a bank, and that was the last place Cade wanted to seek cover. He also knew that he couldn't stay here. So without giving it a second thought, the samurai cowboy stared down his opponent as he cocked his Colt and pulled his shotgun pistol—and he charged.

"I've got you now," he heard the marshal say as he aimed his pistol. But Cade was still crouched low in his attack and fired a barrel at the feet of the horses. The horses immediately jumped up, and the marshal's shot missed again. Then the horses separated a bit, and this gave Cade a good shot—and he took it.

The bullet caught the marshal in the gut, just above his right hip, and the force of it caused him to fall backward. But it didn't kill him, and Cade was in the middle of the street and still advancing to finish him off when he heard the first shot fired from over his shoulder. Then there was another, and when he stopped to see where they were coming from, he saw the six riders charging at full speed toward him with their pistols drawn.

There was no time to think it through, and Cade simply turned back and started running toward the big window of the brothel in front of him. When he was close enough, he dove through the window, and shattered glass and bullets rained in behind him.

A woman screamed as Cade rolled over the sitting couch onto a decorative rug in the center of the room. When he opened his eyes, he saw three scantily clad women—one in the room with him, and two others standing on the stairs. "Sorry, ladies," was all he could say as he quickly pulled himself up on one knee to take aim out the window. But before he could get a look, another volley of shots kept him pinned down and forced him to duck below the window wall.

"Cade Wilson, we have you surrounded!" a voice from outside said as the sound of horses' clip-clopping spread out across the street. "Come out with your hands up, and I promise we'll treat you kind."

It sounded like that last part made a few of those men laugh, and Cade agreed with the joke. Death was not kind—it was only inevitable. But he hadn't come this far to be bested by this lot of bounty hunters.

He listened for the sounds of the horses as he clicked back the hammer of his Colt and of his shotgun pistol. Cade accepted that his chest armor may need to absorb a shot, but it would be worth it if he could identify the leader and take him out. That was his plan just before he heard the first rifle shot—it was Joanna!

The shot had come from behind the bounty hunters, and it sounded like she got one of them when a man began to wail about his leg. Wherever she had shot him, it worked perfectly and provided the distraction Cade needed. He rose up above the shards of glass still in the windowsill and took aim with his pistol at the first horseman looking back at him—and fired a round into his chest.

As the first man fell off his horse, all the other riders turned circles in complete confusion. They fired back at Cade in the window, and behind them in Joanna's direction behind the fence.

Cade was taking aim at another bounty hunter when he saw an arrow hit the man in the back. It was Red Sky from his position on the roof! *Nice not to be alone in this fight*, he thought as he took aim at the next closest man on a horse.

But he was a little too careless when he stood still too long to get a better aim, and when he exchanged shots with the bounty hunter, he felt the sting of a bullet graze his left leg while his bullet caught the rider in the gut. Cade grimaced, then aimed his shotgun pistol and fired the second barrel into the man's chest to finish him off.

He quickly spun to his right to take cover behind the wall as two more shots were fired in his direction. Cade took a second to assess the gunshot wound to his leg. It was only a flesh wound in his mid-thigh, but it was bleeding, and it hurt like hell when he put any weight on it.

The last three riders must have realized they were the ones completely surrounded, and Cade was still behind the window wall when they fired the final volley of shots back on his position. He took a minute to reload his shotgun pistol and was disappointed to hear they hadn't taken out the leader.

"Regroup!" a familiar voice shouted, and without firing another shot, he heard three horses circle about before taking off in the direction they originally came from.

As the trailing sound of the riders grew quieter, Cade peeked out of the window. The street was now clear, except for three dead men on the ground and their wandering horses. Then Cade looked to his left to spot where he'd shot the marshal, but he wasn't there. As he peered a little closer, he saw the spot trail of blood on the ground. One of those horses in front of the brothel must have been his, and he must have ridden off during all the shooting.

Cade looked up to see Red Sky on the roof of the building on the corner. The building from across the street was definitely a bank—and from Cade's experience, any shoot-out in front of a bank was nothing but trouble. When Red Sky acknowledged him, Cade waved at him to get down off the roof and head to the hotel.

Then he looked to where Joanna was hiding to give the same signal and was surprised to see her already walking the horses down the street toward their meeting spot. So he tipped his hat to her and leaned back against the wall before he slid slowly down to the floor.

He was inspecting his leg when the woman who was with him in the room stepped forward. She handed him a white kerchief before she reached behind her head to untie the black ribbon from her hair. After pulling the bow loose, she slowly shook her head and let her thick auburn hair fall down around her shoulders. Gazing at him, she offered the ribbon to Cade and then looked at the wound on his leg. He holstered his weapons to take these from her and fashioned a bandage with the ribbon.

The ribbon was long enough to wrap twice around his leg wound before he fastened it. Though it wasn't much, it would have to do, and hopefully the ribbon would be strong enough to keep the bandage tight.

"Thank you, and sorry about the mess," he said as sincerely as he could, and offered her a gold coin from his coat pocket.

"Don't mention it, darlin'," she replied with a seductive smile. "But if you do come back this way again, just use the door next time."

•••

Sideways

The first two gunshots were enough to draw the attention of everyone on the street, including the entourage of travelers making their way to the train station. And since the group with him was closer to the station than the hotel, Whitmore ushered everyone inside the heavy wooden doors of the completed portion of the building.

When the shooting continued and a fight broke out on the street, it was impossible to ignore what was going on, and curiosity seemed to infect everyone at the same time.

"Sounds like there's a bit of trouble brewing this fine

morning," Sinclair said to Whitmore, breaking the silence. "I wonder if our friend is in town?"

"C'mon now," Whitmore said with his arms extended to corral and direct everyone inside. "Let's stay inside and remain clear of whatever's going on out there," he continued while looking to his shadow riders and personal bodyguard. "I want you four to cover our back. And Toshi, I want you with me."

"Is it Viper?" Toshi asked.

"It doesn't matter! He's not why we're here," Whitmore said. "Your loyalty is to me. And if he comes, then I will expect you to kill him. But it will be easier to defend ourselves in the station, and we need to be on that train with the governor. Do I make myself clear?"

Toshi nodded, but Whitmore knew he didn't agree. "Yes, I am loyal to you," Toshi replied. "But if that is Viper, there is no defense we can mount here that will stop him."

"Don't be so sure of that, old boy," Sinclair said after eavesdropping on the conversation. "I wagered much thinking he would come north looking for Mr. Whitmore. Dangerous men with a price on their head do dangerous things. And now I'm about to collect on that bet."

Whitmore shuddered at the thought of Viper being here of all places, and he couldn't bring himself to say his name. After the first couple of shots were fired, it didn't take much convincing to usher the Carmichaels and their staff into the station. When the six men on horseback showed up and the shooting continued, he took one last look over his shoulder— and that's when he saw Viper running in the street and diving through a window.

He had confirmed his worst fears but didn't know the outcome of the fight. It didn't really matter if Viper was wounded or still alive, Whitmore wasn't taking any chances. "Hey, Sinclair, maybe you could keep watch on the street and tell me if you see anything," he asked politely.

"What's going on out there?" Victor asked point-blank. "Do you have a hand in this, Whitmore?"

Whitmore didn't bother to answer, and instead just gave Victor a stern look. The kind of look that suggested this wasn't the time or place to hash out the story of his vendetta with Viper. But as an additional measure, he did address his men. "Shadow riders, I want you to fan out and be prepared to defend our position. And that means keeping watch on what's going on out there, too."

Then he turned to his business partner to ask what really mattered. "Bruce, where is the governor?"

Bruce pulled his pocket watch from his vest pocket, and the smooth brass cover reflected a glint of light from the morning sun pouring through an east-facing window. "It's a quarter past nine. The governor should be making his way from his hotel," he said, pointing across the tracks in the other direction.

Whitmore was feeling more anxious by the second, and he couldn't believe what was happening. "This whole deal will go sideways if this trouble with Viper persists," he said to Bruce in a muffled voice that only he could hear—and then he made his way across the room to the boarding platform with a clear view of the building's west-facing side.

At first glance, five men appeared to be standing in front

of the hotel across the tracks. With a more distinguished eye, he was able to make out Stanwick and his travel partner, Mr. Tobin. Based on how the other three men were dressed, Whitmore assumed one of them was the governor.

But something looked wrong. Even though the gunfight had happened on the other side of the tracks, the five men were just standing there—and they were not walking toward the train station. Instead, they seemed to be turning to go back inside the hotel. When Whitmore saw Stanwick look back to the train station, he tried to get his attention by waving his arms and motioned for them to come on.

Stanwick just shook his head and waved his open hands a few times in front of him. Whitmore could read his body language to see that the answer was no, and then Stanwick followed the governor back inside the hotel while the other two men guarded their retreat.

"No! No! No!" Whitmore shouted in frustration. "This can't be happening! After all the work I've put into this deal, the governor isn't coming out because of a gunfight in the streets?"

"Listen to yourself, man!" Victor Carmichael said loud enough for everyone to hear. "Of course the governor is not going to risk being out in the open while men are shooting each other in the street."

Whitmore glared at Victor, but he knew he was right. And even though the shooting outside had stopped, his anger had boiled over, and he wanted blood. So he yelled across the room at the bounty hunter who was just standing there looking out the window—doing as he requested. "This has gone on long enough. How about you go out there and earn your money, bounty hunter. Or if it's not too much to ask… could you please go out there and kill Viper, now!"

Sinclair looked back at Whitmore with a sarcastic grin. "I don't think I need to go out there to kill him. He's coming this way."

CHAPTER 12

9:30 a.m.

As he made his way down the main street, Cade walked gingerly, feeling the pain in his upper thigh. Even though it was a short distance to the hotel where he'd rally with the others, he cursed every step he took and his carelessness for getting shot in the leg.

The random number of scattered people now gathering in small crowds told Cade the gunfight must have drawn the attention of all the townsfolk. Even some of the people who had ducked for cover emerged, and it was evident that everyone was now taking notice of him.

Cade couldn't hear all of their whispers, but he could imagine they were recalling the details of it all. At least one person said, "Someone needs to get the sheriff." But Cade wasn't going to wait around for the sheriff or try to explain what happened. The dead men in the street were someone else's problem. They shot first and paid the price. Dust to dust.

He followed behind Joanna and watched her tie up the horses on a post in front of the stagecoach near the hotel entrance. When she looked back to him with her rifle in hand, Cade cocked his head to the left as a silent instruction for her to enter. Hopefully, they would be able to take some shelter there without any more surprises. As Cade stepped through the front door of the Prairie Moon Hotel & Saloon, he saw Red Sky coming right up behind him.

Joanna was there to greet them in the lobby, which also served as the restaurant and bar. Only two other people were in the room, and one looked like the hotel manager. But he didn't approach or say a word as the three quietly took a seat at a table by the window.

"Thanks for your help back there," Cade said with a grin, shaking his head. "That didn't really go as planned, and I think everyone in Colorado knows we're here. Now how do we get over there?" he asked earnestly and pointed out the window to the train station.

"Could we please get some coffee?" Joanna asked the hotel manager, which shook him out of whatever daze he was in. Cade just gave a nod and watched the man turn to fetch some without argument.

"I saw many men from the roof. They all went inside the train station, and it would be easy to defend. It would be death to try and attack them straight on," Red Sky said.

Cade agreed. The station offered a well-fortified position. Even if catching the train was no longer a priority, they couldn't let his Benefactor, or Joanna's mother, get on board either.

A young boy emerged from the kitchen with three cups

and a pot of coffee. The rich smell of it as he poured was a welcome experience. It had been a while since Cade had a hot cup of coffee, and for a moment it transported him back to Rocky Creek and fond memories of breakfast at the Johnson Ranch.

As he turned to the sunlit window and closed his eyes, he imagined Lucy sitting over him in her bed with her hair and face surrounded by a bright, warm glow—and she was smiling at him. It gave him a pleasant feeling inside for a fleeting moment. Before he could enjoy the thought of being with her again someday, he needed to settle the business at hand.

The three friends sat quietly around the table, all deep in thought. They were so close to accomplishing what they came all this way to do, but the two hundred feet between the hotel and the train station seemed like two hundred miles of open street with no cover or way to advance on the building without being shot.

Then the piercing sound of a train whistle disturbed their peaceful moment and brought everything back into focus. And as they watched the train pull into the station, in advance of its scheduled departure, Cade was quickly reminded that whatever they were going to do next, time was working against them.

But watching the train pull into the station gave Cade an idea, and he suddenly became interested in one of the only other people in the room. A customer who was standing silently at the bar and minding his own business, but curiously drinking a glass of whiskey for breakfast.

"Excuse me, sir," Cade called out to the man at the bar. "Are you the driver of that stagecoach out front?"

The man seemed to nervously finish his drink and swallowed hard before answering. "Yes, why do you ask?"

•••

Fearful Memories

Joanna heard the clock chime ten times, and as the three of them were still huddled around the table, ironing out the final details of their plan, this was a timely reminder that the train would be leaving for Denver in an hour.

She looked out the window at the station. Aside from a few people making their way inside, there was no sign of her mother or the Carmichaels. But she knew they were inside or on the train because there was nowhere else for them to be. And for the first time in days, she began to worry about crossing paths with Spencer.

Joanna remembered how she felt that fateful afternoon. The foul smell of his breath as she was pinned under his weight, and how that look in his eyes changed from lust to fear and surprise when she took his knife and stuck him with it.

When she saw Spencer and his father in the street, the hate in her heart was temporarily assuaged by the sight of her mother. But it also became clear that her quest to see her mother again would not come without crossing paths with the Carmichaels. Then a mixed swell of emotions hit her like a flood—and for a moment, she felt like she would drown in them.

Her heart beat loudly in her chest, and she could hear the blood pulsing in her ears. Then she began to feel like it was hard to breathe, and she needed air. She was suffocating at the thought of Spencer ever touching her again.

Cade must have taken notice because he put his hand on her arm, which brought her attention back to the conversation at the table.

"Joanna, are you going to be okay?" he asked.

At first, she pulled her arm from his grasp, but then realized he was just trying to calm her down. His voice was soothing and peaceful, and like her father, she knew he would never do anything to hurt her. And in that moment, she also realized how much she still missed her father, too.

"You may not believe this, but I get anxious every time before a fight," Cade continued. "And there's something I do whenever I feel that way, and it helps me become centered and focused on everything around me. Would you like to try it?"

Joanna could only nod. She was still feeling too short of breath to speak, but she was willing to try anything to calm herself down.

"Good. Now first, get comfortable in your chair, and look straight forward," Cade began. "Focus on a spot on the wall or at something that will help clear your thoughts, and take a deep breath. Now close your eyes.

"Listen to the sounds of everything around you. Feel the weight of your body in the chair and pay attention to the smells in the air moving around you," he continued, and she did her best to oblige. "Are you feeling more relaxed?"

"Yes," she replied. While doing as he instructed, she

could hear sounds coming from the train, even though it was across the street. A familiar smell of food came from the kitchen—and it smelled like bacon. Then she could feel the energy from Cade and Red Sky sitting at the table with her.

"Now focus on what you need to do," Cade instructed. "You've come this far to see your mother again, and nobody is going to stand in your way. Can you imagine that for me?"

Joanna struggled with this at first. She already felt vulnerable, and now even more so with her eyes closed. As she began to imagine things just as Cade had described, images of her mother danced slowly around her mind and mixed with the awareness of her immediate surroundings. Then the face of Spencer Carmichael appeared in the swirl.

But this time, she was not afraid. Instead, she felt angry at the sight of him—and it was a hate that burned deep in her soul. If he tried to stand in her way, or touch her again, she was going to do more than stick him with his knife.

"Yes. I'm beginning to see," she replied. "I saw my mom. I could sense the room around me… and then I saw the face of the devil. That bastard killed the first man I ever loved and ruined my life, but I'm not afraid of him anymore."

"That's good. Now take another deep breath and open your eyes," Cade said while shifting in his chair. "Because what we're about to do is extremely dangerous. But if we stick together, we might just survive this day and get what we came for."

Joanna blinked her eyes open to see Cade and Red Sky looking back at her, and she smiled. Whatever haunting memories had caused her to feel anxious and afraid were now washed away. Now more than ever, she felt lucky to have these two men as friends.

"I'm ready," she said, sounding a little more confident than she probably really felt. But at least she was ready to face her fears.

Cade smiled back. "You're a brave young woman, Joanna. But now you need to get mean. Stay focused on why we're here and on finding your mother once we get inside the train station. And if anyone tries to stop you—"

"I'll kill them," she said.

• • •

Stalemate

"What are they doing in there?" Whitmore asked, not really expecting an answer. His frustration with the situation had not abated, and neither had his disdain for the man who was ruining everything. And that man was last seen entering the hotel across the street.

"I don't know, boss," said Lester, one of his most trusted shadow riders. "Viper, some girl, and an Indian have been holding up in that hotel for half an hour," he continued while taking a break from his lookout position.

"Well, I'm not going to wait around to find out," Bruce said. "I think we need to call this a day. I'm getting on this train and heading back to Denver." He grabbed his leather duffle bag and joined all the other passengers who were already on the train or anxious to board.

Victor also stepped forward to address Whitmore. "I agree. Whatever is going on out there has nothing to do with our family or our business deal. And right now, I'm more than ready to put this whole situation behind me."

"But, Dad… I saw Joanna Carter out there, too. I don't know why she came back, but if I get the chance, I want to kill that girl myself!" Spencer said from behind his father, and he said it so loudly that Whitmore sensed there was something more to that story.

Victor turned to his cast of servants and then to his son. "We're getting on this train. All of us, now! And we're going to let these hired guns finish this. Do you understand me?"

Spencer nodded somewhat defiantly, and the Carmichael entourage started gathering bags and moving to board the train. But Whitmore wasn't ready to concede the day as a complete failure just yet.

In an attempt to cut them off, Whitmore fast stepped his way in front of his business partners on the boarding dock. "Hold on now. This train's not leaving until eleven o'clock. Why are we running? There's got to be something we can do?"

"Joseph, this isn't running. It's common sense," Bruce replied as he stepped in close. "Let's get on the train. Once we get moving, we can smooth this over. If it makes you feel better, you can leave a few men here to cover our back. But you've got to accept this situation for what it is. The governor is not coming out of that hotel. We're not having a meeting this morning. And being on the train is better than waiting for whatever might happen here."

Whitmore didn't like it, but in his heart, he knew what Bruce said was true. He also trusted Bruce, and he had to accept that today was not going as planned if there was any possibility of salvaging this deal.

The look on Victor's face was also easy to read—he was a man who didn't like anyone telling him what to do in front of his son or his people. Whitmore conceded that the best thing to do was to step out of the way, and so he did. As he let everyone pass, he began to reconsider his position, too. Maybe he was better off getting on the train and letting his hired guns finish the job—just as Victor had said.

"Sinclair, what are you prepared to do if Viper tries to get on this train?" he asked the bounty hunter who, up to this point, had been quietly following along and not interfering in their business. But now it was time to play every card in the deck to win this hand.

Sinclair was still standing in the corner and keeping watch at the window. "I'm going to wait right here for him to come," he replied without looking at Whitmore. "That man has come this far, and I don't think he'll stop short of coming to get you now."

"What do you mean?" Whitmore asked, seeking clarification on being the hunted. "Are you suggesting that Viper has been planning to come after me all along?"

"Yes. That's exactly what I'm saying," Sinclair replied. "You don't really believe it's a coincidence he's here, do you? He's likely been making his way north for about a week to get here—but why? Why risk heading north or coming all this way to find you if he stole your gold and had every chance to run?"

Whitmore was dumbfounded. *Why would Viper be pursuing him?* He couldn't answer this question, and it continued to frustrate him. But somehow, he sensed the Englishman was right.

"He's been coming for you, and you want him dead," Sinclair continued. "Don't you see? Your fates are somehow intertwined, and today is the reckoning. I don't know much about this fellow, but after observing you the past few days, I get the sense that Viper is a very dangerous individual who won't stop until he gets what he wants. Much like yourself.

"So, I'm going to continue waiting for him to make his next move. Because I'm just as certain as I was when I met you in Denver—this 'Viper' is a man of purpose. And to beat him, I'll need to be close to those he's after, or those he loves," Sinclair said and revealed his ultimate strategy.

Whitmore had heard enough. It was painfully obvious that everything was falling apart today, but now he couldn't even get a straight answer from a bounty hunter.

"Suit yourself," he said, screwing up his face. "But if you're looking to get paid for his death, you better kill him before he gets to me."

Then he turned to Toshi—his most trusted bodyguard—the samurai who trained Viper. "Toshi, you know this man better than anyone. You trained him. What does he want from me?"

"His freedom," Toshi replied.

...

Viper Must Die

Toshi knew that his Benefactor didn't understand Viper the way he did. While Falcon was driven by hate and Scorpion by the need to belong, it was hard to say what sense of purpose guided Viper—and so it had taken Viper longer to reach his potential as a warrior.

As a warrior, Viper wasn't as strong or as lethal as the other two, but he was smarter and more cunning. He was the finest of the three students because he possessed the greatest potential for wisdom.

In this moment, and after hearing the bounty hunter's observations, Toshi began to realize that Viper's sense of purpose was now completely guided by his integrity and the virtuous traits that were always a part of his character. This was bigger than revenge, or greed, or something so obvious that it was easy for a teacher to challenge and unleash a student's potential. Righteousness was a purpose that had to be free and unbound to be fulfilled.

Toshi remembered his conversations with Viper, and how Viper began to question the morality of being a samurai and of wielding weapons of death in servitude to their Benefactor. There were questions that troubled him when what he was tasked to do was in conflict with his heart and "protecting the innocent," and these questions persisted. He was seeking wisdom beyond servitude, and so it was inevitable that Viper might eventually question his loyalty.

Viper's questions and soul-searching also reminded Toshi of the personal conflicts he experienced when he was set free by his master. At first, Toshi couldn't understand why everything he stood for had to change. He had spent his life in servitude to his lord and sacrificed everything for glory and to fight for him—and to die for him, if that was the way. Being free and without obligation was a concept he couldn't understand.

Toshi had thought it was the ultimate punishment for his transgressions because he ultimately strayed from the Way. When he was young, he didn't want to marry or have a child, but as he got older, he did both when he found love. And while love didn't cloud his judgment or his conviction, it began to influence his sense of purpose and eventually broke his spirit when he lost them both.

Shortly after the deaths of his wife and son, and before he left Japan, his master had summoned all his samurai warriors to inform them they would be disbanded. The new emperor wanted to modernize the military and the way of the samurai would be replaced by advanced guns, powerful cannons, and other new weapons of war. He felt like a lost man in the New World, as he couldn't imagine not being a samurai—like his father had been, and his father before him. And this was why he came to America. To him, freedom was his desire to find the Way again.

Now he served his new Benefactor, a man driven by pride and ambition. Whether he agreed with him or not, he was honor-bound to serve him. And he also knew what would be asked of him.

"What do you mean, he wants his freedom?" Whitmore asked. "I've given him everything, and he was supposed to be loyal to me."

"Yes, but his spirit was breaking," Toshi replied. "Too many times he began to question his existence at the fort. And unlike his brothers, he would be the first to know things that exist… and that which does not exist. In the void is virtue, and no evil. Wisdom has existence. Principle has existence, and the Way has existence."

"Are you telling me that Viper developed a conscience? He's just an orphan of an otherwise wasteful and pointless war that left him on my doorstep. Your training was supposed to mold his spirit and turn him into a samurai warrior," Whitmore said with a sarcastic laugh. "As his Benefactor, I've been very generous and only asked for loyalty in return. And now you're saying he wants to be free?"

Toshi looked his Benefactor in the eye. "Yes. That's what I'm saying. And in his mind, he is already free of you… and the spirit of who he once was is now nothingness. To be free of him, you will have to release him, or kill him."

He could see his Benefactor thinking about everything he just said, even if he didn't necessarily understand it.

"So be it," Whitmore said with a sigh. "Toshi, I want you and Lester to come with me." He pointed to the remaining shadow riders. "You three will stay here for now and cover our back until they announce the final boarding. And if Viper comes, you will not stop shooting until that bastard is dead. Do you hear me?"

Toshi shook his head. "Viper was my finest student. Not because he is a great warrior. Because he is a survivor," he said as he sensed the shadow of death surrounding the men asked to stay behind. "He has already bested Falcon and Scorpion. These men won't be able to stop him."

His Benefactor just sneered back at him. "Maybe you're right. And if it comes down to you, then let me make my expectations clear. Whatever happens, Viper must die!"

CHAPTER 13

10:30 a.m.

The train whistle gave a long howl, immediately followed by three clangs of a bell. Even if the sounds and their symbolism were a mystery to someone who had never been on a train, Cade knew it was time to make their move.

Red Sky and Joanna were in position to make their way out the back door when Cade gave the signal. He wanted to make sure anyone watching from the train station would see him leaving the hotel. If all attention was on him, the plan should work.

Cade stepped out the door and passed behind the stagecoach driver. He stood there for about a minute and let the driver untie the horses and get up into the seat before he made his next move.

"Remember now, all you have to do is ride by the station and drop me off in front of the train. After that, I would suggest you get the heck out of there before all hell breaks loose," he said to the driver, then handed him a gold coin.

The driver just smiled back, a smile barely visible through his overgrown beard, and gave a nod. "Whatever you say, mister."

Cade tipped his hat, put his finger and thumb inside his mouth, and gave a loud whistle before opening the door to the carriage and climbing in. The coach's interior was surprisingly accommodating, but he struggled to fully appreciate the pillowed seat covers across the hardwood benches while feeling very confined in such a small space. At least the cushions were quite comfortable to sit on, even though the ride wasn't going to last but a moment.

"Get 'er up!" the driver said with a quick snap of the reins, and the coach jumped to life. The four work horses up front made quick time of getting out into the street, then made a big sweeping turn to the right. When the driver passed in front of the station as instructed, Cade knocked on the roof for him to slow and drop him off near the engine up front.

When the stagecoach came to a stop about a hundred feet farther up the street from the station, Cade made sure to exit out the opposite side—out of sight from the only visible windows of the station. He figured the men inside were expecting a frontal assault on the building, and were not prepared for him to come at the building from the front of the train.

But to Cade's surprise, somebody was waiting for him as he stepped in front of the horses to remain out of view. Three men stood across the street, about ten feet apart in a fenced line. The two men on either side were carrying rifles in each hand, and the man in the middle could only be the local sheriff, as the badge of justice shone brightly on his chest in the late morning sun.

"I've heard about you, Cade Wilson," the sheriff said, speaking loud enough for anyone in his audience to take notice. "And I've been told the three dead men in the street shot at you first. So here is what I want you to know. I'm here to keep innocent people out of harm's way… and to protect the governor."

Then the sheriff tilted his hat back a little with his left hand, and Cade could almost see his eyes as he slowly lowered his right hand to the Peacemaker on his hip. "And if your business causes a problem between you and me, consider yourself warned," he said with the conviction of a man here to handle his business if necessary.

Cade had nothing to say in return, but they exchanged a nod to show they had an understanding. Then, after surveying the activity around the station, Cade ran straight to the front of the train engine, so he could cross the tracks and make his way up the other side.

• • •

Heart of a Warrior

Joanna waited with Red Sky in the alley by the hotel's side wall. When she saw Cade run from the stagecoach to the train, she knew it was time for them to cross the street and make their way to the tracks and come up from the back.

While running to the tracks, the distance seemed farther than she had imagined, but they were able to make it across and all the way to crouch behind the last car on the tracks without being shot at. Cade must have drawn any attention away from them.

The last car on the train was a stock car for animals, and she had seen one like this before. This one had two horses tied up on the front side, and there were a dozen hogs fenced in the back. The smell of the pigs was more than she could bear, but the back of the train provided some cover to stop and look around.

"I don't think anybody saw us," Joanna whispered as they remained crouched behind the last car, observing the activity at the station. "And I don't see anyone standing on the platform."

"Let's go. Follow behind me, and be careful," Red Sky whispered back.

Red Sky led the way with an arrow lightly pulled back in his bow, and he hunched down as he walked up the side of the train. Joanna was right behind him with her rifle in hand as they approached the coupling and the next car on the track.

This one was a freight car, and through the semi-open door she glanced inside. The contents looked like tools, crates, and demolition equipment—the same tools her father would use as a surveyor. Seeing this equipment triggered a painful memory, but she quickly shook it off as they needed to keep moving forward to the passenger cars. Then Red Sky suddenly stopped, and she almost ran into him.

"What's wrong?" Joanna asked.

"Look up ahead," Red Sky replied over his shoulder.

Joanna tried to get a better view by craning her neck around Red Sky to see, but still remain low and hidden. It was hard to make out what everyone was doing, but she did see three men in gray coats scrambling around to defend their position—and the position they were taking wasn't against the two of them.

"They must have seen Cade," she said.

Then Red Sky perked his head up in a different direction. He looked back to scan around them, then turned quickly and pulled his bow. "Behind you!" he shouted in alarm.

Joanna looked behind her as a bullet splintered the wood of the freight car just above her head. The three remaining bounty hunters were back—and they were shooting while riding their horses straight at them.

There was nowhere to duck for cover as two more rounds burst against the side of the freight car. But Red Sky steadied himself and took aim before he let the arrow loose. The arrow struck the closest rider just under his neck in the upper part of his chest, and the horse continued to charge forward as its rider fell to the ground.

"Dammit all, shoot the girl! I'll take the Indian." the leader told the other rider, then he pulled his horse to a stop and tried to aim his pistol at Red Sky.

Joanna stood and tried to take aim at the second rider with her rifle, but she hastily pulled the trigger and missed as the bounty hunter dismounted his horse. When his feet hit the ground, he quickly took aim and looked ready to shoot.

She was still trying to reload as she stared down the barrel of his pistol. But just as the bounty hunter pulled the trigger, Red Sky came diving in between them while throwing his tomahawk. The warrior's axe struck the man in the face, and he wouldn't get another shot off as he fell to the ground.

Red Sky collapsed at Joanna's feet and did not move. She immediately dropped her rifle and fell to her knees. As he lay there motionless, she put her hands on his shoulder and his hip to roll him over. When she got him on his back, she could see the blood where the bullet had hit him just below his left shoulder.

When he blinked his eyes open, Joanna saw him wince. "Are you okay?" she asked—but he didn't answer. Instead, his eyes grew big and wide as he was looking over her shoulder. That's when she heard the sound of the horse coming up behind her and the click of the hammer.

Without a second thought, she pulled the pistol from Red Sky's holster—the pistol she had not seen him use—but it was just like the one her father had. And she reared back with the gun in both hands and pulled the trigger.

Her shot missed, but the horse was startled enough that the leader fired his bullet into the dirt. Then he was mumbling something to himself as he tried to settle his ride before attempting to take aim.

Joanna was surprised by the kick from the pistol, but nothing she couldn't handle. In her panic, she was upset with herself for missing—and she knew the next shot needed to count. She took careful aim at the rider as she pulled the hammer back with her thumb, and the gun fired again.

The second shot made her ears ring, and all she could hear was the dull, steady hum that followed as the smell of gunpowder lingered in the air. She locked eyes with the bounty hunter, almost waiting for him to shoot her back. But then his eyes rolled over white, and he slouched forward in his saddle. As the horse began to walk away, the leader of the six riders fell to the ground.

She felt like the world around her had ceased to exist; for a moment, she couldn't even remember why she was here. Everything that had just happened seemed so surreal that it almost slowed the passing of time.

She looked at the pistol in her hands and realized she had just killed a man—and that man was her first kill. She shot him before he could shoot her, and he would have, if given the chance. As she processed the depth of what had just happened, the pistol seemed so much heavier than before.

But then she heard Red Sky's voice bring her back. "Nice shot," he said.

Suddenly remembering her wounded friend on the ground, she turned her attention back to Red Sky. "You're still alive?" she said. "You saved my life!"

Her eyes welled up with tears of joy, and she knelt over him and hugged him. "Thank you," she said before pulling back to reexamine the wound. She placed her right hand near the bloody spot on his chest, then she poked at it to apply some pressure—but that made more blood seep from the wound. So she reached down to the bottom of her dress and tore a piece off to serve as a bandage.

"That's good," he replied. "But it hurts. I can feel the bullet in my shoulder."

She didn't know what else to do, but she realized they were out in the open, and they couldn't stay here. "Can you move?" she asked. "We need to get you back to the hotel."

"No!" he said firmly as he sat himself up. "Leave me. I'll watch your back. Go find your mom. Help Cade."

Thoughts of her mom and Cade reemerged. "You're right," she said as she snapped back to the plan. Then she handed the pistol back to Red Sky. "Here, you might need this."

As he took the pistol from her hand, the next thing Red Sky said to her rolled through her mind like a wave of emotion—as both a reminder of what had happened, and a foretelling of what was to come.

"Be brave," he said.

Joanna nodded back as she stood and picked up her rifle. "I will," she replied.

•••

Smoke & Steam

The stack from the locomotive was billowing black smoke and soot. And as noisy as it was, Cade still heard the gunshots that came from the other end of the station. As he made his way down the opposite side of the train, he passed the steam engine and the coal car to come up low behind an empty flatcar.

The next car in line was the first of two passenger cars,

and those were too big to get caught behind. But the empty flatcar offered cover and a vantage point where he could see the shadow riders scrambling to locate him. The three of them looked like they were caught completely off guard—and Cade appreciated that everything was going according to plan. But something was confusing him, too. *If the shadow riders were looking for him, who was doing all the shooting?*

Whoever it was, it provided a perfect distraction because the shadow riders had turned their backs; they clearly didn't know which way the fight was coming from, either. And that's when Cade cocked his Colt and shotgun pistol and advanced to a good spot to attack.

In one quick jump step, he put his left foot on the coupling and tried to spring up to the flatcar's open platform. But the gunshot wound on his thigh painfully reminded him that his left leg wasn't at full strength, so instead of landing flat-footed, he had to roll through his landing and pop up on one knee.

The move was still quick enough to surprise the shadow riders, and Cade took aim at the closest one first. He was standing behind a stack of crates against the wall of the station, but a blast from the shotgun was enough to splinter the crates and startle his target into view. Both were quick to fire their pistols at each other, but Cade's shot found its mark in the shadow rider's chest, while the return fire only caught a piece of his left shoulder armor.

Now Cade was out in the open on the flatcar, so he quickly ran toward his attackers and jumped from the flatcar to the ground while taking careful aim at his next target. But again, a jolt of pain stabbed through his left leg when he landed on the dusty wooden planks of the platform. This threw him off-balance, and he had to limp quickly to the same stack of crates he had just shot at for cover.

As he stepped over the body and settled behind the crates, he found cover just in time to avoid two shots in his direction. As soon as he was able to put his back to the wall of the station and steady himself, he popped out to fire at the shadow rider standing near the boarding area of the passenger car.

The pistol shot caught the shadow rider in the right side of his hip, forcing him to stumble into the open on the boarding platform. Cade wasn't going to miss from this range with his shotgun pistol—and the blast planted the shadow rider against the side of the passenger car before he slowly slid down in a pool of blood.

Another shot splintered the crates, and Cade had to retreat behind them. His shotgun pistol was empty, so he holstered it, knowing he still had four rounds in his pistol. Hopefully, he could get a shot off on that third shadow rider and buy some time to reload.

But when he peeked around the corner of the crate, he could see the third shadow rider standing behind a big wooden post in the center of the boarding platform. And before he could take aim, another shot forced him back.

Cade cursed himself for being so foolish. He didn't like this position and felt trapped behind the crates with a considerable distance to cross to get back to the train. That shadow rider had great cover and a vantage point to fire at him if he tried to run for it. And with his wounded leg, he knew he couldn't move as fast as he would need to.

He closed his eyes to reset his senses, then he tried to get a better sense of his surroundings and his next move. After a long exhale, he tried to remember his time with the Johnson family and the prayer they had said to keep him safe.

"A little luck would be nice, too" he said quietly to Red Sky's spirits, or whoever was listening.

•••

Catching a Fly

Sinclair was initially drawn out by the action coming from behind the train, which seemed to catch everyone else in the passenger car by surprise, too. Then the shooting from the front of the train started, and the attack plan seemed pretty clear to him and the last shadow rider on the train.

"They are attacking from the front and the back," Lester told Whitmore, but loud enough for everyone in the passenger car to hear. "What do you want me to do?"

"Stay with me," Whitmore snapped back.

"I think you owe us an explanation, Mr. Whitmore," Victor said as politiely as an ultimatum could sound. "Being around you is putting our lives in danger, and doing business with you is becoming a sour proposition."

"If you want to ride in the other passenger car with your servants, go right ahead. But whatever explanation you think you deserve right now is the least of my concerns," Whitmore said with a sneer, before turning to the bounty hunter. "Is this where you finally get involved?"

Sinclair just smiled and tipped his hat. "Time to go to work," he said and checked the rounds in his ivory-handled Colt. "And if you don't mind, please keep an eye on my belongings if we get separated," he added, nodding at his saddlebags.

He loved chaos as much as he loved a challenge, and the only thing better than a challenge was getting paid for it. Besting Cade Wilson and collecting the bounty would go a long way to building the reputation he coveted as a quick-draw shooter. Yet as he was about to step out of the car to get a better look, he was able to see a young woman making her way up the side of the train while her native warrior companion was still on the ground and in no shape to come up behind her.

"Joanna Carter, I presume," he whispered to himself as he waited for her to get closer. A few seconds later, the girl tried to slip around the corner of the second passenger car and enter the boarding area—and Sinclair kicked the rifle out of her hands and pounced on her.

As she fell on her backside on the boarding platform, fear and embarrassment washed over her face. But she was quick to try to stand up while reaching for a big knife that was tucked in the rope belt around her waist.

Sinclair quickly pulled his shiny pistol and clicked back the hammer. "You'll be dead soon enough, but not right now. Take your hand off the blade," he said, pointing the barrel directly at her face and waiting for her to acknowledge him. "Now be useful and come here," he added, and he reached out with his left hand to grab her by the wrist and pull her off the ground.

At first she resisted, but Sinclair was deceptively strong, and he pulled her arm while spinning her around, so her back was against his chest. And after he readjusted his grip on her right arm, he pinned her against his body while pointing the barrel of his pistol to her temple.

"You're quite the wild thing," Sinclair said to the disheveled girl firmly in his grasp. "I need you to introduce me to your friend, Mr. Wilson. But please allow me to do all the talking, if you please," he added with a condesending chuckle.

Joanna continued to struggle, but it was no use. Sinclair had placed her between him and the man he assumed was attacking from the front of the train. And as they slow-walked their way up the boarding platform, they eventually arrived a few paces behind the remaining shadow rider, who had taken cover behind the post.

"Where is he?" Sinclair asked the shadow rider, trying to assess the situation.

"I've got him pinned down over there behind those crates," the shadow rider said, sounding confident in his position. "If you can draw him out, I think I can get a clean shot at him."

Sinclair twitched his mouth from side to side as he quickly calculated his options. Then, without warning, he took aim with his pistol and shot the shadow rider in the back.

"Sorry, old boy, but that bounty is all mine," he said as the shadow rider fell to the ground.

Then he put the barrel back to Joanna's temple and pulled the hammer back again. "Now let's take care of business, shall we?" And after they sidestepped a few paces to take cover behind the same post, Sinclair kicked the dead body out of the way and hollered out to the man called Viper.

...

Vengeance is Mine

Cade heard a single gunshot and continued to listen for more, or for advancing footsteps, but none followed. Then a man's voice broke the silence.

"Mr. Wilson… I've heard so much about you, and now we finally get to meet. My name is Sinclair, and I have a friend of yours with me. Someone who would appreciate it very much if you came out to see us," the voice boomed out across the boarding platform.

Cade opened his eyes. Everything around him seemed cast in vibrant color. The steam engine sounded like unbridled power getting ready to charge any moment now. His leg was still sore, but he knew he had to press on. The man calling him out by name had his attention.

"What do you want?" Cade called back. Given his position and this unexpected situation, he thought it was best to ask before he planned his next move.

"I want you to step out where I can see you," Sinclair replied. "There's a bit of money on your head, and reportedly in your possession. Or so it's been said by your former employer." Then he twisted Joanna's forearm until she let out a little scream. "And I'd like to have a little conversation with you before I have to shoot this poor girl."

Cade didn't really have much of a choice. He couldn't hold out from here, and now there was a new wrinkle between him and his Benefactor—and Toshi, too. So he slowly emerged from behind the crates with his Colt in hand. Once he could see the look on Joanna's face and the man holding her hostage, he stepped up on the boarding platform and prepared to take a shot if he had to.

"Here I am… now what?" Cade asked very bluntly while noticing the other dead shadow rider on the floor.

Sinclair offered up a thin smile. "Well, you certainly look how I imagined, given your reputation. But I would first ask that you lower your pistol. You wouldn't want to shoot your friend by accident," he said, giving Joanna's arm another twist.

Joanna winced and then turned slightly to the man using her as a shield. "I swear, if you hurt me again, you're going to regret it."

"She's a feisty one, isn't she?" Sinclair said with an over-confident grin, and he gave her wrist another twist. "I'm sure we could exchange pleasantries all day, but let's get down to business. There's a story about some gold I'd like to hear about. But for now, I'd like for you to holster your pistol."

Cade shook his head. "How about you let the girl go and I'll tell you whatever you want to know?"

"Oh, we'll get to that," Sinclair replied. "And I promise that I'll give you a chance to prove how fast you are with that pistol. But for now, I want you to holster it and show me your hands so we can talk. Do it now… or I'll put a bullet in her head."

Cade could sense this man was not making idle threats, and that the secret he still held about the gold was about to serve him again—at least for the moment. So he slowly holstered his pistol then presented both hands out in front of him.

"Good," Sinclair said, sounding increasingly confident about his control of the situation. Then he surprised Cade by slowly holstering his pistol, too—but he remained carefully shielded behind Joanna. "Now we can chat and tell stories. I love stories. Let me go first.

"As you may have guessed by my accent, I'm not from the States," Sinclair said very casually. "But I've made a name for myself, and I've earned a few dollars here and there as a big game hunter. The kind of hunter that builds a reputation tracking dangerous men like you. As chance would have it, I've recently met up with Mr. Whitmore, or the man you call your Benefactor. I've also met Toshi, the man that trained you. And I've heard stories about the men you've bested and something about ten thousand dollars in gold. So now I have to ask the person who knows firsthand. Is all of that true?"

Cade was in no mood to verbally fence with this guy or tell stories. His tailored look and shiny pistol made for a nice display, but to Cade it was just fancy curtains on another gun for hire. Instead of playing along, he took a poke to see if he could get into the head of his overconfident opponent.

"Funny thing about stories… the people that spread them usually heard them from someone else. So what's your reputation, bounty hunter? Shooting people in the back?" he asked with a head tilt to the shadow rider lying on the dusty planks between them.

"Now, now," Sinclair replied. "There's no need to get personal. I happen to be known for being what you Americans call 'quick on the draw,' which I've found to have a double meaning, but they both describe me," he said with a dry laugh. "But as for that poor chap," he continued while briefly acknowledging the man he shot in the back. "He just happened to be in the wrong place at the wrong time. And since it's bad for business to share reward money, it was a necessary decision to—"

The loud crack of a bullwhip against the wood floor interrupted the bounty hunter and commanded everyone's attention. Marshal Blackburn stood in the doorway with the late morning sunlight streaming in behind him. He carried a shotgun in his left hand, and the Widowmaker in his right—and he casually switched the aim of his shotgun from Cade, to Sinclair and Joanna, and then back again. There was a torn rag tied around his gut as a makeshift bandage, and the gunshot wound in his hip made his movements look very pained but determined. As he slowly limped forward on the platform, he dragged his right leg and left a red-stained boot print in his wake.

"You and I can agree on that, Englishman," the marshal said in a gravelly voice. "I've tracked this man for many days. He put this bullet in my hip, and that girl you're holding burned my partner. So now you're in the wrong place at the wrong time… because this man's blood belongs to me."

CHAPTER 14

Enemy of My Enemy

The train whistle howled again, and the men in the engine car were arguing and sounded anxious to leave. If there were any formalities with getting underway, they must have been abandoned after the shooting started and everyone clamored onboard. But the windows of the passenger cars were all filled with faces peering out at the spectacle on the boarding platform.

Cade knew he was out of time. He either needed to be on that train—or figure out how to get his Benefactor off it. There was no other way. He knew that if he missed this opportunity, it would be a huge mistake.

The only good thing was that everyone was now out in the open on the boarding platform. But Marshal Blackburn had the drop on him, and the foreign bounty hunter was still holding Joanna hostage. It wouldn't be an easy choice to focus on just one opponent. The marshal was wounded, but he looked handy enough with that shotgun to punish a reckless move. More of an unknown was the Englishman. If Sinclair was as quick as he made himself out to be, the marshal wasn't going to get off two shots with Joanna caught in the middle. Knowing he needed to change his odds, Cade gambled on the gold once more.

"You still want to hear that story about the gold?" he asked Sinclair, but loud enough for the marshal to hear.

Sinclair peered back at Cade from the corner of his eyes. "Yes, I do," he replied.

"Yes, let's hear that story," the marshal said while aiming his shotgun at Cade.

But Cade wasn't dealing with the marshal just yet. "Let the girl go," he said, trying to negotiate with Sinclair. "Let her go, and I'll tell you where it is."

Before Sinclair could answer, Blackburn spoke up. "Nobody's going anywhere," he said, reminding everyone that he was currently in control of the situation. "I like having all of you where I can see you."

But Sinclair seemed willing to deal as he slowly pulled Joanna over to his left and let go of her wrist. "I don't know who you are, but the girl will be dealt with soon enough," he said to the marshal. "I want to hear what Mr. Wilson has to say."

Cade watched as Joanna peeled away from the bounty hunter and stepped slowly backward toward the train. If this would be a contest of speed, at least he'd have a clean shot with Joanna out of the way. But the marshal still had a shotgun pointed at him.

"The girl is free. Now tell me about the gold so we can

get on with this," Sinclair said to Cade then lowered his right hand near his holstered pistol.

"You stay right there, little lady. We've got a score to settle," the marshal said to Joanna before addressing Cade directly. "Now enough of this. You tell me where the gold is, and I'll make this painless," he said while twitching his whip, and Cade sensed the one-eyed bounty hunter was ready to make good on his promise.

Cade steadied himself and tried to predict which of them would shoot first. He sensed they might be doing the same as the three of them stood locked in their standoff. Facing two enemies would put them at odds against each other—and so he would have to draw first, or wait for the first one to flinch.

"The gold, where is it?" Sinclair insisted. His outburst drew the marshal's attention, and the aim of his shotgun. Then the locomotive let out a big burst of steam and it was the opportune moment Cade needed.

"*Agua de vida!*" Cade shouted back and went for his pistol. With the marshal wounded, and distracted, it made sense to take out the unknown opponent.

But Sinclair was faster, and Cade had barely pulled his gun from his holster before he heard the gunshot and felt the bullet hit him in the chest. His chest armor stopped the slug, but he felt it all the same as the force of it knocked the wind out of him.

Cade fired an off-target shot as he staggered slightly off-balance and a jolt of pain reminded him of his leg wound. Then he saw Sinclair produce a derringer from his left sleeve with another impressive display of speed, and watched as he turned slightly and shot the marshal with his two bullet pistol.

The marshal took the bullet on his left side and flinched at the pain. But he was big enough to stand his ground and was able to fire a barrel that blasted Sinclair's right foot.

Sinclair groaned and dropped to one knee with pistols still in both hands. Cade had also dropped to one knee to make himself a smaller target, and because he was still short of breath and trying to regain his composure when he saw Sinclair raise his Colt to take aim at him.

But the crack of a whip echoed through the station as the Widowmaker wrapped around Sinclair's right wrist. He fired the shot, but it missed—and Cade could hear the bones in Sinclair's arm snap as he dropped the pistol and wailed in pain.

"You rat bastard… how do you like that?" the marshal asked while twisting his whip to release it. And as the whip coiled back, Cade saw the marshal turn in his direction. "Your turn."

Cade had caught his breath enough to raise his pistol and fire a shot at the marshal, and the slug caught him in the left side of his chest. The marshal began to stumble, and he fired the second barrel from his shotgun harmlessly into the floor. But again he stood his ground, and Blackburn did not go down from Cade's single shot.

Pressing the attack, Cade got to his feet and faced down the man who had strangled him—and he would give no quarter for that to happen again. As he walked straight at the marshal, he peeled back the hammer and fired two more shots into the marshal's chest. And when his Colt clicked empty, he holstered it and pulled both swords.

Surprised that the marshal was still standing, even while the light in his eyes was fading, Cade went low with his attack and slashed the marshal's legs to drop him to his knees. Then in two swift moves, he stuck his left sword through the marshal's heart and brought his right sword full circle with both hands and sliced it across his neck.

After a brief moment, Cade pulled his left sword from the marshal's chest and stood back. Then he popped his arms out to each side as blood dripped from the blades. With his swords at the ready, he watched the marshal's body collapse and his head roll off onto the dusty floor.

Then Cade turned to Sinclair. The bounty hunter was still on one knee and staring at his right hand, which was hanging limp from his broken wrist. The look of pain and shock on his face was evident, as if he was still trying to process what had just happened.

"Bloody hell. How are you still alive?" Sinclair asked, looking up to Cade. "I was faster than you. I shot you first. I saw the bullet hit you in the chest. How?" he asked again. When Cade didn't answer, Sinclair straightened himself up and tried to raise the derringer in his left hand to take his last shot.

But the shot that rang out from the two-round pistol missed its mark, and Sinclair's body fell to the plaform with a thump.

Behind the bounty hunter, Cade saw Joanna standing there with a vengeful look in her eye. She had picked up her rifle and cold cocked him with the stock. And after she composed herself by brushing some of the hair out of her face, she said her final piece to the man on the floor. "I warned you," she whispered.

• • •

A Mother's Love

"The train is about to leave. Go find your mom!" Cade said to Joanna without acknowledging what just happened, and she nodded back without saying a word.

She turned to make her way to the forward passenger car, because Joanna assumed her mom would be with the "commoners" and other low-fare ticket holders. For as long as she'd known, the Carmichaels traveled in the finest accommodations available—and their servants and her family did not.

When she reached the forward passenger car, she grabbed the cool metal handle and stepped up into the entryway. The familiar smells of people, leather and wood, and the Hopper, all brought back plenty of memories—some good and some she'd rather forget. After stepping through the entry, she was at the rear of the car and looked anxiously for her mother through the crowd of passengers just staring back at her.

It hadn't occurred to her that everyone in this car was watching what had just happened. But as she stood there holding her rifle, it dawned on Joanna why they were all waiting for her to do or say something.

"Mom!" she called out—and through the sea of faces,

there was one at the front end of the car that made her heart burst.

Everyone else became a faceless blur as she made her way through them. And then the woman in the same paisley blue dress opened her arms and took Joanna in.

"My darling girl, I've been so worried about you," her mom said while they embraced.

Joanna was enraptured. She basked in the smell of her mother's clothes and the warmth of her arms, and it was the best she had felt in a long time. Something she had foolishly taken for granted over the past couple of years was now the most incredible thing in the world, and she wished this feeling could last forever.

"But you shouldn't be here," her mother said, and the moment was gone. Then she placed Joanna's head in her hands and made eye contact—just as she had always done when she had something important to say. "After what you did to Spencer, you shouldn't be here," she said.

That's when Joanna saw the bruise on her mother's cheek and the dark circle around her eye. "Who hit you? What did they do to you?" she asked angrily.

Her mother looked away and didn't answer. Joanna could tell she was ashamed to say. Victor Carmichael had a temper, and so did Spencer. It was easy enough to imagine that what Joanna had done had caused those men some pain and suffering, and they took that frustration out on a woman who had never done them wrong a day in her life.

"Spencer came at me, Momma, that's what happened. He trapped me in the tent and came at me. He forced me on the ground, and—" Joanna tensed up, thinking about how to word this. Because the tears welling up in her mother's eyes were already breaking her heart.

"And that's when I stuck him. I stuck him with his own knife… and I ran. I ran, Momma," she said, pulling away slightly. "I didn't know what else to do."

The look on her mother's face reminded Joanna of when her father was killed. The wrinkles around her eyes and pursed lips meant her mom understood what happened but was struggling with how to deal with it. Joanna then realized she didn't know what to do either.

Then the nerves in Joanna's belly tingled, and she sensed that they didn't have time to sort this out right now. "Momma, come with me. Let's get off this train and never look back. We can make a new life somewhere, anywhere."

Her mother's eyes blinked nervously and darted back and forth from Joanna to the other people she worked with in the passenger car. Then she put her hands on Joanna's shoulders and pulled Joanna's face to hers. "No, baby, I can't leave. My place is here," she said. "I can't leave. But you can. You're so much younger than me… stronger than me. You need to be your own woman, now. I know you can make it without me, because you already have," she said with a proud smile that also seemed like a dam just strong enough to hold back her tears.

Then her mother's lip quivered, and Joanna prepared herself for what her mother would say next.

"I saw you hit that man. I would've never guessed you capable of that, or what you did to Spencer. You don't belong here, but I do. I need you to know that in your heart. And I need you to know that I will always love you, but you have to go. Go now, and keep running until you find a safe place. Because they won't stop until they find you. And know in my heart that I love you," her mother said, visibly heavy with all the emotion, and the dam finally broke as she began to sob.

Joanna tried to understand, but a creeping frustration made it hard to believe. She had come all this way to see her mom again, and now her mom was telling her to leave. She was trying to think of something else to say to convince her otherwise, but her mother's eyes had become wide as her gaze was now fixed on something else over Joanna's shoulder.

"Oh no," her mother said softly. "It's too late."

· · ·

11:00 a.m.

The clock chimed eleven times, even though it was barely audible with the random sounds and noise generated by the train and the voices surrounding Whitmore. But it was a welcome sound, because Whitmore wanted nothing more than to get this train moving.

He felt a headache coming on. The kind that would start up behind his eyes and could last for hours. But this headache had a name and a place associated with it. After he just witnessed Viper survive another fight with two men as deadly as the day is long, he began to feel something else that he hadn't felt in a long time—a crushing feeling that could upset his stomach and cloud his judgment. He was afraid. And he lashed out at others in spite of it.

"Why isn't this train moving?" he screamed at the porter. He needed to take his anger and frustration out on something, or someone—and the only man in the parlor car who was there to accommodate passengers was an easy target. "It's eleven o'clock. Did you not hear the bells?"

Then he turned to the last shadow rider in his company. "Lester, I want you to cover that entrance over there, do you understand me?" he said, pointing at the parlor car's back entrance. "And I want you to shoot anyone who tries to get on board."

"Toshi, I want you to—" He looked around, but Toshi was nowhere to be seen. "Where's Toshi?" Whitmore asked to everyone around him.

Everyone in the car stared back at him blankly.

"Where's my son?" Victor replied.

•••

The Teacher

Toshido Hasegawa stepped off the train into the warm autumn sun. The smell of progress was full of smoke from machines that bothered his senses. And in this moment, he longed for the lush green mountains of Japan and the more familiar smells of fruit trees and soft winds blowing in from the sea.

He closed his eyes and wished he was far away from here, and far away from what he had to do.

Since the death of his son, he had removed himself from attachment when teaching others in the way of the samurai. The pain and emptiness in his heart could not be filled by another. And when he came to America, he sought a new master to serve and to find peace and honor in the life he had always known. Instead, he found himself tasked with training young warriors once again and trying to instill whatever wisdom he had left to share.

Now his finest student in this new world was standing in front of him. He'd grown into a man before his eyes and become a deadly warrior with instincts the other two had either ignored or did not possess. And now he would have to face his student as an opponent in this unceremonious place. The student he had failed to not get attached to.

"Welcome, Viper," Toshi called out to his student and gave a bow. "You have bested many opponents and earned my respect. You are a deadly samurai and no longer the donkey."

Viper bowed in return but then shook his head. "There doesn't have to be blood, sensei. I don't want to fight you, or anyone else for that matter," he said, keeping his swords lowered. "That's why I need to speak with our Benefactor. This is between him and me. I want to be done with him, and all of this," he said, motioning for Toshi to look at the bodies lying around them.

Toshi didn't want to look, and he stood his ground without saying a word. He'd seen enough carnage in his life. Walked too many battlefields where flies feasted on the blood of the dead. He knew that looking around would only make today more difficult than it already was.

"Please let me by. I just want to talk to him. I can get his gold back. I'll give everything back. I just want to be free. There has to be some way we can work this all out," Viper said.

Toshi shook his head. He understood what his student wanted, but freedom wasn't anything he could give. "My loyalty, and my place, is with our Benefactor. Something you should have remembered and honored from your training. Your place was with us. But now my place is between you and him. And so now it shall always be."

"But I'm not the same person I was," Viper replied. "I've seen things—experienced things. Experiences that have changed me since being away from the fort.

"The pain of every life I've taken is starting to weigh on my soul. To become Viper, I had to kill my best friend, just to prove my loyalty to our Benefactor. And yes, I was honor-bound to defend and fight for him. But I won't kill out of servitude anymore, and I won't be a murderer.

"I also want a life outside the fort and to start a family of my own. And knowing what I know now, I can never go back. Don't you see?" he asked.

"Yes," Toshi replied while pulling his swords. Then he stepped into a fighting stance and prepared to attack. "I know that you can never go back… because our Benefactor wants you dead."

CHAPTER 15

Wrath

"Joanna Carter!" A familiar voice boomed from the opposite side of the passenger car, and it pierced through whatever conversations were floating around. The crowd of passengers parted down the middle so the man who made his presence known could further announce his intentions. "We've got some unfinished business."

Joanna knew the voice without turning around. Spencer was the last person she wanted to see right now. Her heart was broken, having come all this way to hear her mother refuse to go, even after all the abuses she had suffered. But her mom was right. The anger in her heart had kindled a new flame, and that fire grew stronger every day she spent away from her old life. She was tired of being hurt and pushed around by bullish men—and she was becoming less afraid of anything or anyone.

She picked up her rifle and spun around to face her enemy—the man who had tried to have his way with her, and then put a bounty on her head. And if Spencer was looking for another fight, he was going to get one.

"No, we don't have any unfinished business. There's nothing between us, and what's done is done. Now leave me be, or so help me, I'll shoot you dead right here in front of all these people," Joanna said, feeling the sting of anger in her heart give her energy and focus.

Spencer's eyebrows creased his forehead and he stood there in the entryway, looking surprised to be confronted. That's when Joanna sensed maybe he hadn't really thought this through—and she wasn't the same timid little girl he may have thought he knew.

The crowd around them was deathly silent. They were just the audience for whatever feud was about to play out in this theater. Joanna didn't care. She thought there was still a chance to get her mom off the train, and the only person she could see was the devil at the back of the car. There was nobody standing between her and Spencer, so she held the rifle loosely by her hip and pointed it at him—ready to shoot if he came at her.

As Joanna was locked in their standoff and trying to think of how she might back out to the front of the car, the train suddenly lurched forward. The jolt caused her to stumble, and when she stepped to stop herself, she accidentally pulled the trigger.

But instead of hearing a gunshot, the hammer just clicked.

"You're empty," Spencer said with a sinister tone and pulled a shiny new knife from his belt. "I'm so glad you came back, and I could just shoot you right now and be done with it. But that would be too easy. I've been dreaming about this moment for a long time.

"The doctor who stitched me up said I was lucky after what you did, and that I might still have children someday. But you won't. Because I have a new blade, and I'm going to enjoy cutting you nice and slow," he said, then positioned both hands in front of him and took a step forward.

Joanna stared coldly at Spencer and dropped the rifle. She had lost count of her rounds and didn't reload before making her way to the train. It was useless now, and the sound of it hitting the floor didn't even register to her. Even as the train began to pick up speed, everything around her seemed to slow down as she casually traced her hand across her rope belt to the blade that had returned to its owner—and she was more than ready to give it to him.

"Have you forgotten your old knife? Let's see if it remembers you!" she screamed as she pulled the blade and charged.

• • •

All Aboard

Toshi stood between him and the train, and Cade didn't know what to do next. His teacher was confronting him like any other deadly opponent, and he was wearing the light-gray battle coat fashioned similarly to his and his former brothers'. Both of his swords were drawn in a battle stance, and the blades shimmered in the light.

Cade had imagined this was a possibility and would have been a fool to think otherwise. His recent vision wasn't exactly like this, but it arrived at the same conclusion. Toshi was their Benefactor's personal bodyguard—a companion who traveled with his master wherever he went. Now he wasn't just here to stop Cade from getting on board; he was here to fight to the death.

Toshi stood firm in his defensive position in front of the train, blocking the entry to their Benefactor's passenger car. In response, Cade started moving to his right at an angle toward the front of the train. There was more than one way to get on this train with an entryway on both ends of each passenger car, and he was moving cautiously so as not to be the one to provoke the fight.

Then the engine let out a burst of steam and the loco-motive came to life. The entire train lunged forward about a foot, and then another as it began to move. Cade realized that any thought of slow-walking across the platform was now pointless. He had to move now!

Cade quickened his stride toward the unguarded steps of the forward opening, and he moved as fast as his left leg would let him. But Toshi was quicker, and he ran up swiftly to cut Cade off with an attack.

He raised his left sword in defense, and the first clash of blades with his sensei was quickly followed by another strike that he had to defend with his right sword. Then they both stepped back and stared at each other.

Cade was still trying to separate fighting his teacher from fighting another opponent. This fight was the last thing he wanted. But much like his first kill—his best friend, Paul—he would need to be completely removed from his feelings to survive this fight. And the conflicting thought of having to kill Toshi to get his freedom was still clouding his judgment as his teacher's next attack came swiftly.

Toshi used his left sword to strike high, and spun around quickly to go low. But Cade defended it and was able to spin the opposite way to avoid the attack at his legs. Then he tried to catch Toshi with a counterstrike across his exposed back. But Toshi was faster than Cade realized, and he easily blocked the attack.

Again, the two separated, with neither gaining an advantage. But it also seemed that Toshi was primarily focused on keeping him off the train that was starting to roll down the tracks, and Cade couldn't help but notice the second passenger car was almost past them.

Sensing the urgency, Cade stepped quickly forward and launched his first attack. The two exchanged a parry of slashes and counterattacks that were some of the best moves Cade had in him. But the attack did not produce a strike, and all it did was keep him from getting on the train.

"Very good, Viper," Toshi said with a smile. "You have been practicing your two-sword technique." Then, as if the compliment was a distraction, he immediately launched into another attack.

This time Cade was able to block the strike to his face, and the follow-up on his left side, but then the tip of Toshi's left sword jabbed forward and stuck Cade in the chest.

As Toshi pulled back with some surprise that his sword

didn't penetrate, Cade was forever grateful for the chest armor he had acquired from Falcon. It not only saved his life again; it also gave him an opportunity to counterattack and stick Toshi in the gut with his right sword.

Toshi winced as Cade removed his blade. It wasn't a fatal strike, but he could tell that it caught his teacher completely by surprise. Toshi took two steps back, and both warriors stood quietly looking at each other before a familiar voice echoed throughout the station.

"Toshi, get on the train!" the voice shouted. It was their Benefactor. And as the train was picking up speed, the coupling between the freight car and the stock car was quickly making its way up the track.

Toshi slid his right sword in his belt scabbard and jumped for the hand ladder at the tail end of the freight car. After he grabbed the handle, Cade watched as his sensei was whisked away while still trying to secure his footing.

Cade saw the last passing car moving quickly and sheathed his swords. Then he looked for something to grab on to as he ran along side the stock car as fast as he could with his injured leg. But he would not be able to keep pace with the speed of the train for long, and he would soon run out of platform. So when the car began to pass him, he saw the little hand ladder on the back and lunged at the only rungs he could grasp.

The power of the train was incredible as it pulled him off his feet. While he had a solid grip on one handle of the ladder, his body banged against the side and back of the car while his boots dragged across the railroad ties with a steadily repeating thump. The smell and grunts of pigs were in his face, and he wouldn't be able to maintain his grip much longer. But after pulling his knees up to gain some leverage, he was able to reach up to the next rung with his right hand.

Now he was able to pull his right leg up and find a toehold at the base of the car. With a few more coordinated moves, Cade was finally able to climb up the back end of the train—and he took a series of deep exhausted breaths as he pulled himself up to the flat top of the stock car and rolled onto his back.

The sway of the train was something Cade had never experienced. His first attempt to roll onto one knee and stand was a little wobbly, but he soon gained his balance and looked to the front of the train. Black soot from the engine trailed all the way back to where he was standing. Its smell permeated the air and choked out the fresh scent of the cedars and pines.

But now that he was on the train, he needed to advance. As he slowly walked his way up toward the front end of the car, he saw Toshi's head pop up over the top of the freight car.

By the time Cade reached the coupling area between the two cars, Toshi was standing on the other side and looked ready to defend his position. But he also seemed to be struggling to find his balance on this moving train, and Cade could see a small trail of blood dripping down his left leg.

"I'm sorry about that," Cade said with a gesture to Toshi's wound, even though he knew it was in vain. It didn't serve him to continue having feelings for his opponent, but he couldn't help it. So he tried to focus on the fact that Toshi had already tried to stab him, too. If it weren't for his chest armor, he wouldn't be here now. But Toshi was still standing between him and the man he needed to reconcile with—and the life and love of a family he wanted. That made Toshi the next person he had to fight, but he still believed that he didn't have to kill his sensei to get what he came for.

Cade stood at the car's leading edge and looked down at the space between. He guessed the coupling area's gap was at least four feet or more. It wouldn't be a long way to jump, but given the strength in his leg and Toshi defending the other side, the distance was daunting. The ground passing beneath the cars provided an alarming vision of what could happen if he didn't make it.

"You have made me proud, Viper," Toshi called out, which surprised Cade. "Your skills with the sword and the fight in your heart have made you a deadly samurai. And being a survivor with a sense of purpose has made you stronger than any warrior driven by hate, or revenge, or greed."

During all his years of training, Cade had never heard Toshi say he was proud of him. He was always the taskmaster. Firm and sometimes punishing in his teaching methods. And now that they were facing each other as opponents, it was the last thing he thought he'd hear. Especially after turning against their Benefactor and killing Falcon and Scorpion.

"But I have the advantage. What will you do now?" Toshi asked, letting him know the fight was not over.

Cade's first instinct was to load his pistol. It was the most logical thing to do, but again, Cade felt strained. It would be shameful to resort to guns against his teacher. A shame he wouldn't want to carry the rest of his life. He also didn't want to shoot Toshi to get to their Benefactor—but he still had to make the jump to the next car.

Then he thought of an alternative and backed up about six feet. He pulled his left sword and the knife from his right boot, then he braced himself in an attack stance, knowing he had to time this perfectly. As he felt the sway of the train, he noticed a slow rhythm in which it moved down the tracks. When he thought the moment was right, he took a running start and threw the knife at Toshi, jumping at the same time.

The knife seemed to surprise Toshi even though he easily defended it and cast it aside. But that was the point. The act of defending the knife throw allowed Cade to make the jump and even stumble a few feet past his teacher to secure his position on the car.

"Clever," Toshi said as he returned to his attack stance. "Your warrior instincts and willingness to sacrifice serve you well."

Cade pulled his right sword and gave a nod, but he was not happy about sacrificing his knife or feeling overconfident about what he had gained. All he did was advance up the train—and now the fight with his sensei could resume.

...

A Familiar Sting

Joanna screamed as she came at Spencer at full speed, and he looked ready to stand his ground with his knife out. But instead of running straight into him, she went into a feet-first slide along the floor just after Spencer lunged to intercept her charge.

Spencer looked caught by surprise, but Joanna was exactly where she wanted to be. And with her right boot reared back between his legs, Joanna kicked Spencer in the same place she'd stuck him not so long ago.

"Bitch!" he shouted as he hunched over and stumbled backward, clutching his hand over his crotch. When his back was up against the railing of the entry area, he swiped the knife wildly back and forth, defensively cutting at the air between them.

Joanna got back on her feet and slowly approached Spencer like a wounded animal. He was in pain but still capable of killing her. And when he switched the blade to his left hand, Joanna sensed he would go for his pistol.

She pounced at him, and Spencer defended himself. She was only an arm's length away from him, and she twitched the knife in her hand, looking for an opening to cut him. The sway of the moving train accentuated her movements, but she knew this standoff couldn't last. And when Spencer did try to go for his gun, he left himself open and Joanna lunged.

But Spencer was quicker than she thought, and her attack with the knife was clumsy. She hadn't come at him strong enough, and he was able to swat her strike away with his right hand. Now her failed attack left her open, and Spencer came back at her.

Joanna was leaner than Spencer, and when he stabbed back, she was able to move aside. But the train was building up speed and she fell off-balance; her momentum carried her into him. As they collided, she was close enough to smell him again and immediately felt repulsed. The sway of the car kept them engaged as they grappled with each other, and he tried to stick her with the knife in his left hand. But she saw it coming and reached across to grab his wrist with her left hand and stop him.

When she caught his wrist, they turned in the entryway and she tried to stick him with the knife in her right hand. But he reached over and grabbed her wrist and their arms became intertwined as they tried to outduel each other. She could feel how much stronger he was, and the more they grappled like this, Joanna knew she couldn't win this fight without getting nasty. So she leaned in and pulled her right arm close to her mouth. Then she locked her teeth into Spencer's right hand—and she bit him so hard between the knuckles that she could taste blood.

As Spencer screamed in pain, he released his grasp on Joanna's wrist—loose enough for her to pull her right arm free and then thrust forward to stick her knife in his gut.

Being this close to Spencer was making her angry, and she noticed that stabbing him now was much different from shooting the bounty hunter, or from the last time she stuck Spencer with a knife. She could feel his body reacting to the blade, and she was close enough to look deep into his eyes and smell the chaw on his breath as she continued to press it into his gut.

"Take that, you bastard," she said spitefully, and the pained expression in his eyes said enough back. Then she twisted the blade in his belly and used her position of leverage to move Spencer in front of the steps and railing leading into the car. "That's for Tommy," she said while giving Spencer a shove off the train.

But as she pushed him, Spencer grabbed her wrist and the hand still holding the knife. And as he fell backward off the train, he pulled Joanna along with him.

Falling off the moving train was completely unexpected and both of them hit the ground with a hard thud that kicked up a small cloud of dust. Somewhere during the fall, Spencer released his grip on Joanna, and she let go of the knife as she rolled a couple times on the hard ground before coming to a stop.

Her thoughts were spinning as she lay on her back covered in dirt and sweat. Then she felt all the pain. Some of it was the dull ache of bruises on her hips and shoulders. Others were sharp pains, like the one on the back of her head. It took a concentrated effort, but when she was finally able to sit up, she reached back to find the spot that hurt to the touch. When she pulled her hand back from her matted hair and saw the blood, a dizzy wave of nausea washed over her.

As Joanna rolled over onto her hands and knees, she could see the blood-covered rock on the ground that must have hit her head. And after she vomited up whatever was in her stomach, she looked up to see the train pulling away and fading from view—with Cade and another man with swords standing on top of it.

She tried to think through everything that had just happened, and the feelings of nausea were replaced with a deep sadness. It was a different kind of ache, associated with a feeling that she had failed. She couldn't get her mother to come with her, and she sensed that she would never see her again.

Then Spencer's coughing brought her thoughts back to the moment. He was about forty feet away from her, hunched over and spitting blood from his mouth. But still very much alive and holding the knife he had pulled from his gut.

"I hate you," he said as he slowly pushed himself up. His right arm was limp at the shoulder, and it looked like it was barely connected or dislocated from his body. There must have been a cut somewhere under his hair line, because there was blood and dirt all over his face. But he seemed determined to get up and, eventually, he rose to his feet. "And I'm going to kill you if it's the last thing I do," he said as he staggered forward and pointed the blood-covered blade at her.

Even with one arm and a gut wound, Spencer looked menacing. He was a strong young man fueled with spite and malice, and Joanna realized she would need to finish this fight—but she didn't have a weapon.

She watched Spencer come toward her, and she braced herself for his attack. That's when she noticed he wasn't holding the other knife. The shiny new knife. *Where is it?* she thought, looking around. Then she saw the sun reflecting off the blade lying in the dirt about twenty feet to her right—and in the space between them.

Spencer stopped for a moment to see what she was looking at and glanced at the knife. Then he slightly changed his angle to try to cut her off.

He was still staggering. Joanna knew she had to get to

that knife before he did, but she lacked the strength to stand. So she began to crawl on her hands and knees in a race to see who would get there first.

Both of them were moving as fast as they could to get to the discarded blade, and Joanna paid little attention to the pain in her fingernails as she dug into the dry earth. She could taste the dust and sweat in her mouth as she closed the gap to within striking distance of the knife—and when she sensed he was closing in on her, she dove for it.

She grabbed the handle of the knife with both hands and rolled over on her back. Spencer lunged at her in the same moment Joanna held the blade out in front of her and screamed. She continued to scream as she closed her eyes and felt the weight of him fall on her. And as her wail ran out of air, there was silence.

When Joanna opened her eyes, she saw the blade in the center of Spencer's chest, and the fading look of anger in his eyes. It was over. She winced at the effort it took to push his body off of her. That's when she noticed her left arm had been stuck with the bloody knife just below the shoulder.

She sat up, then she tore off a piece of her dress to wrap around the wound and stop the bleeding. Her arm hurt when she tried to raise it, but given the circumstances, she was grateful to be alive.

When she saw Spencer lying there with his shiny new knife still stuck in his chest, the sea of rage and hate she felt toward him slowly subsided. For a moment, she almost felt sorry for him. He had everything in life, and she had nothing.

But here they were—and now he was dead, and her mom was on a train heading to Denver with his father.

Joanna began to laugh at the irony of it all as she crawled over to Spencer's body and pulled the knife from his chest. It was a heavier blade, and she liked the weight of it in her hand. There was also a nice sheath to go with it, so she wiped the blood off on Spencer's shirt and claimed it as her own.

She also thought it would be handy to have a pistol, so she undid his gun belt and pulled it off. Then she stood and slipped it around her waist and fashioned the sheath on the left side. Being a lot thinner, she cinched it the best she could around her waist; the pistol holster sat perfectly on her right leg, and the knife on her left hip.

The last thing she cut was the rope belt around her waist before putting the blade into its sheath. She held up the rope and then tossed it on Spencer's corpse. It was a perfect symbol of where she'd come from, but not who she was now.

That's when she heard horses coming up from behind her. *Now what?* she thought. All she wanted right now was a moment of peace and a drink of water.

"Are you okay?" a familiar voice asked.

Joanna turned to see Red Sky with their horses, and she felt so relieved it was him that she offered up the best smile she could muster. "I'm better now," she replied.

CHAPTER 16

Dynamite

"What the hell is going on?" Victor asked Whitmore, not waiting for an answer. "I just saw my son fall off the train with the girl that used to work for us. We need to stop—"

"Nobody is going anywhere, and we're not stopping this train," Whitmore shouted.

Whitmore already felt like everything was going wrong, and stopping the train was the last thing he wanted to do. But even though whatever was happening to Victor's son and that girl was the least of his worries, he was equally curious about what was going on outside their passenger car.

"Everyone stay here, I'm going to take a look," he said, and almost nobody seemed willing to argue. Victor was the only person now yelling at the porter to stop the train, but Whitmore tuned out that discussion as he walked to the entryway door and slid it open.

All of the sounds from the train and the views of the

passing landscape were magnified and more visceral outside the car, but there wasn't much else to see from where he stood. So he stepped down to the bottom steps of the entryway and pulled himself up by the handle. Once he could stand on the railing, he was able to peek over the top of the car behind him.

It was a risky move and harder than he thought as he attempted to secure his footing on the rail. But as the train made a nice, slow turn to the right, he was eventually able to see Toshi and Viper squaring off on top of the freight car behind them.

"Damn, that man has nine lives," he whispered to himself.

After he climbed down from his perch and was safely back in the entryway, he reentered the car to find that Bruce, Victor, and the other few random passengers were all looking at him.

"What did you see?" Bruce asked plainly. It was an obvious question, and he seemed to be speaking what was on everyone's mind.

"Toshi is fighting Viper on top of the train, and I don't like the looks of it," Whitmore replied.

"Did you see my son?" Victor asked, visibly shaken and desperate for information.

Whitmore shook his head. "No, I'm sorry. I did not," he said. He could appreciate Victor's feelings for his son, but his main concern was the fact that Viper had killed everyone in his path—and now only Toshi remained. And if Toshi couldn't stop him, he would have to kill Viper himself.

"Hey, boss, look what I found in that bounty hunter's saddlebag," Lester said aloud to get his attention and produced three sticks of dynamite bound together with a long fuse.

"Sinclair wasn't kidding about being prepared for any situation," Whitmore said to himself and smiled. Then he turned to the porter with a curious thought. "How hard would it be to disconnect that car behind us?"

...

Iron Horse

The top of the freight car had a center beam and slits across it in sections. It wasn't completely flat either, as it sloped gently from the center beam to the sides like a pitched roof. These footing challenges and the movement of the train were going to make it hard for Cade to fight and maintain his balance.

He also didn't have to wait long for Toshi to attack, and his sensei wielded both swords in a fluid, crossing motion as he advanced on Cade's position.

Cade struggled to defend the attack. He didn't have much experience in two-sword fighting techniques, and he was trying to remember what he did know while being mindful of his surroundings. Because as he defended the attack, he took two steps back that put him almost at the side of the car and looking over the edge.

"Stop!" Cade yelled at Toshi, hoping that he might actually relent—and he did, which was a surprise. But then he sensed that Toshi only stopped to express his disappointment.

"After all of your training, have you not learned? There is no other way for a samurai but death," Toshi said, sounding very disheartened. "You turned your back on the Way and brought dishonor to the house of our Benefactor. Now only one of us can remain… and I'm prepared to die before I would shame myself. What about you?"

Cade struggled to agree with his teacher. The philosophy of the samurai was as pure as the sunlight glimmering on Toshi's blades—and Cade knew Toshi would fight to the death. His loyalty to the Way was unwavering. But he completely underestimated the fight he would need to win against his former teacher, or that his sensei might let him survive this day.

Other thoughts of doubt began knocking on the door of his mind. It was the first time he really considered that coming here, seeking a pardon or a parlay, was a big mistake. Their Benefactor was never going to set him free, no matter what he offered or bargained in return. It was also a mistake to think he could persuade their Benefactor to change as a person or to stop sending bounty hunters to make things right, however he felt wronged. It would be a dishonor to his house and everything he had built, and a small price to pay if he, or Toshi, had to die for him.

Cade shifted his focus back to the fight and slowly sidestepped closer to the center beam while also putting some distance between himself and his sensei. Then he briefly closed his eyes to reset his senses and imagine Toshi as just another man and the deadly opponent he was.

He thought about Toshi's possible weaknesses, and that he preferred close fighting because of his size. Then he tried to remember *The Book of Five Rings*, and Cade thought of Water.

The instruction he tried to recall was a simple strategy.

When struggling blade to blade with an enemy, it is important to wait until he breaks or withdraws—then Cade could expand and spring forward with his sword to take advantage of his reach. It worked earlier on the platform, and he could try this again.

Cade instigated the next attack, but he didn't charge. He used his reach with his left sword to push Toshi back. When Toshi blocked and countered, they exchanged another quick parry to reestablish some distance between each other. But this time, when Toshi withdrew, Cade pressed forward with a double thrust to the chest and followed with a slashing strike to Toshi's left side.

But Cade's attack was easily defended. "Your attack lacks conviction," Toshi said in his teacher's tone. "If you are simply trying to cut me, you will lose," he said as he pressed a counterattack to Cade's face and slashed at the side of his torso to force a retreat.

"Ask yourself, what is essential in terms of purpose and discipline?" Toshi preached over the sounds of the train. "It is to have a mind that is pure and lacking complications. Now stop trying to cut me and finish it!"

Cade couldn't believe that Toshi was daring him to strike, but he understood the challenge and that he needed to tap into the ferocity it would take to kill his opponent and attack with full force. He advanced and slashed at Toshi's face with his right sword, then he followed with a thrust to his abdomen that was defended but left his opponent open—and Cade used his right boot to kick Toshi in the chest and send him flying backward.

Sensing his first advantage in their fight, Cade pressed the attack and charged after his stumbling opponent. But Toshi was quick to roll through the kick and come up on his knees to take a defensive position. After another parry of slashing strikes and defensive counters, Toshi scored a cut just above Cade's right knee and then made a surprising move. He sprang up from his crouched position and spun around in the air, slashing Cade across the face. This forced Cade to withdraw, while Toshi landed lightly on his feet.

The cut across his right cheek wasn't deep, but it caught Cade by surprise, and he could feel it bleeding. The same with the cut above his knee. Toshi seemed to change his strategy to match Cade's, and he was going to inflict a cut after each parry.

As he realized this, Toshi was already pressing his next attack and this time slashed with both blades across Cade's left side. As Cade defended the attack, he was able to deflect one strike with his forearm armor—but the second one slashed across his abdomen.

When he sidestepped, it allowed Toshi to pass him to the left and gave Cade the opportunity to spin and score a slash across Toshi's back. It was the same move he had been taught years ago, and—knowing Toshi—he doubted he'd get a chance to use it again.

Bloodied and wounded, the two samurai faced off again as the iron horse continued to roll down the track. The longer they fought, the more Cade's respect for his sensei swelled inside him. And all the doubts or fears he had about this confrontation were fading as he continued to hold his own against the deadliest warrior he knew.

But as he absorbed the pain from his new wounds, he wondered how much longer he could continue like this. If he and Toshi exchanged cuts with each pass, eventually one would prove to be fatal.

"Toshi, come here!" the voice of their Benefactor ordered. The command completely disrupted their fight, and Cade looked over Toshi's shoulder to see Whitmore's head poking above the top of the freight car.

"Master Toshi, you have my respect," Cade offered up as he wondered why Whitmore was calling out to him or would risk showing himself. "I can't match your skill with the sword, and I refuse to use my gun. But the fight I seek is beyond you, so I'm going to ask you one last time—"

"Toshi, come here, now!" Whitmore shouted and Toshi took a step back to look in his direction. "You will get on this car and defend it, do you understand?"

Toshi retreated, reluctantly at first, but then acted on the instructions as ordered. Without a word, he turned his back to Cade and quickly stepped to the edge before he leaped to the passenger car ahead of them.

The top of the passenger car was a little more rounded from the center to the edges, making it even harder to stand on. But once it looked like Toshi found his footing, he turned to face Cade and resumed a defensive stance.

Cade knew he had no other choice now, and with no immediate threat, he sheathed his swords. He was lucky to make the first jump, but there was no way he would be fortunate enough to do it again. So he pulled his pistol and began to reload as he limped forward.

The pain in his leg was more noticeable now, and the ongoing motion and smell of the train exhaust made him feel a little woozy. But he pressed on, knowing this fight wasn't over, and accepted that he would have to shoot his way to the next car—and likely to the final confrontation with his Benefactor.

He finished loading his Colt and gave the cylinder a quick spin as he stepped to the front edge of the freight car. But as Toshi stood on the passenger car ahead of him, it suddenly seemed farther now and it continued to pull away.

"Goodbye, Viper!" Whitmore yelled out from the safety of the entry area, but then quickly ducked inside the car.

Cade cautiously stepped to the edge and looked down. The cars had been uncoupled, and now the space between them was almost twenty feet and growing. As he looked at the ground and the track passing underneath them, he also saw the dynamite and the burning fuse.

There was no time to think, and the last thing Cade saw before he turned to run was the look of anguish on Toshi's face.

•••

Death & Dishonor

The sound and force of the explosion rocked the entire train—and in an instant, the freight car behind them became a ball of fire and smoke as boards and other parts of it filled the air and rained from the sky.

As the rest of the train continued to pull away from

this destruction, it was hard to imagine how anyone could have survived that blast. After the last two cars crashed into a crumpled mess behind them, the only sound that followed was the wheels of the passenger car clicking along the tracks.

"Did you see that? That's how you get rid of a problem!" Whitmore said aloud to every onlooker in the parlor car. The big smile on his face and the tone of his voice was full of amazement and confidence in his victory. Seeing Viper blow up on a train was the best he felt all day.

"What have you done?" Bruce asked in a very sober tone, and Whitmore could tell that his business partner was more concerned than celebratory.

"Like I said, I took care of a problem. That man was a menace. You saw him. He's killed more than two dozen of my men, shot up a town, and he was coming for us. He needed to be taken care of," Whitmore replied without remorse.

"Coming for us, or coming for you?" Victor asked. But Whitmore just sneered at him and didn't answer.

"That car was probably full of demolition equipment—expensive demolition equipment. And your recklessness has no bounds," Victor continued. "You can consider any business between us over... and my son better be alive, or so help me God—"

"Don't you dare threaten me." Whitmore stared at Victor defiantly. "Whatever happened between your son and that girl was your business, not mine. And whatever that precious equipment might have been worth, it can surely be reimbursed. But that man had to die, whatever the cost."

Toshi reentered the parlor car and he looked like a samurai

who had just survived a fight to the death. His wounds were still bleeding as he passed Whitmore without saying a word, and he walked straight to the bar and poured a glass of whiskey.

"Toshi, are you alright? What did you see?" Whitmore asked curiously.

Toshi drank the glass of whiskey and set it peacefully down on the bar. "Yes. I am alive… and I am ashamed," he replied.

Whitmore was confused. "Viper is dead. It didn't happen by the sword, but you served me well and you're still alive. Why are you ashamed?"

Toshi shook his head. "There is no honor in what you did. Death comes for us all, but Viper did not deserve to die like that. That is not the way of the samurai."

Whitmore's frustration quickly returned. Everyone, including his personal bodyguard, was turning against him in his moment of triumph.

"There's something I need everyone here to understand," he said aloud for all to hear. "My grievance with Viper may have been my own, but how he died is of little consequence. That he is dead is just the way of the West. And that's the last I want to speak of him today… or his memory."

"But did you see him die?" Bruce asked.

•••

Heaven's Door

The blast from the explosion echoed across the landscape, and Joanna had come riding up along the tracks with Red Sky to see the devastation.

Only the stock car was recognizable, and it was turned sideways and off the tracks. The horses and pigs inside were wailing and trying to get out, so Joanna jumped off her horse, slid the door open on its hinges, and climbed inside.

The smoke from the resulting fire was thicker than the train exhaust, and the pigs ran by her as soon as the door was open. But the horses were still tied to their posts, and Joanna pulled her knife to cut them free. After she freed all the animals and walked out behind them, she looked around for Red Sky.

"Where are you?" she said, coughing as she called out through the smoke and ash.

"Over here!" Red Sky replied, and Joanna tried to track his position. His voice sounded like it came from the direction of the creek bed on the other side of the tracks. She made her way over, and from a distance she saw Red Sky kneeling over a body lying on the ground. Sensing it was Cade, Joanna ran as fast as she could to get to them.

As she got closer, her worst fears were confirmed. It was Cade, and he was just lying there while parts of his clothes were singed or still smoking from the explosion. But what scared her was that he wasn't moving—and Red Sky turned Cade's body over as Joanna knelt down on the other side.

Cade's eyes were closed, and his face was covered in soot and blood. Joanna couldn't tell if he was still breathing, and she grabbed him by the shoulders of his coat.

"Cade, wake up!" she screamed as she tried to shake the

shadow of death from his body. "You can't be dead. Please, wake up," she repeated as she collapsed on top of him and began to sob.

With her head against his chest, she could hear a faint heartbeat. So she reared back and started beating on his chest with her fists. "Wake up!" she screamed again. Then Cade opened his eyes, gasped for air, and coughed violently from the smoke in his lungs.

As Joanna and Red Sky looked down at their friend, he blinked, slowly regaining consciousness and awareness of his surroundings. Then he slowly shook his head and pursed his lips together while trying to sit up.

"Are you okay? What do you need?" Joanna asked with a nervous, happy smile.

"Water," he replied.

CHAPTER 17

Long Road Back

Cade and his friends traveled slowly north about two miles up the creek from the explosion, and as far from the train tracks as they could get for the time being. Cade assumed the train accident would draw a lot of attention, so he suggested they get out of the way and wait until dark before making their next move.

For now, they were all wounded, dirty, and bleeding. So when Red Sky found a nice spot with a pool of water to wash up, they all took advantage of it.

They all needed a bath even though the water was late September cold, and there was no place for shame or embarrassment as they removed most of their clothes. And after they washed themselves and some of the stains from their clothes, they laid them out on warm rocks to dry in the afternoon sun.

Cade had taken off his battle coat and removed the chest armor to take his creek bath. Having the extra weight off of him felt great, and he enjoyed a big deep breath of fresh mountain air. Taking a moment to examine the two breast plates and the four smaller abdomen plates all linked together with a meshed chain, he traced the pits with his finger and took inventory of all the bullet holes and the one cut where Toshi's blade had been stopped. The leather folded over the steel plates had proven its worth again, and he was grateful to have it.

The hem of Joanna's dress kept getting shorter as it was used to make fresh bandages, but they needed more than bandages to tend to the bullet in Red Sky's shoulder.

Cade made a small fire of twigs in the crevice of a rock formation and tried to keep it from smoking as much as possible, but they needed the flame to help cleanse and seal their wounds. Their spot was downwind from the train derailment, so hopefully their day camp would go unnoticed.

"Sorry, I wish we had some whiskey… and I know you're not going to like this, but I think this will help with the pain while we treat your wound," Cade said to his friend and referred to his stinger. He strapped the stinger holster back on his left forearm, then he flicked his wrist to make it protrude past his closed fist. And with his right hand locked with his friend's, he gently stuck the stinger into Red Sky's shoulder a few inches from where the bullet went in.

Red Sky's body seized up and Cade knew the toxin was beginning to take effect. Since his pants were drying in the sun, he pulled his belt and put it in Red Sky's mouth. His friend seemed to know why as he clenched it between his teeth.

"Get ready to pull your knife from the fire," he said to

Joanna. But as Cade moved Red Sky's arm to test his mobility, he noticed that the bleeding had slowed.

"It looks like the bullet didn't hit anything major, but this is still going to hurt. I'm going to try and find the bullet with my finger," Cade said to Red Sky, and his friend blinked as if he understood.

"Do it," Red Sky muttered between his teeth, and bit down on the leather belt.

Cade cleaned up his little finger the best he could and rolled it in a small tin of salve ointment he had received from the doctor in Rocky Creek. Then he nodded to Joanna and she pulled her blade from the fire—holding it just above Cade's hand.

Cade poked his little finger into the wound and went as far in as he could. He pushed past the soft flesh until he could touch the bullet with the tip of his finger and feel it against the bone. The bad news was that they didn't have anything on hand to pull it out. But the good news was that the bleeding didn't increase when he removed his finger.

"This is what my old colonel would call a battlefield wound. We don't have the tools to pull it out, and I think it might be best to leave the bullet in and cauterize it," Cade explained. "It doesn't seem to have cut anything major, and might do more damage to try and dig it out."

Red Sky winced in agreement, and Cade proceeded.

He pushed some additional salve in and around the wound, and then guided Joanna's hand with the hot knife. When the blade touched blood and skin, it produced the familiar scent of burned flesh. Red Sky screamed through the belt in his mouth, and Cade pulled the knife back and immediately applied some more salve to the burn. Then Joanna began wrapping a bandage from her dress around his shoulder to cover it.

"Hopefully this will hold until we can get back to the old woman," Cade said, revealing his intentions for their next move. "She'll know what to do, and it would be a good place for us to heal. We should rest here for now and then head south when it gets dark."

Red Sky just nodded, and Cade pulled his belt from his friend's mouth. Then he and Joanna finished treating him before they used some of the salve on each other while the effects of the toxin on Red Sky wore off.

Cade knew the cut on his cheek would scar, as would the cut above his knee and the gunshot wound to his leg. The slash across the side of his abdomen was shallow, but almost in the same place he'd been cut by Falcon. Toshi had learned from the fight at the station that he had the chest armor, and must have known where to cut the next time.

He also knew that his past was doing more than catching up with him. It was killing him—slowly and painfully with each fight. The opportunity to bring an end to his pain had slipped through his fingers when his plan to negotiate his freedom ended in an explosion on a train. The scar on his face would be an ever-present symbol of this failure, and a painful reminder of what happened when he turned against his Benefactor and his teacher.

But this wasn't the time to dwell on it, as Cade sensed that Red Sky and Joanna were as exhausted as he was. After a quick look around, he found a nice soft spot of ground to sit and rest. For the remainder of the afternoon, they all sat peacefully and enjoyed the soft autumn breeze that occassionally showered them with golden leaves and a welcome sense of calm. They were hungry, too. So he rationed out whatever jerked meat they had left and tried to start a conversation about what happened earlier in the day.

"What happened to you? Did you get to see your mother?" Cade asked Joanna, and the pensive look on her face implied a painful story would follow.

"I asked her to come with me, but she said no. She believes her future belongs to someone else, and before I could try and change her mind, Spencer Carmichael showed up," Joanna replied with a deep sigh. "I charged him, and I don't think he was expecting that. Then the two of us fought it out and fell off the train. But I killed him. I killed him with his own knife," she said solemnly while drawing pictures in the dirt with a stick.

"But before that, Red Sky saved my life," Joanna said abruptly, as if to change the subject and acknowledge their friend. "And that bullet in his shoulder was meant for me," she added with a smile of appreciation.

Joanna continued with her story of the three bounty hunters, and then Red Sky added the part about Joanna's courage and how she saved him, too. Cade appreciated listening to them bounce around the details and found himself being entertained by their recounting of events.

"I shot that man before he could shoot us... that's all," she said humbly.

"But the leader of those men was your first kill, yes? You've taken the most significant step in a warrior's journey," Cade replied. "And you saved me from that English bounty hunter, too. Thank you," he added with a slight bow of his head.

"Well, he had it coming. I warned him, and he was about to shoot you," she said bitterly. "But who was that guy you were fighting on the top of the train? Was that your sensei?"

Sensing it was time to tell his version of the day's event, Cade started to recall everything that happened to him. "Yes. That man was my sensei. My teacher. And I was foolish to think I could reason with him or confront my Benefactor. But fighting my former teacher taught me an important lesson. To be ready to confront either of them again, I will need to train harder to be physically and mentally prepared. Because I have to accept that it will be a fight to the death."

"How did you survive that ball of fire?" Red Sky asked curiously.

Cade told the story of his fight with Toshi on the train and the big explosion. His friends listened intently and began to better understand his connection with his sensei, but they were still surprised he survived.

"I remember Toshi's face and running away after seeing the dynamite, but everything during or after the blast is a blur. I can't believe the explosion didn't kill me. And since you found me down by the creek, it must have thrown me pretty far," he said.

That's all he could piece together before the last image of Toshi's face danced through his memories. It was a look that

Cade could only associate with sadness—and it was a look he only saw from his teacher once before.

"Maybe everyone thinks you're dead?" Joanna said, and the comment brought Cade's thoughts back into focus.

"Yes, and maybe that's a good thing," he replied. "It would be nice to stop looking over our shoulder for a bit. And besides, there's no way we can go to Denver now. Any element of surprise is gone, and we're in no shape to fight like that again," Cade continued while looking to the south. "We need to get back to Moira's cabin. Maybe she'll have a vision for what to do next. Because right now, I'll be honest and say that I don't know what to do or where else to go. But I do know that we need to get somewhere we can rest up and avoid being hunted."

The last part of what Cade said lingered in the air with the smoke from their dying fire, and the three weary warriors silently sat back and rested until the sun set over the mountains. The day was over, but their long journey south was about to begin—and the future was uncertain.

•••

Frost

Red Sky guided them by night and the glow of the moon was bright enough to put some distance between them and the train tracks. But after a few hours of riding southeast away from the mountains, the cold, thin air made it hard to press on any farther.

Finding a place to camp would be hard, too. There were fewer trees and areas for cover in the open plains. But Red Sky's tribe once roamed this land and knew it well—so he quietly called on the voices of his ancestors to help him find a place to stop for the night. And his call was answered when they arrived at a small watering hole, and the night sky reflected off the surface as wind-blown ripples occasionally blurred the light of the stars.

Water was a gift when traveling across the plains, and Red Sky gave thanks while Cade and Joanna walked up their horses. They made a small fire with grass and sage brush that didn't offer much to help them stay warm, but it would do until morning and they could travel faster by day.

He could feel the bullet in his shoulder every time he moved his arm, and the cold made the dull aching pain that much worse. But he was still alive, so he had to believe that his sense of purpose must still be true. As he looked to the faces of Cade and Joanna staring quietly at the flame, he thought back to how they all met and how far they had come.

It felt good to close his eyes and sleep, but the glow of the morning sun came quickly since they had traveled until late in the evening. And even though they had rested, everyone was still very fatigued.

"We should get a move on," Cade said as the sun finally crept over the horizon. "Hopefully we can continue our way south without being noticed."

"Yes. But we should continue toward the rising sun a bit

longer before heading south," Red Sky replied and noticed that Joanna didn't say anything. She was probably too cold and weary to offer any argument.

For another day they continued south and tried to remain as far from any outposts or towns as possible. They hunted along the way and were fortunate enough to survive on some prairie rabbits and any water they found or had to cross along the way.

On the second day, Red Sky continued to lead them south across the flat, open land. But by mid-afternoon something wasn't quite right, and he couldn't put his finger on it until they stopped at the high point of some rolling hills. That's when he shook his head at the painfully familiar sight, and the rancid stench of death and decay surrounded them.

There must have been one hundred or more buffalo lying dead and scattered among the grassland. Their bodies had been left to rot in the sun as swarms of flies buzzed around their bloated carcasses.

"What happened here?" Joanna asked, and Red Sky forgave her for not knowing what he and his people knew all too well.

"This is why we fight," Red Sky replied as he looked at all the dead buffalo with sadness and disgust. "The white man kills the buffalo and leaves nothing for my tribe to hunt. They take land and everything on it as if it belongs to them, and then they tell us where we can live."

"It's not right," Joanna said softly. "It reminds me of those men at The Stockyard."

"Those men don't know how to respect the land or the

buffalo. The spirit of these animals belongs to the plains, and the plains belong to them. There were once so many that my tribe could hunt them for food and skins to survive the winter. But now, they are few, and we are few," Red Sky said while continuing to survey the landscape with a deep sadness in his heart. "And they call us savages."

"There is no way for me to apologize for the actions of other men," Cade began. "Men without honor or respect for the land we share. But I am truly sorry for what happened here, and for the things I've done to push people around and tell them where they can or can't live. I promise to continue fighting alongside you, to make amends for those sins, and defend the innocent seeking justice."

"*Haitse*," Red Sky said to his friend. Cade was the first white man he'd met that appreciated others and treated him like an equal. His words spoke true and there was iron in his actions. And he respected Cade—and Joanna, too. It gave him hope that things could change some day, if there were others like them.

"Let's keep going. There is nothing for us here," he said to his friends and the three pressed on through the field of death. For the remainder of the day, they rode in silence.

On the morning of the third day, they woke up to a cold dusting of frost on the ground. Red Sky was a child of nature, and this was a sign that they needed to reach Moira's cabin soon. His shoulder still hurt, and they were out of salve. Getting back to the cabin represented so much more than just reaching a destination, and he thought they could make it by the afternoon if they rode hard.

"Follow me," Red Sky said to his friends. "We're almost there."

•••

The Wreckage

Joseph Whitmore II was having breakfast in the Frontier Hotel with Bruce, but he was not enjoying it. He had grown tired of Denver, and he wanted to put Colorado behind him as soon as possible. But he was waiting for news from the governor about his decision, and from the sheriff and other officials who were to decide what he may be held accountable for.

"When do you think we'll hear?" Whitmore asked. He knew his business partner was well-connected, and here they were again—waiting for information.

"Soon, I expect," Bruce replied, but his wrinkled brow indicated he really didn't know. "I sent a wire to Bradley Stanwick yesterday morning. Hopefully he'll get back to us sometime today. But timelines might be the least of their concerns right now. I'm pretty sure they're still stuck in Colorado Springs until they repair the rails and clean up the mess."

"Right, the mess. You saw what that man could do. He had to be stopped," Whitmore said and then took a sip of coffee. Whether he really believed it was an act of self-defense or not, the last thing he wanted to be reminded of was the mess he was in and the one he caused. The meeting with the governor never happened, the Carmichaels were out of the picture, and—given everything he had invested in his long-term plans—he would still have to tell his father what happened.

"That's not for me to say," Bruce replied. "How's your friend, Mr. Toshi?"

Whitmore appreciated that Bruce cared to ask, but that was another topic he didn't want to talk about. He looked to his bodyguard sitting with Lester at the table across from him. "He'll be fine. The doctor was able to stitch him up, and he's been reminded of his position."

"Mr. Akers, a message for you," the hotel manager called from across the lobby as he approached Bruce with a piece of parchment in his hand. After handing it over, he promptly clicked the heels of his polished shoes together and left.

Bruce had just opened the folded paper to look it over, and Whitmore was already anxious to know what it said. "Well, what's the news?" he asked.

Bruce handed the paper over to Whitmore without saying a word—and when he read it, he knew why.

MR. AKERS

GOVERNOR PROCEEDING WITH MOUNTAIN
PASS ROUTE.

SPENCER CARMICHAEL FOUND DEAD.

VIPER'S BODY NOT FOUND.

B. STANWICK

Whitmore crumpled the parchment in his hand. It was the worst news he'd ever read in three sentences, and it confirmed that his long-laid plans had failed to produce the deal he envisioned.

"Viper's body wasn't found. What do you think about that?" Whitmore asked Toshi.

Toshi looked at Whitmore and seemed reluctant to discuss the matter. "I don't think anything about it. It was no way for a samurai to die," he replied.

But Toshi didn't seem surprised that Viper's body wasn't found. Maybe Viper was able to jump off the train or somebody took his body away? It was all a mystery, but Whitmore knew Toshi had a better vantage point, so if he had witnessed something he didn't—he wanted to know.

"Tell me, Toshi. What did you see?" Whitmore asked firmly, and his samurai bodyguard eventually said something that cut to the core of his pain.

"I saw the explosion, and no ordinary man should have survived that. But Viper is no ordinary man. I believe he could still be out there. And if he is… then we are not done with him yet," Toshi replied.

"If he's still alive, my samurai friend, it's because you failed to kill him," Whitmore said in anger, and his accusation silenced the room as he pushed his chair back and rose to his feet.

"No. He's alive because of the armor you made for Falcon," Toshi responded in defiance.

"Enough! I've grown weary of your defiance and I'm

tired of waiting," Whitmore said as thoughts of loss, fear, and revenge swirled through his mind. "Now go get our things. We're returning to the fort, and we're leaving in ten minutes."

•••

Shelter from the Storm

Cade could smell the smoke from the chimney before he could see the cabin. The breeze had shifted during the day, and now it was blowing in from the south. As they drew closer to the foothills, the barn and the humble structure came into view.

"Do you think she's expecting us?" Cade asked Red Sky, and his friend simply cocked his head in doubt.

Cade smiled. "Of course she is, but maybe not all three of us," he said with a chuckle.

It was a long day of riding, but they finally arrived about an hour before the sun would dip below the mountains on the western horizon. Cade raised his hand to stop his two friends as they dismounted and tied up their tired horses. "Let's not surprise her. I should go first."

The dog was still lying in the same spot on the creaky front porch, and it didn't bother to bark, just like before. It just looked at Cade with indifference as he went to knock on the door. But before he tapped the door with his knuckles, Moira's voice called from inside. "Welcome back, death rider. Please come in," he heard her say.

He pushed the door open and saw the old woman sitting

in her corner chair with a thin yet welcoming smile, and her pet pig lying at her feet. "I see you saved the girl," she continued as Cade entered.

In the dimly lit room, there were familiar smells coming from the dutch oven hanging in the fireplace.

"Hello, Moira, it's good to see you again," he said, motioning for his friends to come to the door. "And yes, this is Joanna Carter. We met her on our way to Denver, and she's come here with us when things didn't go as planned."

"Yes, I know. Now step inside, child. Let me take a look at you," Moira said to Joanna, who then entered and approached the old woman. Cade stepped out of the way and watched as Moira stood from her chair and casually walked around to size up the new houseguest. "She's a strong young woman. You did well, Cade Wilson," she said.

"Thank you, ma'am. It's nice to meet you," Joanna said.

Cade sensed Joanna was trying to make the most of this awkward introduction, and she just stood there frozen and confused but willing to play along.

"And to you, young child… welcome to my home," Moira said with a smile and opened her arms to offer a hug.

Joanna smiled back and happily accepted.

When Moira broke from that embrace, she turned to Cade. "Now you," she said and offered a hug. Cade stepped into the old woman's arms, and he'd never felt so much weakness in his body and strength in his heart at the same time.

"Thank you," Cade said softly into her ear. It was all he could say. Everything he felt in that hug was just what he needed.

"But she'll need some new clothes," Moira said quite bluntly as she pulled away from him. "Where's Red Sky?"

"Right here," Red Sky replied from the doorway.

"Well, get over here and give me a hug," she said insistently. "I'm so happy to see you again."

As Red Sky received his welcome hug, Cade thought it would be polite to state why they were here and what they needed. "Moira, we're tired and hungry, and we could use some of your healing herbs. Could we please stay awhile until we are strong enough to continue our journey?" he asked humbly.

Moira laughed with the cackle of a wise old soul amused with herself. "But of course. I've already got supper in the pot. Now c'mon inside and let's have some tea. I want you to tell me everything."

CHAPTER 18

Whispers & Stories

A cold gray sky hung over Rocky Creek this morning as Lucy Tucker was tying up her wagon in front of the general store.

She watched Eli making his way to school and got a little shiver as fall leaves blew across main street. It was only late October, but she was starting to believe it was going to be a hard winter. All the signs were there, and she could feel it in her bones.

Lucy grabbed the only crate from the back of the wagon and shared some pleasantries with a few folks on the street before she made her way up the steps and entered the store. The little bell above the door announced her arrival, and Daniel stopped talking to a customer to come fetch the crate.

"Good morning," he said with his usual smile. Lucy could only offer a tired grin in return. Her brother was always in a good mood, and she could swear that he must have been born that way. That's what made him a natural businessman.

"Here's everything we have for now," she said, addressing the crate's inventory. "The fruit has all been picked, and we're trying to preserve everything else we can."

"Of course. Thank you," Daniel replied and walked the crate back to the storeroom.

Lucy was enjoying the warmth of the store and the aroma of coffee brewing on the little hot stove. Since she had stopped to come in today instead of a casual drop-off, she hoped her brother might offer her some when he returned. But as she looked casually out the window, she could see Jon Cobb crossing the street and coming toward the store. Suddenly she regretted being trapped in the store and wished she hadn't stopped at all.

The little bell above the door chimed again, and she knew Cobb was going to make his presence known to everyone in the store. "Hello, Ms. Lucy, it's so genuinely nice to see you this morning," he said and pulled off his hat to cover his heart in some odd form of symbolic greeting.

"What do you want, Cobb?" Lucy replied. Things had been a little better between them lately, mostly because they'd had no reason to speak to each other. Since Cade had left and the judge told him to leave her family be, it had been strangely peaceful in Rocky Creek—but she still never appreciated his presence trying to occupy hers.

Cobb readorned his hat and pulled a folded piece of parchment from his coat pocket. She could tell he was about to make an announcement. "I received a bit of news yesterday from a business associate of mine. I told you that someday there would be a big future ahead for our valley, and that day may have arrived!" he said with a big smile. "It sounds like there are plans to bring the railroad through the mountain pass and then right through Rocky Creek," he continued without waiting for her to ask.

"Good for you, Cobb. You're going to be even richer now," Lucy replied indignantly.

"Not just me," Cobb countered. "It's going to be good for everyone, including you. And if I may be so bold, I would ask that we put the past behind us and that someday you might reconsider my marriage offer. We could join our land and make this an incredible opportunity for us… as a family."

Lucy wanted to laugh in his face, but that would seem rude given they were standing in the general store—and her brother had just come up behind her while attending to his customer. As she stepped aside to allow the customer to approach the counter and pay for her goods, Lucy gave Cobb the same "go to hell" look she gave him every time he asked.

"I will never marry you. Can't you get that through your head?" she said as firmly as possible to break through whatever stubbornness lingered in his mind about her.

But Cobb didn't look at all like he was prepared to back down, even when Daniel walked his customer out and joined the two of them to intervene.

Cobb continued. "I'm sorry to hear you say that. Because I have some other news, too."

Lucy wondered where he was going with this.

"I've heard from the same business associate in Colorado that Cade Wilson is dead. He was blown up on a train…

completely blown to bits with dynamite. They couldn't even find his body," Cobb said matter-of-factly.

Cobb's words began to swirl in her mind, and everything after "Cade Wilson is dead" seemed initally irrelevant. But after a moment of shock, Lucy snapped out of the haze and recalled everything he had said in order.

"Who told you this? Who said Cade is dead?" Daniel asked from over her shoulder, and Lucy appreciated that he was thinking about the same thing that was on her mind.

"Sources," Cobb replied. "Trusted sources."

"But you said 'they couldn't even find his body,' so how can this be?" Lucy asked. She wanted so badly for everything Cobb was saying to be a lie, and so she desired more answers.

"They say he must have completely blown to bits. And it must be true because this happened almost a month ago and nobody has seen hide or hair of him since," he added, softening his voice a touch.

Lucy's heart sank into her stomach, and the weight of her grief was almost suffocating as she pushed past Cobb and walked out of the store. As she breathed in the cool air, it was like the rest of the world had become still. She became oblivious and numb to everything going on around her—even the voice of her brother calling her name from over her shoulder sounded like it came from miles away.

As if guided by her subconscious, she walked to the middle of the street and looked to the north. Beyond the church and the school at the top of the hill were the mountains that separated the territory from Colorado. The mountains and the pass in the distance were blanketed by the same gray clouds that stretched across the sky, and they did nothing to assuage her worst fears and the heartache in her soul.

So many thoughts continued to run through her head, including how she would tell Eli and Pa that Cade was dead—and that Jon Cobb could go to hell. But what prevailed was how much she tried to warn herself that something like this could happen. That she should have kept herself from caring about a man who may never return. She had already lost a good husband and father, and now she seemed damned to repeat those feelings of emptiness and loss.

Then a soft breeze blew in from the west and some autumn leaves trickled across the street. The sound of them dancing across the earth spoke to her in a voice she couldn't understand, but something about it resonated with her all the same. They whispered for her to ease her mind and to have faith that everything was going to be alright. Until she knew for certain, she decided she wasn't going to believe he was dead.

"I love you, Cade Wilson," she said softly into the wind, hoping his spirit was listening.

...

Teach Me the Way

Days turned into weeks at Moira's cabin, and Cade lost track of time. He was on the mend and felt stronger every day. It was the most rest in one place he'd enjoyed in a long time—including his time at the fort. And even though it was just a bunk in the barn, it was nice sleeping under a sheltered roof again.

Red Sky and Joanna were also getting healthier and seemed to be enjoying their stay. For room and board, the three of them worked the land and helped Moira with some chores and repairs that must have been outstanding for some time. Even though she never said it aloud, Cade sensed that Moira appreciated having them around, too.

The angle of the sun told its own story, and Cade knew it must be late October by now. He also knew the seasons would change dramatically any time now, and it wouldn't be pleasant.

If his Benefactor thought he was dead, then the best thing he could do was to hold up here for the winter. It was more than a matter of being helpful around the place and having nowhere else to go. He didn't want to risk bringing any more trouble and pain to the people he cared about.

The winterizing was done a few days ago, and Cade and Red Sky were finishing some repairs to the roof of the barn at that time in the afternoon when Moira would make every-one stop for tea. She was very insistent that teatime must be observed, and this usually meant sitting around the table and telling stories. But today was different.

Today they were celebrating Cade's and Joanna's birthday. Even though they didn't have a calendar, his birthday was the 20th of October, and hers was the 28th. And tonight would be the night of the hunter's moon that appeared late in the month.

"Happy Birthday, Joanna," Cade said with a smile. She had cleaned up well since their time here at the cabin, as Moira had cut her hair and fashioned some new clothes. The new look was more than just replacing her torn and tattered dress; it was intended to help her look more like a fighter and less of a target—and because it was very likely that she still had a price on her head, too.

"Thank you. And to you, too!" Joanna replied. "I never imagined this is where I would be when I turned seventeen, but I couldn't be happier to be away from life on the railroad."

"What happens on your birthday?" Red Sky asked while he sipped his tea.

"Well, typically you receive a special gift on your birthday. And it just so happens that I have something for you, Joanna," Moira said. Then the old woman stood to reach behind her and produced Falcon's crimson battle coat. "I didn't think Cade would mind," she said while handing Joanna the coat. "You're about the same size as the previous owner of this coat, but I had to take it in in a few places, based on your measurements."

Cade could sense Joanna's surprise as she took the coat from Moira and held it in her hands. Then she looked to him as if seeking approval, and he just smiled and gave a polite nod. "Go ahead. Let's see how it looks on you," he said warmly.

Joanna slipped her arms into the sleeves, then pulled the coat closed and began to button it. "Wow, this is great!" she said. "I love it!"

"Oh child, it almost looks like it was made for you. And since you needed a coat, it seemed to be the perfect gift," Moira said as she smiled. "I got the idea after I sowed up all the cuts and holes in your coat," she added and gave Cade a wink.

Cade smiled back and no longer felt the ghost of Falcon around him. The fight between them seemed so long ago that seeing Joanna in his old coat didn't bring back any haunting memories. Instead, he appreciated seeing it on her and hoped it would help protect her. "I agree. It looks really good on you," he said. She was a very beautiful young girl, and she seemed so healthy and happy since arriving here.

"Thank you, so much," Joanna said and gave Moira a big hug.

"What about you?" Red Sky asked Cade. "What do you want for your birthday?"

Cade never really celebrated his birthday, but it didn't take long to answer the question. "I've already asked Moira for what I want, and she already agreed," he said, nodding at Moira. "I'm going to stay here for the winter and focus on my training.

"I will eventually need to confront my Benefactor again, because I can't run and hide forever. And I'll need to master my own two-sword techniques to face Toshi again."

"I'm staying for the winter, too," Joanna said excitedly, and the big smile on her face continued to shine. "And after the snow melts, who knows where I'll go? Maybe try and make my way to California."

When Moira and Joanna settled back around the table for tea, it was time for a more somber announcement.

"Are you still leaving tomorrow?" Cade asked Red Sky.

Red Sky nodded. "I need to get back to my tribe. I've been away for so long, and I should be with them to help get through the winter."

Cade felt a lingering sense of guilt for what happened on their quest to capture his Benefactor away from the fort—and failing to help Red Sky get his revenge. "I'm sorry for dragging you with me across Colorado, and I understand that you must return to be with your people. So I want you to have this," he said while reaching behind him and then presenting the broken tip of Scorpion's spear. "You may not be a samurai… but you are a man of honor, a fierce warrior, and a true friend. I trust that you'll be able to restore this weapon to it's former glory and that it will serve you well."

"Our fight isn't over," Red Sky replied as he accepted the gift. "The men who had my people butchered are still out there… and the fight with them is still out there."

Cade nodded in silent agreement. The past few weeks had been restful and they all needed some peace in their life—even if it was just for a short while. But there would be nowhere for either of them to run or live in peace as long as his Benefactor was alive.

"We're going to miss you," Joanna said sadly, and Cade felt that her sincerity spoke for everyone at the table.

"I'll return before the trees begin to bloom," Red Sky said in reassurance. "And then we'll take our fight to the fort," he added as he moved his right arm in a circle. Perhaps he was conveying the passing of time, or to continue strengthening where the bullet was still lodged in his shoulder.

"Let's not worry ourselves about that right now. Today is a celebration!" Moira said. "Now let's finish our tea and afternoon chores so we can enjoy a nice supper tonight," she added.

"I agree," Cade replied and took a sip from his cup. "So tell me, Joanna, is there anything else you would like for your birthday?"

"Yes. I want you to train me how to fight like a samurai," Joanna replied.

•••

Bullseye

On the cold distant horizon, a lone rider approached a fort sitting atop a hill.

He had been riding for many weeks to eventually arrive here, and the place looked like the fabled stories he had heard about it along the way. As he approached the front gate, a man standing guard in a gray coat came out to stop him.

"What is your business here, bounty hunter?" the guard asked.

The rider looked up slowly from under the brim of his hat. The left side of his face was horribly scarred, and he could tell the guard was taken back by the sight of him. "What gave me away?" he asked with a grin.

"We get plenty of bounty hunters around here," the guard replied as he spat on the ground. "But we don't take your kind at the fort. So I suggest you just turn yourself around."

"No. You're going to take me to your boss because we have some important business to discuss." The rider could tell the guard was put off by his insistence but willing to waver on his orders rather than stand here and argue out in the cold.

"Alright, I'll take you to the main house, but don't say I

didn't warn you," the guard replied, and then motioned for the rider to follow.

As they got to the big house in the middle of the property, the guard went inside, and the rider waited patiently outside on his horse. When the guard returned a few minutes later, he was followed by a man who was handsomely dressed but not happy about being imposed upon.

"My name is Joseph Whitmore II, and this is my property. Whatever you have to say, bounty hunter, it better be good," he said from the front porch.

"Whitmore. That would make you the man that put a bounty on Cade Wilson, yes?"

"Yes," Whitmore replied impatiently. "But Cade Wilson is dead, and the bounty is void. I blew that bastard to the moon about a month ago, so if that's what you're here about—"

"No disrespect, sir," the rider said. "But I don't think that's true. I don't think Cade Wilson is dead or I would've found his body. And dynamite didn't make two swords and ten thousand dollars in gold disappear.

"You see… my old partner was the best hunter from here to Texas. He taught me everything I know, and I've been tracking the man who killed him for some time. Cade Wilson and his friends also gave me this," he said, using the back of his hand to point out the burned skin that scarred his face. "Everywhere I go, the stories about him get bigger and the whispers get louder. But nobody has seen the man with two swords, or the Indian and the girl that were traveling with him.

"In fact, nobody outside of some scattered folks and a family in Rocky Creek have seen any of that gold… and not a single coin since the train explosion. After all my searching, the only remains of Cade Wilson that I've found is this here knife that might have belonged to him," he said, pulling the foreign-looking blade from a strap on his saddle. Then he threw the knife at Whitmore's feet and it stuck in the wooden deck right between his legs.

Whitmore sneered back at the rider, visibly agitated by this conversation. "You have about one minute to turn your horse around and ride on back to wherever you came from. I don't like being threatened or called a liar. Especially by the likes of you," he said with a glare and snapped his fingers. And when he did, the man who was standing guard put his hand on his pistol, but the rider was unafraid and unaffected by this little display.

The guard also seemed to realize that his posturing wasn't going to change the situation, and he would have to do more than threaten to use his pistol. But before he could pull his gun, the rider quickly pulled his and shot the guard's hat off his head.

"You're not hearing me, friend," the rider said while the guard slowly holstered his pistol and pulled his hand away. "That man killed my partner and cut his head off at the train station in Colorado Springs. And I do believe that you were there to bear witness, so I want us to come to an understanding. I'm going to have my revenge… and I will collect my reward."

The rider could tell he had Whitmore's attention now, so he made his proposition. "The man you call Viper is still alive. And with your help, I mean to flush him out along with the gold that he stole from you. And when I do, I want to be the one to kill him. But until then, I would appreciate it if you could offer me some accommodations," he said with a glance over his shoulder at some dark clouds and a threatening sky. "My horse and I could use a rest."

Whitmore reached down and pulled the knife from the wood. The rider could tell he recognized it, and then he nodded and motioned for his guard to stand down and pick up his hat. "I'll entertain you long enough to rest and hear your plan. But if I don't like the sound of it, it will take more than some fancy shooting to save you," he said plainly.

The rider holstered his pistol before tipping his hat. "Much obliged," he replied.

"What's your name, bounty hunter?" Whitmore asked.

The rider leaned back in his saddle and answered the question with callous indifference. "My name is Bill Swift, but you can call me Bullseye."

References

- Musashi, Miyamoto. *The Book of Five Rings.* Bottom of the Hill Publishing, 2010.

- Tsunetomo, Yamamoto. *Hagakure: The Book of the Samurai.* Kodansha International, 1979.

Acknowledgments

A very special thank you to everyone who supports the dream and helped me share this story: Sherrie and Max Wagner, Janis Bosley, Judy Moore, Deborah Harmon, Chuck Garcia, Bruce Kral, Brian Dibblee, Lee and Leslie Langan, the Porter family, Jayson and Tedd Gibson, Jim McCall, Chris Mohn, Leor Lapid, Thiery Talia, Andrew Hodges at The Narrative Craft, the team at Paper Raven, and all of my fans and readers.

The Author

Nate Wagner is an independent author with an overactive imagination and an affinity for westerns, science fiction, thrillers, and horror. And with future novels in the works, his dream is to publish novels in each of these genres.

Before he began writing fiction, Nate spent most of his career in marketing and advertising; writing and pitching creative content and campaigns. Nate is also a Navy veteran that has traveled the world and called many places home—but now he resides in Arizona with his wife and son.

Nate is the founder of Creative Refinery LLC and is passionate about developing ideas and characters for future stories. As a mentor, he enjoys helping other first time authors share their stories from conception to manuscript, to becoming self-published authors.

Follow Nate Wagner,
learn more about the series,
and get a sneak peek at
Way of the Ronin:
The Samurai Cowboys - Book Three

thesamuraicowboys.com